The Man in the Moss-Colored Trousers

By Mary Bringle

The Man in the Moss-Colored Trousers

MARY BRINGLE

PUBLISHED FOR THE CRIME CLUB BY

DOUBLEDAY & COMPANY, INC.

GARDEN CITY, NEW YORK

1986

Verse excerpt reprinted with permission of Macmillan Publishing Company from "An Irish Airman Foresees His Death" from *Collected Poems* by William Butler Yeats. Copyright © 1919 by Macmillan Publishing Company, renewed 1947 by Bertha Georgie Yeats.

Library of Congress Cataloging-in-Publication Data

Bringle, Mary.
The man in the moss-colored trousers.

I. Title.
PS3552.R485M3   1986   813'.54   86–6213
ISBN 0-385-23555-0

First Edition

This book is dedicated to Andrew "Scobie" Drummond,
who will not feel the need to read it.

Ring-a-ring-a-rosie,
As the light declines,
I remember Dublin City—
In the rare auld times.

The Man in the Moss-Colored Trousers

ONE

The dog's name was Wolfe Tone. He was medium-sized and of some mixed breed which did not invite speculation. Nobody could think why his owners had named him Wolfe Tone, since they were not known for having Irish Republican sentiments, and the truth was that Terry, the oldest and cleverest of the Brannigan children, had claimed that the dog, viewed in certain lights and at particular angles, resembled a wolf's cub.

Wolfe Tone was not at all popular in Gilligan Crescent—he savaged the rubbish bags, habitually, on collection day. Nobody was unkind to him— although Mrs. O'Rourke had once chased him from her flower bed with colorful curses—and for the most part he was ignored, and led the life of a dog of no distinction.

His status rose abruptly one day late in May when he became, briefly, a sort of celebrity. Terry Brannigan, just back from school, found Wolfe Tone in an agitated and highly nervous state. He whined and made dashing movements in the direction of the old racecourse, looking back over his shoulder to see if Terry was following. As Terry later told it, the dog had finally loped to the low stone wall surrounding the racecourse and set up a constant, furious barking. Since barking was one of the few vices Wolfe Tone did not indulge in, Terry had decided something was amiss. He had joined his dog at the wall, looked into the lupine, pleading eyes, and when Wolfe Tone leaped the wall, Terry followed after.

Several other children, loitering near the bus stop, climbed over too, sensing excitement. Gervaise Doherty, who had been doing something nefarious in a gully surrounded by overgrown weeds, came along with them. They ran panting after Wolfe Tone, speeding over the uneven, hummocky terrain of the abandoned racecourse, and now they were joined by Janie Keane, a studious girl who appeared from nowhere, her Irish language textbook in her hand. In the end it was quite a band of children who were allowed to share the dog's discovery.

He took them all the way to the hulk of the derelict grandstand, where they had all been forbidden to play. His imperious barks turned, there, to the uneasy whimpering Terry had first heard on his return from school.

The man's clothing was such that he blended in quite well with the wild grass and weeds that grew in the confines of the grandstand, and it was dark inside. The dog led them nearly to him before any of them noticed him. It was the pale shape of one of his hands, flung out at an odd angle, that attracted Terry's attention. He wore moss-colored trousers and a grayish cotton shirt, and the sparse hair covering his head was, so Gervaise later said, the hue of Chef's Sauce. They could not see his face, which was pressed against the earth, and they stood in silence until Janie began to sniffle.

Although the secluded grandstand would have been an ideal spot for a tramp to sleep, the children never doubted that he was dead.

"Should we turn him over?" Gervaise whispered, as if they were in church.

"Never," said Terry with authority. "Don't you know you're not supposed to touch anything until the cops arrive? Haven't you watched enough television to know that now?"

"Those are American shows. You're just afraid to touch him."

"Would y'ever shut up?"

"What if he's someone we *know?*" whimpered Janie.

"Then we don't know him anymore," said Terry unkindly, stung by the entirely true assertion that he was afraid to touch the man.

All of their fathers were at work at this hour, and it never occurred to them that their mothers might be useful. This was a serious matter, requiring male authority to determine who the man in the moss-colored trousers was. Had been. There was no Garda station in Balgriffin, the closest was up in Howth, and the only Garda officer whom they knew personally was at work in Dublin. Furthermore, as Gervaise was quick to point out, Mr. Scully was not a detective. He was in charge of the lost-and-found department.

A boy called Matty Keegan provided the proper solution. He was originally from Belfast and had become nervous at mention of the police—he had good reason to distrust them. "Will we go to the pub?" he asked in his mournful Northern accent.

Terry considered, or pretended to. He was usually the leader, but he recognized that Matty's statement, disguised as a proposal, contained the appropriate solution. Tom Mulligan, the barman, would know what to do, whom to call. He was a strong, astute, kindly Sligo man who bore the proper stamp of authority.

Normally children were welcome at the pub only on Sunday, following the last celebration of Mass, but this was obviously a special occasion. They turned from the gloomy shambles of the grandstand and retraced their steps across the racecourse. The black-and-white cows who grazed at the far end had drawn in a bit closer than usual, and Wolfe Tone, trotting along beside his master, threw a contemptuous look in their direction.

All of the children who had discovered the dead man lived, like Terry and Wolfe Tone, in Gilligan Crescent, a group of tiny, cream-colored, attached houses designed to resemble a community of Georgian mansions in extreme miniature. The Gilligan in question had been a famous golfer who had heaped glory on the town of Balgriffin when it was little more than a fishing village some seven miles north of Dublin's City Centre. The once splendid racecourse and the champion golfer were Balgriffin's only claims to fame. Although it was considered a part of Dublin and had a Dublin address, the village was by no means a true part of the capital city. Just as the Georgian architecture of Gilligan Crescent was not really Georgian, just as Wolfe Tone did not *really* resemble a wolf—so Balgriffin was not truly a part of Dublin. One could say, and some did, that Balgriffin was where Dublin ended. Beyond the derelict and haunted-looking racecourse, not used for a decade now for horse racing, there were only fields and marshy plots of land which were periodically submerged beneath the waters of the estuary.

On a fine day, when the tide was in, Balgriffin assumed a picture-postcard beauty. The steep summit of Howth guarded the easterly curve of the estuary, and floating dreamlike in the middle, glimpsed now as an island and again as a greenish protuberance of rock mysteriously attached to the coast, lay Ireland's Eye, around whose waters Brian Boru had done battle with the Vikings.

Far out, between the lip of Howth Harbor and the Eye's rocky, east shore, the open sea declared itself in shades darker and more dangerous than the pale green of the estuary. Balgriffin seemed protected from the murderous sea, yet each year some reckless child would soldier out at low tide, intent on adventure, and be caught by the turning tide, and drowned. The milk-white church of St. Peter and St. Paul—it stood at the very apex of the village, on the sea road and diagonal from the pub, its cross and lightning rod at odds—would be full of mourners, but generally the casket was empty. An old legend stipulated that the bodies of Howth fishermen were never found, and although the drowned children were not fishermen, and not from Howth, their bodies were rarely recovered.

Tom Mulligan was not thinking of the tragedy of the drowned children when the Brannigan boy appeared in the door of the public bar; in fact, what he had been thinking of was the deteriorating state of old Cats Phelan who earlier had appeared to be in a sort of swoon, slumped almost beneath the bench under the TV. When he had approached Cats, however, all solicitous and anxious, Cats had snarled at him. "Eff off," was what he had said. "Can't you see I'm attending to something?"

And, indeed, he had been performing an act of what Tom thought of as personal hygiene—paring his toenails. It was all very well, at that slow hour of the afternoon when there were so few customers, but what would Tom do if Cats took to the odd pedicure when the place was full? It was the problem of it, the *diplomacy* that might be required, he was thinking of when young Terry's self-important face peered round the door.

"Can we come in?" the boy asked. "We have something to tell you."

Tom paced to the end of the bar and saw a regular band of kids huddling in the entrance. There was the Doherty boy, and a little girl he'd seen cycling along the sea road, and the poor lad from Belfast—something to do with plastic bullets, there—and several others, all about the age of his own son. Twelvish. His father's heart, prepared for bad news always, quickened with apprehension, and he told them to go round by the saloon bar, where he would meet them.

He stepped through into the empty, adjoining bar—intended for groups of ladies or courting couples who did not want the hilarity of the public bar in the evenings—and met his deputation coming through the door. They did not sit in the plush red seats of the booth nearest the entrance, but remained standing, ill at ease. The little girl looked close to tears, and the boy from the North seemed shifty and pale.

"Well now," Tom said, "what have you to tell?" He spoke jovially, with a heartiness he did not feel. It was partly the barman's habitual good cheer, and partly out of a desire to fend off calamity.

Terry cleared his throat. "There's something on the racecourse," he said in a rapid, low voice. "We found it when my dog was acting strange."

"What was it, then?" Instantly, his mind had envisioned a cache of arms —a half-buried trunk containing neatly stacked Uzis or Armalites, rounds of ammunition, grenades—who knew? In the small industrial estate of Balgriffin, in one of the warehouses, just such a shipment had been discovered. People had assumed it had come from America, intended for the IRA, but it had turned out to be a contribution from Australia.

"It's a man," said Terry Brannigan. "In the grandstand."

Now he thought of a child molester. He had a daughter of fifteen, and such thoughts came naturally to him. Mightn't a man of that bent perceive his tender and innocent Nuala, with her bristling Mohawk and jaunty knees, as a natural prey? "What sort of a man?" he asked carefully, looking at the little bespectacled girl with concern.

"Dead man," said Terry.

"He's dead. We could tell," said the Doherty boy.

"For sure, he's dead," said the little girl. "He's lyin' awful still, Mr. Mulligan, with his face in the dirt and all."

"Thing is," said Terry, "we thought you'd know who all to call."

Tom stared incredulously at the children; although he knew they were in earnest he thought they might have misunderstood what they had seen. "In the grandstand, you say? Now, wouldn't that be a fine place for a—" He stopped. He had been about to say "tinker," a word now thought too insulting to use. "Traveling person," he amended. "Maybe some of that lot has staked out a place to live in the ruins?"

"No," the child from Belfast said. "Just the one man, Mr. Mulligan. There's no camp, and he's not just asleep or anythin'." He paused, perhaps feeling awkward about reminding them of his intimate, and superior, acquaintance with death. "I'd say he's been shot," he said.

Tom asked if they had seen any blood, but the wretched look on the little girl's face made him sorry. "No blood," the Northern boy said briskly, "but then, we didn't turn him over."

"Good man," said Tom, resting a hand on the boy's shoulder. "I'm going to ring up to Howth and report this. They'll send some men down to investigate. I want you to go home, and stay away from the racecourse. Just go straight on home. I'll take care of it."

"But they'll need me," Terry said. "They'll need me and Wolfe Tone to show them where he is, won't they now?"

"Wolfe Tone's the wee dog," the Belfast boy said, comprehending Tom's confusion and relieving it, man to man. "He nosed him out."

"It's out of our hands now," Tom told them. Frantically, he ransacked his mind for the perfect phrase which would make Terry understand. "It's a matter of footprints," he told them, remembering an old segment of "Kojak" he had once watched with his wife, in Sligo. "If they have too many prints, it'll muck things up. Leave it to the professionals and go along home."

"Yeah, okay, he's right," said Terry, hiding his disappointment.

Tom gave them each a packet of crisps, on the house, and told them again to go straight home. He stood at the side door and watched them trudge away on the sea road, turn inland at the church, and disappear from sight. The tide was out. The estuary's bed looked dismal—cluttered here and there with little piles of rubbish—and yet another band of children were playing on it, rolling an old pram over the dark sand and causing a black-and-white dog to bark in alarm.

He went back to the public bar to call the Howth station, and as he was lifting the receiver, he noticed that Cats Phelan had fallen asleep.

When Matty Keegan returned home, he found his mother having coffee in the kitchen with Mrs. Kennerly from number 32, just across the way. He removed his book bag quietly, savoring the sight of her when she didn't know he was looking. It made him weak with happiness to see his mother laughing and chattering away, like in the old days. She was beginning to look pretty again, too, and he shuddered, remembering how her glossy dark hair had been when she stopped caring about it—lifeless and dry, like the pelt of a dead animal.

Today she was wearing a blue blouse and a darker blue skirt, and she had tied her hair back with a scrap of scarlet yarn. The blouse matched her eyes, calling attention to them, and the bright yarn made her look like a teenager, even though she was, he knew, thirty-two.

"Matty!" she cried, seeing him there in the door. "You gave me a start. You're late, son. And say hello to Mrs. Kennerly. And you'll find a lovely slice of something on the counter."

This was his mother's way when she was happy. She talked in rapid, scattershot bursts. He said hello to Mrs. Kennerly, who was drinking something he suspected was not coffee, and thought of how much he had missed his mother's verbal patterns during the bad time. She had hardly spoken at all, and when she did, her voice emerged in a hollow, listless way that had terrified him. It was as if, while he had been in the hospital, someone had put a stranger's voice box in his mother's body.

On the counter he found a generous portion of lemon crumble. He asked permission to take it out into the garden, and his mother smiled and said yes, of course, and wasn't it a lovely day, and why were she and Imelda sitting inside when they could be out in the sunshine? Nevertheless, the two women reached for fresh cigarettes and made no move to get up.

In the miniature garden—made even smaller by the concrete toolshed his da had constructed—Matty settled near the bed of spinach and began to eat his crumble, reflecting on how much this new situation was or was not likely to upset her. Back home (home to Matty was Belfast, despite what had happened, and he considered his comfortable life in the Republic as a sort of way station), his da had explained it to him.

"It's the drugs, son," he had said. "The doctors have her on a lot of tablets. That's why she seems to be sleepwalking, like, but she'll get better."

In the end, though, his father had taken a more radical solution than any of the doctors. He had moved his family out of the war zone, over the border to safe Balgriffin, in the Free State. And Nora Keegan, who left behind her relations and friends of a lifetime, and who was surrounded by strangers, miraculously did improve. She complained of the unfriendliness of the Free Staters, suspected her accent put them off, but little by little she lost the taut, strained air of perpetual anxiety and began to come back to life. She had made a few friends in the Crescent, and she was taking pains with her appearance. Best of all, she didn't need the tablets anymore.

An unmelodious sound suddenly filled the air. His sister, Maureen, was practicing her clarinet. He could see her, in profile, in the window of her bedroom. He had no sense of their house in Gilligan Crescent as being small, or cramped. He had always lived in small houses—the Victorian redbricks of the Falls Road—and the Crescent houses seemed quite grand to him.

Very soon now, his mother would find out about the body on the racecourse.

Matty calculated. If no one told her, she would likely find out when she watched the evening news. He heard Wolfe Tone's name being shouted by one of the Brannigans, and decided to go out in front so he could at least watch for the Garda car to arrive.

"I'm puffin' like a train," Mrs. Kennerly was saying, lighting yet another cigarette. His mother laughed and fiddled with the scarlet bow of yarn.

At the front door, Matty could see Terry and Gervaise and the others, all sitting on the low wall in front of their houses, staring in the direction of the racecourse. No car had arrived yet. He joined them in their vigil, hoping his mother would go on laughing.

He knew a killing in their town wasn't the same as what had happened in Belfast, but a dead body was a dead body, and death was what his mother had come South to get away from.

TWO

Although people who lived in Balgriffin liked to talk about the crime wave sweeping Dublin, not much in the nature of serious crime had ever touched the village. The older teenagers might be seen lurking outside the Youth Centre, trying to hitch rides to Dublin or Portmarnock, and perhaps some of them experimented with drugs there, but in general it was a quiet place. There were rumors of joyriding and auto vandalism among the younger set, just as there were rumors of marital infidelity and broken marriages among their parents, but crime, so to speak, had remained a rumor blowing in from the heart of Dublin. Somewhere near Clontarf it seemed to lose its momentum, and by the time it tried to muscle in on Balgriffin, it had grown listless and feeble.

By late evening of the day of Wolfe Tone's discovery, Balgriffin saw more detectives swarming about its environs than it had ever believed possible. Dozens of them moved about on the racecourse—humbler gardai as well, and a few whom Terry Brannigan claimed were Special Branchmen. They prowled over the ground which had once resounded with the thud of Irish thoroughbred hooves and now lay tangled and overgrown, dotted with wild buttercups; the familiar old hulk of the deserted grandstand, rising jaggedly against the darkening sky, took on a sinister shape as the night drew in. Everyone in Gilligan Crescent saw the odd-looking black bag in which the dead man was conveyed to an ambulance, and almost all of them had the same thought: it looked much like the large lawn bags Wolfe Tone was fond of examining on collection day.

All the Crescent people waited for the sound of official fists to crash against their flimsy doors, but at this early stage the only door to be so favored was that of the Brannigans. Kathleen Brannigan assured her neighbors that the detective-gardai had merely asked Terry to confirm the rumor about his discovery, and to say whether he, or any of the other children, had touched or altered anything in the vicinity. Then they had gone away, promising to return when more was known.

Finola Doyle, who did the photographs for the local paper, the Balgriffin *Weekly*, came by to take a picture of Terry and his noble dog, and that, for the first day, was that. Everyone who could adjourned to the pub, where there was endless speculation, and Cats Phelan, who grew irascible when there was too much noise, shouted that he wished the body had been his own.

Kate Brannigan rose, the following morning, with a two-edged feeling. One edge contained exhilaration, because today the police would return and make a nice break in the monotony of her day; the other was all guilt—something she was so familiar with it seemed like an old friend. Surely it was wrong to feel elated at the prospect of a police interrogation, especially since a man had been killed. If she were truly a good woman, she would be appalled and heartsick at the thought of a fellow creature's body lying so close to her tidy little house.

And it *was* little, dear God, little was the operative word, with five children and three bedrooms—sometimes it felt as if they were living in each other's pockets. Dressing in the tiny bathroom, so her husband could savor his last few minutes of sleep, she thought enviously of Mrs. Keegan, across the way, who had only the two kids.

Kate enjoyed the moments at the beginning of the day, when everyone was still asleep and she could feel alone. Soon they would all be conscious, and consciousness would bring them to the realization of certain wants and needs that only Kate could satisfy. Their voices would form a little orchestra of demands, her husband's baritone pleading for a fresh shirt while the baby wailed a soprano lament for her breakfast. It did sometimes seem too much to bear, especially since they would all, except for the baby, clear out after breakfast and leave her to a day of spectacularly dull expectations. In the circumstances, who could blame her for looking forward to a chat with the police?

She looked in the mirror, well pleased with what she saw. Childbearing ruined so many women's looks, but nature had reserved one of its little surprises for Kathleen Brannigan, and with the birth of each child she had become prettier. The pale, carroty-haired, angular, knob-kneed girl she had been—the girl Brian Brannigan had inexplicably fallen in love with—was now a well-rounded, honey-toned woman of thirty, whose physical presence in a room was considerable. "Hah!" she whispered spitefully, before leaving the bathroom. "That's one sin you never thought to warn me of, you old terror." She was carrying on a running battle with Sister Michael, a nun who had made her school days miserable with cautionary tales about the wages of Intellectual Pride. Michael had apparently thought the child Kathleen too poor a specimen to indulge in the sin of vanity, and now that she was dead, and her former pupil grown beautiful, it was too late.

Downstairs, Terry slept peacefully in the pull-out in the sitting room.

Wolfe Tone came crowding up to Kate when she entered the kitchen, a look of mute supplication in his yellow eyes. Kate let him out into the garden and began to heat water for the boiling of eggs. When she had plugged in the kettle and cut the bread, she turned her little kitchen radio on low and prepared to hear about the tragedy on the racecourse on the morning news.

The announcer told her about the devaluation of the American dollar, a six-car collision in County Longford, a missing trawler up in Donegal, and a bombing over the border, in Newry. There was nothing about the dead man in the grandstand.

The bombing in the North made her think, automatically, of her neighbor, Nora Keegan. Mrs. Keegan's boy had been one of the band of children who had discovered the body. Matthew, that was his name. Matty, an odd little creature he was, and on the few occasions when Terry had brought him home she had felt uncharacteristically shy and bumbling. For one thing, she couldn't understand the boy, his Northern accent was deep and impenetrable, and she found herself smiling and acquiescing to everything Matt Keegan said. For another, she felt in awe of him.

A year ago, when he was only eleven, Matty had been a casualty in the war. He was an unlikely survivor—the only one she had ever met. He never talked about it, but in Balgriffin it was impossible to conceal anything, and Kate knew all the details from the moment the Keegans moved in across the Crescent. The part of her that was all compassion and softness wished to solace Matty Keegan and his small family, but the other quarter or half argued that his presence in the village could only stir up trouble.

Pale, stern, Matty Keegan had descended upon Balgriffin to remind the villagers that a part of their country was under siege, and it was a reminder which nobody welcomed.

Nora studied the photograph the Garda detective had handed her, trying to control the trembling of her fingers. It was no use. Her hands shook helplessly, and at this display of panic and confusion, the younger of the two detectives straightened expectantly. He thought, of course, that this particular housewife, unlike the twenty-four they had already interviewed, recognized the dead man and was quivering with emotion. Nora put the photo down on her kitchen table and studied the face looking up at her. She clasped her hands together in her lap and considered this man who had been photographed in death.

He had a longish face, and rather high cheekbones. The lower lip was unexpectedly full, and the staring eyes long and of a pale grayish color. She wondered if he had died with his eyes open, or if a police photographer had propped them open somehow. She looked up at the older garda and shook her head.

"Are you sure, Mrs. Keegan?" the younger one asked in transparently polite tones. "Because at first, there, when we showed you—"

"My hands, you mean," Nora said. "Yes, I know. But it wasn't because I recognized him. I have a wee problem with this sort of thing."

"Mrs. Keegan is from the North," said the older one. And then, to her, "How long have you and your family been in Balgriffin?"

"Six months, just. My husband works for Guinness, and I've the two children in school here." Why was she babbling? These men were not like the police at home—she wasn't looking at the nose of an SLR and being made to feel guilty for simply being alive. When would she learn?

As if he could read her mind, the older one smiled and said, "You've nothing to fear from us, Mrs. Keegan, but I know how it must be. I have a daughter who married a man from Fermanagh. I know."

Nora smiled at him gratefully. She answered the remaining few questions easily and in relative comfort. She knew of no feuds raging in Balgriffin, could think of no mortal enemies dwelling within its confines. She didn't know many people yet, and was sorry she could be of so little help. The men released no information, and it would have surprised Nora to know that she was the only woman in the Crescent who had asked no questions.

They left behind a poorly reproduced black-and-white picture of the photograph she had seen, made up like a poster seeking the whereabouts of a bank robber. *Height:* Five feet, ten inches. *Weight:* Fourteen stone. *Identifying marks:* Crescent scar on left upper thigh. *Hair:* Brown, thinning. *Eyes:* Gray or blue. *Age:* Estimated late forties. They also left a card, imprinted with the name *Sean Lynch,* together with a number where he could be reached anytime.

"Which of you is Mr. Lynch?" Nora asked.

"Myself," said the older one.

"I knew a man, Sean Lynch, back home," she said.

"It's a common name, Mrs. Keegan," said the pleasant detective.

"Oh, aye, to be sure," said Nora. She said good-bye to them at her door and watched them cross over to Mrs. Brannigan's house opposite. Kathleen Brannigan had the door open before they'd even rung her bell, and Nora saw, to her amusement, that her neighbor was dressed as if for an afternoon party, and fully made up.

All up and down the Crescent women were loitering in their doorways, or sitting on the low stone walls, watching the progress of the police with eager, furtive eyes. Nora knew she could easily join them, gossip with them, and be taken into the fold, but she had a horror of prying. She shut the door and went back to the kitchen, annoyed with herself for being amused at the Brannigan woman's expense. Why shouldn't wee Kathleen be excited by the prospect of a visit from the police? The poor girl was run off her feet with the five children, and she had every right to welcome a strange, new experience. It would make a nice break.

Nora lit a cigarette, vowing for the thousandth time to cut down. She had not smoked while the police were in her house because she knew how her hands would tremble when she tried to convey the point of the cigarette to the flame at the end of the kitchen match. She inhaled with pleasure, and thought of Sean Lynch's daughter, married to a Fermanagh man. How had they met, and did the detective travel North to visit his daughter? Or did the couple live, like herself, in the Republic now? Lynch had sought to reassure her, saying he knew what it was like. *I know*. He had meant well, but how could he know?

What she had not told him was that the Sean Lynch she had grown up with, in Belfast, was serving a life sentence.

"By my reckoning," said the young detective to Sean Lynch, "we've done exactly three quarters of that bloody Crescent."

"Good man," said Lynch, extracting a bit of limp lettuce from his sandwich and parking it to the left of his pile of chips. "Do you honestly believe that the remaining quarter will, miraculously, provide the necessary information the three quarters have been withholding?"

They were having their lunch in the pub, both because it was the only place to take a midday meal in Balgriffin and because Lynch firmly believed that the repository of all important knowledge in a small town was, necessarily, the chief barman of the local pub. Tom Mulligan had not yet come on duty, and the barman was a young lad who seemed no more than fifteen. He whistled in an aimless fashion as he pulled the pump and dashed into the kitchen and guided them to the buffet laid out in the saloon bar, yet Lynch never doubted that the boy knew exactly who they were.

The younger man chewed his bite of sandwich with methodical precision. "I didn't form an impression that they were lying. *Withholding*. That Brannigan woman, one with the red hair and tight blouse—wasn't she the desperate one to come up with anything? Drug rings and all, she'd got it all worked out."

"No," said Lynch. "I think the ladies of Balgriffin are honestly bewildered. All of them, young and old. The man's a stranger to them. Maybe he just had the misfortune to be passing through this village, maybe someone killed him for his money or his car and dumped him in the grandstand."

"You don't believe that."

"Not a'tall, Frank. But that's what the ladies want to believe. They'd like it if it turned out to be the work of some drug czar from Dun Laoghaire even better, confirm their worst suspicions, but as the old lady in number seven pointed out—why bother to drive all the way to Balgriffin to leave him on the racecourse? Unless, of course, the racecourse itself is meant to be the appropriate final resting place for our deceased friend."

"Something only the killer would know. A private joke."

"The Kennerly woman is quite the joker. Suggested someone had murdered his bookie. Not that there aren't some who'd like to." Lynch got up and went to the wall phone. Frank Browne shook more H.P. sauce over his chips, a habit his wife deplored, and watched his partner speak a few sentences into the phone and then listen intently. His face, as usual, revealed nothing. Observed impartially, Sean Lynch would be seen as a middle-aged, rather heavy man whose thick black eyebrows seemed to say he was capable of brutality. This was not the case, and only when Lynch smiled, as he had at the nervous Mrs. Keegan, was it possible to see that he was basically a sweet-natured man. Lynch had, Frank knew, a passion for Irish traditional music. Well, fair enough, everyone liked the Chieftains, but with Sean it was a scholarly affair. At his house, in Blackrock, he had maybe a thousand tapes, all neatly labeled and cataloged; once he had forced Frank to listen to an interminable, rambling anecdote, told by an ancient man from Inishmore, entirely in Irish. When the man got down to fiddling it was great stuff, he had to admit it, but when Frank had asked why Lynch bothered with the old fella's story, Lynch had looked pained and said, "The story, the fiddling, it's all part of the same thing."

Lynch's children were grown and married themselves now, and he lived in apparent harmony with his wife, Una. There was too great a difference in the two men's ages for Frank and Sean to be true friends, but they liked and respected each other. Lynch knew, for example, that Frank had a secret fear of hornets and wasps—something few people suspected—and Frank knew that the one thing that truly enraged Sean Lynch was any hint of cruelty toward children. When that busty Mrs. Brannigan had given them the details about the Keegan kid, Lynch's outrage was apparent in the sudden, extreme pallor of his face.

"Just one bit of news, Frankie," he said now, coming back to the table. "Our friend's prints are all over the racecourse, walking under his own steam. That knocks out the theory of his being done somewhere else and dumped in the grandstand. He died where he was found."

"Any other prints?"

"Only about a million others. Every kid in Balgriffin plays out there, even though every mother in Balgriffin insists her children are forbidden to go there. And when the littler kids clear out, the teenagers slip in for a bit of illicit love beneath the stars. In the area where the body was discovered there are over two dozen different prints. Some are small, but at least a third could belong to adult males."

Frank sighed and ordered two more pints of Smithwick's. Technically, they were not supposed to drink on duty, but he felt it was uncivil to be in a bar and not buy any of its chief commodity. The autopsy report would be complete at the end of the afternoon, but neither of them expected anything to emerge from it. It was instantly apparent to them how the man had died, and only the Balgriffin folk, who assumed that he had been shot, would be surprised.

While they were waiting for the pints, a tiny old man who looked to be in a state of rage came groping his way in from the public bar. "No effin' peace!" he shouted at them, lurching toward the men's room. "Great, loud, blathering tele*vision* always turned on! A man my age needs tranquillity!"

"Don't mind him, now," said the young barman, putting the pints down with a flourish. "It's only Cats Phelan."

"I take his point about the television in bars, though," Lynch said. "Don't like them myself. Put a drink in for Mr. Phelan, son, would you?"

The boy colored. "Ah, Jesus," he said miserably. "That's good of you fellas, but with Cats, now, it's a bad idea. Old devil might take it in his mind that he was being offered a bribe by the police." His voice had sunk to a conspiratorial whisper. "Once old Mrs. Tighe put one in for him on his birthday, and Cats—well, didn't he go around sayin' she wanted to get in his pants so he would leave her all his money?"

"I see," said Lynch, looking amused. "Here's what to do. Just say you can't remember who bought him the drink. Say it was a rich golfer passing through who bought drinks for the whole house."

This plan seemed to please the boy, who grinned hugely and said, "Right. No problem."

"One other thing," Frank said. "Why is he called Cats?"

"Probably because he used to be a fishmonger," Lynch answered. "Isn't that it?"

The boy nodded. "So I've been told," he said.

On the evening television news it was announced that the body of a man in his forties had been found in the ruins of the Balgriffin grandstand. He had been dead for approximately twenty-four hours, and his identity was totally unknown. Nothing of a personal nature was found—no papers, wallets, cards —to enable an identification to be made. His fingerprints were not in the police records. The same picture the gardai had shown to the Crescent residents was shown on the screen, and a special number given so that anyone with information about the dead man could speak to the police in confidence.

He had been garroted.

THREE

The worst thing about living to be eighty was, in Andy Halloran's opinion, the gradual loss of his sight. He had got to the point now where it was mainly a matter of moving shapes. You knew who had entered a room by the way the shape moved, mostly. At home it was easy. Only his wife, Ellen, was likely to be encountered there, but the pub presented a challenge.

"Now, I believe that's Gerry O'Hara just come in," he would say anxiously to the person who happened to be sitting with him on the long bench. "If I'm not mistaken, that's young Margaret Corcoran who just went past." He was almost always right. On the occasions when he was not, he felt secretly shamed.

He was greatly loved in Balgriffin, and he knew it, but the sly pleasure he derived from his popularity was not enough. They liked him for his quaint old sayings, his genuine wit, and his courtesy, but what he really wanted was to be useful. He had spent a lifetime being useful, beginning with his first job at the age of twelve, and even after he had been made to retire from the work force some sixty years later, his usefulness had continued in the form of small services performed for his wife. He was a good gardener, and he had derived great satisfaction from providing Ellen with cucumbers and runner beans, lettuce and tomatoes.

He had also loved to read, for although his education had been abandoned at an early age, he possessed a quick and curious mind. He had been in the habit of reading *The Irish Times* from front to back, every morning, and now he had to get his news from smug voices on the radio or telly.

It was a matter of torment to him that he could not see the face of the murdered man they had discovered in the grandstand. If no one around him knew the man, Ellen pointed out, then it was unlikely that Andy would know him, either. That was not the point.

"A longish face, you say?" he asked Tom Mulligan, who had come to lower the volume of the television at Cats Phelan's request. It was nine-thirty on the evening after the news announcement, and the pub was full.

"Right, Scobie," Tom called. "That he had."

"Scobie" was his nickname, and had been for half a century. It was the name of either a prize-winning horse or an illustrious jockey; Andy could no longer remember which and Cats, the only man of an age to remember, sometimes said one thing and sometimes the other. Ellen always called him Andy and was no help, either.

"And his eyes, Tom? You can tell a lot by the eyes."

"Not when they're dead!" Cats shouted irritably. Tom had already gone back to the bar. "They're just eyes, Mr. Halloran," came the low, fluting voice of Mrs. Keane, whose daughter, Janie, had been one of the children to discover the body. Mrs. Keane came rarely to the pub, but it was in the nature of murders that they drew the survivors out to commiserate and speculate.

Courteously, he offered Mrs. Keane a cigarette from his good pack. He always carried a fresh pack of Player's in his left jacket pocket, and in his right a package containing butts of varying lengths. He smoked the butts, culled during the long day, and offered the fresh ones.

"Oh, I won't, Mr. Halloran, thanks very much. I'm trying to cut down."

"I do believe," Andy said, "that it's possible to tell a man's character by his face. Studies have been done, if I'm not mistaken. It should be possible to look at this poor fella's face and determine what class of a life he's led."

"Oh, you're a rare one," said Mrs. Keane fondly. "You can afford to believe that because you're still irresistible."

His lips curved up in the obligatory smile, acknowledging the compliment, but inwardly he was perturbed. A shape loomed up, lunging in, and a hand stroked his hair. "Christ, would you ever look at this hair?" trumpeted a youthful voice. "It's the envy of all."

"I believe that's young Bobbie McGrath," he said dutifully, recognizing the abrasive voice of a boy Ellen had told him was now sporting a spiked coiffure, dyed blue.

"Too much effin' noise!" screamed Cats.

"Our Janie," Mrs. Keane said intimately, crowding up close so he could smell her perfume, like it or not, "has been very *nervy* since she disobeyed me and went out on that racecourse. It's a terrible thing for a child to see death like that. She's all anxious and teary, ever since it happened, and if she doesn't improve I'm going to take her to Dr. Quinn's surgery and see what can be done. Isn't that the right thing to do?"

"Thinks he's a bloody film star, the old fool!" Cats murmured venomously.

"He might put her on tablets," Mrs. Keane continued in her worried voice. "And she's so young. Holy Mother, Mr. Halloran, she won't be twelve until September."

"Would she ever eff off?" asked Cats plaintively. "Excuse me."

All the time, until Tom called closing by strolling the length of the bar and bellowing, "Ah, come along, lads, PLEASE," Scobie kept his idea to himself. There was no one worthy enough, or sober enough, to receive it.

Mrs. Keane and her husband, a decent, quiet man, accompanied him up the dark lane. His house lay just in back of the pub, but the Keane woman took hold of his arm, guiding him as if he needed supervision. He had made the brief journey thousands of times, and if he kept to the wall he could manage perfectly, but he did not want to hurt her feelings. Still, it angered him. If he could no longer be useful, at least he could be sufficient unto himself. He had no plans for turning out like Cats, who fell asleep in public houses and spoke out loud when he believed himself to be silently ruminating.

Mrs. Keane was going on about how sensitive Janie was, not like some other children, and he allowed his mind to ramble away and consider the man on the racecourse. If only he could have seen the man's face! There would be certain lines, a look about the eyes, dead or not, that would reveal whether the man had been evil, or merely weak.

He had already decided that there could be only one reason for a stranger to be lurking in the grandstand of a derelict racecourse in the middle of the night, and that reason would have to involve blackmail. There had been a rendezvous—the dead man had gone to meet someone. But which was he? The blackmailer or the victim? Had he been killed because he would no longer pay, or because the one he preyed upon had grown weary of paying?

"Here we are!" cried Mrs. Keane gaily, unlatching his own gate for him. "Behave yourself, Scobie."

He bade them good night and went up the path, shaking his head angrily at the way his eyes had let him down. He never doubted that, his sight restored to him, he would be able to tell which kind of criminal the dead man had been.

Calls came flooding in to the special police number over the next few days. A number of them were crank calls, including one from a psychic in Waterford who announced that the man in the racecourse was a "spoiled priest." The vast majority of the other calls came from women who thought the man might be their runaway husband. Because they had not seen him, in most cases, for many years, each of the women seemed to think it reasonable that the dead man *was* her roving lad, even though the picture didn't look much like the way she remembered him. These calls could be ignored when the runaway was too far advanced in age, but at least half a dozen had to be followed up. The errant husbands were located, some in surprising places like Canada or jail, and nothing came of it.

A smaller, but no less determined, group of callers claimed that the killing had been the result of a homosexual carry-on; half of the callers thought the killer was the unfortunate man's lover, and the other half said he had undoubtedly been done in by a vicious gang of youths who had gone "queer-bashing."

A concerned citizen came into the Fitzgibbon Street Station with a wallet he had discovered in a trash can on O'Connell Street. The wallet had been picked clean of money and credit cards, but it contained two items of interest: a reader's pass to the National Library of Ireland, and a laminated card, blank except for a photograph of a middle-aged man and the name *Henry J. Connors*. The man in the photograph had more hair than the man on the racecourse, but the picture had been taken five years earlier, and the resemblance was close enough to excite interest.

Since the Irish pass had been issued less than a month ago, a garda was dispatched to the National Library. The man in charge beamed with delight when shown the pass and the photograph, and pointed to the table where Henry J. Connors, a visiting American professor, was engaged in Yeats scholarship. Dr. Connors was very grateful to get his empty wallet back. It had been lifted from his jacket pocket while he stood in a queue at the GPO. The other card, he explained, was a British Library reader's pass that had just expired.

The dead man's clothing carried no clues. His pants had been manufactured in England, his shirt in Holland. His briefs and socks were of a sort you could purchase from the Marks & Spencer on O'Connell Street, and his shoes were Spanish. "Jesus," said Frank Browne disgustedly, "bloody Common Market. I've got a vest from *Portugal*."

"Don't go getting insular," Lynch replied. "My wife has a raincoat from Sri Lanka."

The antiterrorist Special Branchmen hovered ominously at the fringes of the police activity, coming and going in their blue Cortinas, bent on their secretive missions. They were convinced, as always, that the death on the racecourse was linked to the struggles in the North. No mention was made of their suspicions, but their presence in Balgriffin did not go unnoticed.

Nora knew she was about to slide into the dream by the peculiar silence that attended her sleep. It was the fag-end silence of just before dawn—the time when the soldiers raided. The setting of the dream was always the same —her father's house off the Falls Road in Belfast—but the cast of characters varied. Sometimes her husband, Paul, was there and sometimes not. Now that she had moved South, some of her neighbors in Balgriffin appeared occasionally. Tonight her father's house was crowded, as if there had been a party, and Imelda Kennerly and Kathleen Brannigan were present. Maureen, her daughter, crouched by the hearth clutching her clarinet case. Matty was at the window, and Nora wanted to call to him to come away, but—as always —everyone was too frightened to speak. Caught in the dream, she was nevertheless aware that she *was* dreaming, and if she could only struggle to consciousness before the soldiers' boots resounded in the street she could spare herself much pain.

Too late. An armored Saracen rumbled into the road, and from that moment she was gripped in panic and no longer knew herself to be dreaming. There were the dreadful sounds of the booted feet running, kicking at doors, the hollow sound of gun butts striking against wood, the brutal, excited cries of the soldiers. When the dreaded summons sounded at their door, Matty unaccountably turned from the window and said, "I'll go." She tried to forbid him to go to the door, but her voice would not function. She was paralyzed. The same seemed to be true of all the others, because no one made a move to stop Matty. He passed within a few inches of her on his way to the hall, but she could not even reach out and touch him. Tears streamed down her face and inwardly she screamed, but she was powerless to save her son.

She heard the sound of the door being unlatched, then a moment of ghastly silence culminating in a single shot. The gunfire released her paralysis and she went running into the hall, weeping and calling Matty's name. He lay on his face, as if he had been hurtled from a cliff, and blood from his head seeped into the carpet. She knew he was dead, but all she could say was, "Oh no, oh no, oh no," until she was screaming the words.

She wakened in her husband's arms, and the tears coating her cheeks were real. Paul was rocking her gently, bringing her to consciousness. "Nora, Nora," he said, "wake up, girl, it's only a dream. Wake now. Everything's fine, love, it's only the dream."

"Oh Christ," she snuffled against his chest, "I never thought I'd have that dream again. I thought I was past it."

He smoothed her hair, kissed her forehead. "Will we go and see the boy?" he asked. In the past, Paul had roused her and led her to their son's room, so she could see the living child, safe in his bed. It was the only thing that had worked. She shook her head. "I'll be all right," she said. "It's probably that business on the racecourse made me dream it. Go back to sleep, love."

She hunkered up against him, spoon style, and waited for his breathing to become calm and regular again. He had work the next day and needed his sleep. When she was sure he'd gone under, she crept from the bed and fumbled for her dressing gown. She went out on the landing and, as she'd known she would do, quietly opened the door to the trunk room and looked inside. The sodium light of one of the Crescent's three lamps revealed her son to her, lying peacefully on his back, his arms to his side with fingers curled as if he planned to catch rain in the basins of his hands. His chest rose and fell.

Downstairs, in the darkened kitchen, she plugged the kettle in and waited for the water to come to the boil. The stars had faded—it was almost the exact hour she had dreamed of—and she suddenly hated the people of Balgriffin for not understanding what a dreadful hour it was. They didn't dream of dead children and screaming soldiers and blood and chaos. Above all, they did not have to look into their children's rooms to make sure they were still alive. This murderous hour before dawn held no menace for them; they snored and burrowed their ways through it in perfect comfort, unaware that one hundred miles to the north whole families were dismembered, irrevocably, while they slept.

As she poured her tea she wondered why her dream was always, more or less, the same. It puzzled her, because it wasn't the way it had happened. Not at all.

Frank Browne was not pleased at the task Lynch had allotted him. It was to drop in at the Sinn Fein office on Parnell Square and pick up the latest copy of *An Phoblacht*, the official Republican newspaper. His reasons for feeling uncomfortable were so complex that he himself did not understand all of them.

On the simplest level, it was strange for an officer of the law to toddle into what was, after all, the bailiwick of the political arm of the IRA. It was *inappropriate*. As he unlatched the little rusty gate and made his way to the door, the roar of buses and commercial traffic deafening at this hour as they sped up the east quadrant of the square, he wondered if he was being photographed by Special Branchmen. The idea gave him an uneasy amusement, because the Specials were always good for a joke. He and Lynch thought of them as Keystone Kops. Paranoid, zealous—able to sniff out *international terrorism* from miles away—and always, for some reason, bungling.

And yet there was nothing remotely humorous about the awesome powers the Prevention of Terrorism Act conferred. Under the Special Powers Act, a person suspected of terrorist ties could be detained for up to seven days, without a lawyer or any other mediator to oversee the interrogation. At the end of the seven days, if the supposed culprit had signed a confession, he was turned over to the "Special" juryless court and sentenced.

The law had been intended for the Republicans of the Six Counties of Northern Ireland, but it had been invoked both in England and here, in the Republic. Frank had once thought of becoming a lawyer before entering police work, and the Draconian shape of the Special Powers Act repelled him. It tainted the pureness of what he liked to think of as Incorruptible Law. The concept, rather than the reality. He was in a very good position to know that those who served the law were all too often corruptible, but that the *concept* should be tampered with remained deeply distasteful to him.

In the Sinn Fein office, pictures of the dead hunger strikers from the long summer of 1981 mutely reproached him. Everywhere he looked he encountered scenes of horror, which was exactly what the rebels wanted. Jesus! Just in front of where a woman sat, reading a dog-eared book, was a stack of pamphlets featuring harrowing pictures of the children who had been murdered, mutilated, or brain-damaged by plastic bullets. Above her head was a huge poster, showing a hooded Provo, aiming an Armalite, in a field in Armagh or Tyrone. The text was something high-flown. Without looking, he knew it would be something Pearse or Connolly had spouted during the Rising of 1916.

He browsed among the books, pretending to read a selection from a life of Bobby Sands. The woman continued to read her book, as if he was invisible, or negligible, as a customer.

At last, he lifted a copy of *An Phoblacht* and laid his money down. It seemed such a paltry sum he selected, also, the pamphlet about the children and the plastic bullets.

"That's a new one, now," said the woman, nodding at him with a hard, cheerless smile.

He arrived at the Parnell Mooney pub five minutes in advance of Lynch. They had arranged to lunch there. Frank spread his copy of *An Phoblacht* across his knees and ordered a cheese sandwich and a Guinness. In the section of the newspaper entitled "War News," he came across two items—in Derry City, the IRA had exploded a bomb involving much property damage and no loss of lives, and in the rural border areas of Fermanagh, they had ambushed some paratroopers and critically wounded two of them.

In another column, he read of a kneecapping performed on a rapist who had told his victims he was a member of the IRA. He had been repeatedly warned, but he continued to maintain that he represented the Irish Republican Army, and for his rapes and his lies—intended to discredit them—they had punished him.

Frank wondered what he thought of this vigilante justice. As a member of the Garda Siochana, he deplored it, of course, but as a man with two small daughters he was glad that *someone* had stopped the bastard. Then, too, he remembered the business called "dirty tricks," an episode a few years back in which a man, captured after robbing a shop, had claimed that he was in the payroll of the Royal Ulster Constabulary. He had been urged to commit a series of petty crimes, posing as an IRA man. Plenty of red faces all around, especially when an officer in the British Army was implicated as the mastermind of the scheme.

In a sort of fit of moral exasperation, he drank off half his Guinness. It was dark and cool in the Parnell Mooney, and the place was beginning to fill with office girls on their lunch break. Because of the clement May weather, they were optimistically wearing pastel summer dresses. By the end of the afternoon, Frank reckoned, it would be lashing rain, and all the pretty girls would be cold and sodden, huddling miserably in the long queues for the buses back to Rathmines and Tallaght and Balgriffin. What was it in the Irish character that made them never learn? Why did they, and he, believe that things were going to get better when, in fact, they only got worse?

When Lynch came in, stopping at the bar to order his drink and sandwich, Frank was feeling almost morose. What in hell had Sean thought could be discovered in the pages of *An Phoblacht?* Had he thought to stumble on an item in which the IRA claimed responsibility for an obscure murder on a racecourse that hadn't been used in ten years? He hoped Lynch had not developed what they had always jokingly referred to as "Branchman Mentality."

"Here's yer effin' Provie rag," he said thuggishly, when Lynch settled heavily beside him. "I don't know what you hoped to glean from it, I swear to Christ I don't. And if there *was* anything, the Special Branch would be on to it and already have every Sinn Feiner in Dublin under interrogation."

"I'm well aware of that, Frankie," said Lynch. "Only thing is—they haven't my lyrical imagination." He took the paper from Frank, who had folded it back at the article about the kneecapping, and picked his way to the pages near the end.

"Here's the good stuff," he said, tapping a long column with his thumb.

Frank peered down and saw the names of the dead. It was a list of commemorations, of Memories of the Dead, signed by *Phil and Rosaleen, loving parents. Always remembered by Patrick and Josie, Bridie and Des, Moira and Frankie, Patsy and Geraldine and kids.*

Before Lynch secreted the paper in his attaché case, Frank read the words: *Mary, Queen of Ireland, Pray for Him.*

FOUR

Because the man who had been killed had not been one of them, the people of Balgriffin were not afraid. They assumed that he had been murdered elsewhere and their racecourse had been chosen by the killer as a good dumping ground. The very fact that the killer had not known how much the old grounds were used indicated that he was a stranger. If they had known what the police knew, they might have been uneasy.

Nora Keegan and Kathleen Brannigan met in Molloy's, the small local shop on the Gilligan Road. Kathleen was selecting some packages of frozen hamburger patties from the small freezer when her neighbor came in for a loaf and a packet of cigarettes. Kate was naturally quite friendly and gregarious, but she had never really tried to talk to Nora. This was because Nora, on first arriving in Balgriffin, had been so withdrawn and austere that she discouraged any attempts at intimacy. Kate had felt rebuffed. Lately, though, Nora Keegan had been looking much more cheerful, and Imelda Kennerly had assured Kate that she was, when you got to know her, good crack.

"Good morning, Mrs. Keegan," Kate said, jiggling the handles of the stroller. The baby had begun to fret.

"How's yourself?" Nora replied smartly. "And what a lovely wee girl she is! I know she's called Juliet, because Matty told me. I wonder is she named for the Shakespeare one?"

Kate clutched her frozen patties in amazement. Nora Keegan had just spoken more words, here in Molloy's shop, than she had ever heard issue from her lips in six months. Perhaps Imelda was right. "She is, you know," Kate said, opening her purse and pawing through it in search of her money. "When I was fourteen, we did the play at school, and I was desperate to play Juliet. I knew I hadn't a chance. Sister Michael wouldn't even let me read for the part. She cast me as Tybalt."

The baby had begun to wail, and Nora bent and calmed her, speaking nonsense words and smiling so charmingly that Juliet forgot her grievance and began to pull at Nora's long, dark hair.

"She's got the touch," remarked Mrs. Molloy, ringing up Kate's purchases.

Kate lingered in the shop so that she and Nora could walk back to the Crescent together. She felt the same exhilaration as she had done a few mornings back, anticipating the arrival of the police. Something new was about to happen! Perhaps she would invite Nora in for coffee, or Nora might invite her.

They strolled down Gilligan Road, the unaccustomed sun warming their shoulders, and quite soon came to the low wall surrounding the racecourse. It was queer, seeing it so empty and devoid of human life. The children were in school, of course, but it would be empty even when they returned, because the gardai had sealed it off. There was no way they could physically seal the vast field, but an edict had been posted, and two young gardai now stood at the main gate, looking bored and irritable.

Kate, who had never had the slightest urge to climb over the wall, now saw the racecourse as a forbidden Garden of Eden. The trees were unfurling their pale green leaves, and the little knolls were studded with white wildflowers and brilliant buttercups. A mysterious column of smoke rose from the farthest end, ascending to the pure blue sky like an arrow. The grandstand today seemed ugly—a black, jagged pile of debris covered by graffiti. Most of it was the paired names of lovers, but on the highest reach someone had spray-painted, in huge white letters, *IRA*. These letters were to be encountered frequently in Balgriffin, mysteriously blooming on walls and rocks and even the sides of Molloy's shop, and Kate had always wondered how they got there.

She didn't want to discuss this phenomenon with Nora, who would be made uncomfortable by any mention of the IRA, and she averted her eyes and said, "It looks so peaceful out there. Isn't it terrible, what happened?"

"Oh, aye," said Nora, without conviction, "death is always terrible." Then she turned and smiled broadly. "I'll tell you something, now," she said. "Don't go breaking your heart about not being Juliet. Your Sister Michael had the wrong play. If she'd been casting *The Taming of the Shrew*, now, you'd have played Kate. Certain. Red-haired girls *always* get to play Kate, it's a rule. In Belfast, Agnes Ryan was Kate, and it got me raging, because she was just not up to it. Life's unfair, you know? And would you like to come to my place and have coffee?"

"Great," said Kate. "I would."

About a quarter of a mile away from the Crescent lay a forlorn area of pitted roads and bleak buildings known as the industrial estate, although it was more a shambles than a thriving industrial park. There were a few small businesses, mainly in the automotive parts line, a publisher who printed Mass cards, and two warehouses. Several lean knacker horses grazed the balding meadowland that bounded the estate, and Lynch thought, bumping over the road that led to Denis McGuire's garage, that he had seldom seen a more dispiriting area.

He knew all about Denis McGuire, although he had never met him. McGuire was the man in whose garage the arms shipment from Australia had turned up. No suspicion had been attached to him, because he had immediately turned the cache over to the police. He claimed that he had been expecting a consignment of parts for Renault automobiles, had discovered an Australian crate inside the domestic one, and been shocked to uncover fifty thousand rounds of ammunition, twenty-five SLRs, and what looked like a rocket launcher. Under the circumstances, no one could doubt his innocence. The whole thing was put down to a break in paramilitary intelligence circuits, and forgotten by everyone but the Specials.

Lynch wanted to see Denis McGuire, not because of the arms, but because he was rumored to be talkative and suspicious of all his neighbors. He was, as he told everyone, a born-again Christian. This state of being, according to the detective who had answered McGuire's initial call, had seemed to fill McGuire not with brotherhood and charity but with a sense of holy contempt.

He rounded a corner, jouncing into a gully and narrowly missing a bony, sullen dog, and saw McGuire's garage dead ahead. It was a cavernous, dun-colored building with McGuire's name hand-painted over the entrance. The legs of someone lean and tall protruded from beneath an old blue Ford; otherwise there was not a soul in sight. Lynch parked his car and got out, sniffing the air for the coming rain. Of the legs he inquired, "Mr. McGuire?"

"Straight on through," replied a young voice.

Lynch wondered if the boy were the one who had briefly fallen under suspicion during the arms affair, or a new employee. They came and went—a rapid turnover with the young lads.

Inside the huge garage it was both cool and close. Several Fiats were in various stages of repair, and a Honda motorcycle. From somewhere he could hear the tinny sound of a radio playing an American pop song of the previous decade. It was something his daughter had liked, but Lynch couldn't remember the name of it. Something about brown eyes turning blue with sorrow.

His own eyes adjusted to the gloom, and he saw a small cubicle-office directly to his left. Inside sat a man wearing a light blue coverall. He was drinking bitter lemon straight from the bottle while he looked through some papers. He had red hair which seemed to have been carefully styled, and directly over his head was a message, black letters on white paper: *Praise Jesus!*

Lynch tapped on the door of the office, which was standing ajar, and introduced himself. McGuire, who had proffered a guarded smile upon first seeing him, looked wounded at a visit from the law.

"I thought that was water under the bridge," he said with a long-suffering air.

"And so it is, so it is," said Lynch heartily, "if you're referring to the Australian crate, Mr. McGuire."

"What then, brother?" His eyes, now revealed as green and oddly translucent, regarded Lynch with earnest, open puzzlement.

"The man discovered on the racecourse," said Lynch.

"Some of your boys have already dropped by my place. I've no idea in the world who that poor soul might have been." His lids dropped, as if in a moment of silent prayer.

"Well, that's my point, Mr. McGuire. Nobody has a clue, he might as well have been dropped from Mars for all that's known of him. It's enough to make a man uneasy."

"The Lord works in mysterious ways sometimes. Yes. Hallelujah! Mysterious ways."

"Are you intending to suggest that the Lord would deliberately obfuscate a police investigation, Mr. McGuire?"

Denis McGuire shook his head suavely, as if the very question begged the point so badly he could not bring himself to answer.

"I am an innocent in these matters," Lynch said. "You may choose to believe me, or not. I have come to you because my colleagues tell me that you are a fount of knowledge. They have assured me that you possess certain powers, powers which are only possessed by the truly awakened."

"Thank you, Jesus," said Denis McGuire, conversationally. It took Lynch some seconds to realize that the man was thanking the Conveyor of those powers. "I don't have any powers different from those our Lord will give to anyone who turns to Him, forsaking all others," McGuire said. "And it's painful sometimes, to be so aware of all the sin and evil in the world, the way you become when you're saved. It hurts to know that the wickedness could be stopped if only, if *only* everyone could see the light!" He smiled—a salesman's smile—and Lynch wondered if he knew that he spoke with an almost American accent when discussing his new religion.

"Surely you don't mean to tell me there's all that much wickedness in Balgriffin? The people here seem a decent lot."

"Decent! Oh, very far from decent, Sergeant, very far indeed! What with the teenagers fornicating on the racecourse and buying drugs in Portmarnock? And their parents are far worse. There are people here so steeped in sin I can scarcely stand to look at them. Mrs. Butler on the Gilligan Road, one who drives an Austin? She has four children, and only two are by her husband. Mrs. Kennerly in the Crescent, now, she drinks like a fish and was once found crawling down the road, stark naked, in the middle of the night. The barman over to the pub, the one from Sligo, once did time in jail, and yer man on the sea road, the postmistress's husband, he's been known to expose himself to women from his back window."

Denis McGuire took a long swig from his bottle of bitter lemon, as if the recitation of so much sinfulness had parched him.

Lynch composed his features so he would appear to be suitably serious, yet dubious. "Yes, it's very grave," he said, "but not the class of the crime committed on the racecourse. I'm sure you would agree that murder is the deadliest sin?"

A sea squall seemed to rise in McGuire's green eyes, a turbulence provoked by Lynch's suggestion that the sins of the people of Balgriffin were not quite up to scratch. To press his advantage, Lynch made as if to leave the cubicle.

"Oh, there's death here, all right," said McGuire in a thrilling, understated voice. "Yer woman from Belfast brought it with her when she came to live here."

"Mrs. Keegan?"

"Mrs. Keegan, whose husband drives a Renault from the Stone Age; 1979 it is, and the suspension shot to hell. When I had my bit of trouble here with that crate from Australia, I never thought of her at all. She hadn't moved into the Crescent yet. Unknown to me, she and her husband were living in Tallaght, waiting for the house to come available."

"The arrival, in Balgriffin, of one woman from Belfast hardly implicates her in a conspiracy to ship arms, Mr. McGuire."

"Not that alone. She's a brother who's gone to live in Australia. Melbourne."

Lynch shrugged. "Even so," he said. "Plenty of people go to Australia."

"But not," said McGuire triumphantly, "straight from prison."

"Are you referring to Long Kesh?" Lynch asked, using the Irish name for the place of internment in the North.

"The Maze," said McGuire. "I don't hold with the Brits, but I'll not call it Long Kesh. That's what them murdering thugs call it, and they give us a bad name. *Jesus. Praise* Jesus!"

The phone rang then, and Lynch nodded his thanks and left the shadowy garage. Just in time, he thought. In another few moments, the profane and pious portions of McGuire might grope together and show him something he did not wish to see. Clinically, it would be interesting, but it would also be beside the point.

He drove out of the industrial estate and back onto the main Gilligan Road. Dozens of hastily erected white stone houses lay grouped in what had once been meadows. They had been built to accommodate the hoardes who were seeking to move from the city's nucleus; detectives had questioned the residents of each one of them, and still had come up with nothing. Not until he reached the Crescent and the racecourse did some semblance of beauty lie over Balgriffin again. The clouds, bringing rain, shifted over the deserted grounds so rapidly that the grassy hummocks appeared to be undulating between light and shadow. The church seemed to float before him, blue-white in the middle distance, and when he rounded the corner he found the tide in, and the sea as green as a pale jade scarf Una had worn on their last holiday.

He stopped to let a procession of children cross. They were all clutching books, on their way to the library—a small, two-room cottage on the seafront. The children made him wince, for only yesterday he had forced himself to read through the book about the plastic bullets. Page after page of smiling children's portraits with the word KILLED slashed across, and a brief account of the circumstances of death. Occasionally a luckier child would have been merely BLINDED, or INJURED. Neither in the plastic bullet pamphlet nor in *An Phoblacht* had he found what he had been searching for among the notices commemorating the dead—a date of death corresponding to that on the racecourse. It had been a long shot, but in a case so peculiar he could not afford to ignore even the feeblest impulse.

He had discovered something, though. Among the children who had been injured—children whom the British Army claimed had been rioting, although the people of the ghettos had said otherwise—was Mrs. Keegan's son. Matty was a curiosity, because he was the only child who had survived a serious head wound who had not been brain-damaged.

The children on their way to the library had passed on to safety, and Lynch drove out along the sea road. Glancing to his right, he saw a man selling vegetables from a van. He was on the inland fork of the Balgriffin Road, just next to the pub. There was a small queue of housewives lined up, and a few loitering children. An old man stood against the wall, smoking, and Lynch saw that the boy talking to him was Matty. He wanted to look at this unremarkable tableau for a long time, but now there was a stream of traffic behind him and he moved on. The houses on the front obscured his view of the vegetable seller and Matty and the old man, but their image remained with him all the way back to Dublin.

"What did you do when the bullets came flyin'?" Matty was saying at the precise moment Sean Lynch had noticed him.

"Hid under the bed," Andy Halloran said. Then his shoulders shook with silent laughter, and he repeated the words. "Hid under the bed."

They had been discussing Mr. Halloran's role in the Easter Rising of 1916, when he was a bicycle messenger boy at the age of twelve. Matty enjoyed talking to Mr. Halloran, whom he met on the days when the vegetable man brought his van around. His mother sent him down to buy lettuce or onions, and Mr. Halloran was always there, smoking and just leaning against the wall. They had met, formally, when Matty retrieved the box of matches Mr. Halloran had dropped.

"Is that young Gervaise Doherty?" the old fellow had asked.

"No, I'm Matty Keegan."

"A new man in town. That's grand."

Normally conversations with the old and infirm were rather a trial, but Matty had instantly decided that old Mr. Halloran was out of the ordinary. He didn't try to worm secrets out of you the way so many grown-ups did, and though he must have known from Matty's voice where he was from, he made no comment. Matty was sick of people saying, "This must be quite a change from what you're used to," or "I guess you had a rough time, eh?"

Then, too, Mr. Halloran said startling and amusing things. Once, when Matty explained he had to go to the shop to buy some Chef's Sauce for his mother, Mr. Halloran had said, "You can polish a brass rail with Chef's Sauce. Comes up lovely. I did that once when I worked at the Great Northern Hotel." Another time he had absentmindedly offered Matty a cigarette from his pack, as if he had forgotten that Matty was only twelve. That had been gratifying.

"The first pint I ever had was after the Black and Tans lobbed a bomb into the Customs House," he said now. "I was thirteen, and sweeping up, and didn't a smallish bomb come whistling in? All the survivors agreed they needed a drink, after, and one of them said, 'This lad must have one, too,' and so I did."

Matty thought their childhoods had been remarkably similar, if you didn't count the smoking and drinking and working at various jobs. "What do you think about that business on the racecourse, Mr. Halloran?" he asked.

"Well now, Matty, I'm greatly hampered. I don't see as well as I once did, and I'm sorry to tell you I never saw his picture on the television."

"I can describe him for you, if that's what you'd like?"

Mr. Halloran nodded soberly. "I know he had a longish sort of a head. I'd been told," he said.

"He wasn't special-looking, or anything like that, you know? He'd a regular nose, not big or small, and he was getting bald. Cheekbones reminded me of red Indians you see in American films. His eyes looked kind of surprised, but I overheard my father say that wasn't anything to the way they must have looked when *it* happened, you see what I mean. The police photographer must have got the doctors to make him look as normal as possible. There's only one thing I noticed. They said he was in his forties, but he looked much older than that. *Much* older."

"Forties is a lovely age, a lovely age," said Mr. Halloran wistfully. "How old do you think he should have looked, Matty?"

Matty realized that his companion was making a mistake, thinking that he, at twelve, did not know how middle-aged grown-ups should look. "What I know is, my da is thirty-seven, and this man looked old enough to be his father."

"Would it be a matter of wrinkles?"

"No. Something else. I don't know what, but he looked all used up, like."

Mr. Halloran laughed softly and said something that sounded like "oh boys, oh boys." Then he thanked Matty very earnestly and said, "You're the only one in Balgriffin with eyes."

"Well, it was nice bendin' yer ear," Matty said, using an expression his grandfather favored. "I have to go get a nice aubergine for my mother."

FIVE

Rain came, and then hail, and it was as if the temperate days of May had never been. The waters of the estuary were gunmetal gray, and sea gulls screamed down the chimneys, and the coalmen who came door to door reappeared. Balgriffin was once more wrapped in its wintertime odor of sweetly burning turf, and the clothes on the line never dried.

"May showers bring August flowers," Imelda Kennerly joked at the bus stop. "If we're lucky."

Nora smiled, standing beneath her streaming umbrella, and cursed her luck that she and Imelda should have chosen the same day to go in to the city on errands. She would have been glad of the company of her new friend Kathleen, but Kate's baby daughter had a cold and could not be brought out. It wasn't that she didn't like Imelda, who had been kind to her right from the first—it was something that had been tormenting her since the murder.

The double-decker came grunting in to the stop, and the two women climbed to the higher level, so Imelda could smoke on the journey to Dublin. They settled in seats near the front, and Imelda immediately lit up. Her glasses were steamed over and her damp hair emitted the odor of Harp Lager, which was her favorite shampooing material. She was a large, rather red-faced woman who possessed two features of extraordinary beauty. She had wide-set eyes so dark they appeared almost black, which in a country of blue-eyed people gave her a distinctly exotic look, and legs so spectacularly turned she wore shorts whenever possible and walked like a queen. Today, with shorts out of the question and her eyes obscured behind the beaded lenses of her glasses, she was merely an untidy countrywoman from Cork who smoked too much.

"I drank the rest of the vodka last night," she confided to Nora, "and when that ran out I broke into Jim's whiskey. I've never been fond of whiskey, but if you put it in with red lemonade it's tolerable. Jesus, didn't I hear it from him this morning? I told him it was inadvertent, said I'd been rearranging the bottles when the whiskey spilled, but that's a stupid story. I could tell the minute it popped out of my mouth—it didn't even make sense —but my head was like a big balloon and I couldn't be troubled to invent another one."

Nora said that liquor, in general, did nothing but depress you beyond a certain point, and that the answer to Imelda's unhappiness lay, not in the bottom of a bottle, but elsewhere. She heard herself and despised the conventional, comfortless nature of her words, but the truth was that mention of Jim Kennerly had touched her sore spot. She knew that Jim was supposed to be having an affair with a young girl who worked in a Portmarnock disco— indeed, she had heard it from Imelda herself—but it was not his infidelity that so troubled her.

She had never liked Jim, right from the start. He was falsely jovial, with his booming, mirthless laugh, and she thought him corrupt, the sort of man who was forever searching out illicit "deals" and cultivating the men who made them possible. The first time she had gone, with Paul and the children, to one of the Kennerlys' barbecues, she had had an unreasonable fear. It was that the black hairs sprouting on Jim Kennerly's knuckles would find their way into her food and poison her.

"Holy Mother," groaned Imelda. "You're about as sympathetic as a backed-up septic tank, you are. I've got ten years on you, Nora Keegan, just ye wait until ye're my age and see if the old salvation doesn't beckon from the bottle. Just wait!"

Nora laughed, which seemed to appease Imelda, and then the young conductor came to take their tickets, and they rode companionably through Raheny, racketing along toward the Five Lamps, and Nora released certain signals which let Imelda know that she was on her side, after all.

And she was. The thing that had been troubling her was, she thought, trivial. Certainly she would never have mentioned it to the gardai, much less the Branchmen. She had been raised in a part of the world where the police were regarded as criminals, and she would not inform, not even for a man who seemed as decent as that Lynch. And still, mention of Jim Kennerly troubled her in a particular way. She had not seen him since the murder, but she had seen him just before it must have taken place.

A man got on the bus at Fairview Park. He did not come up to the top, but both she and Imelda had noticed him waiting in the rain. He had neither umbrella nor raincoat, and his hair was plastered to his skull in long points.

"Yer man's likely a poet or a schoolmaster," said Imelda, a hint of contempt in her voice. "One thing I'll say for Jim—he's always aware of his appearance. He's never caught out."

"Would he iron his own shirts if he hadn't you to do it?" Nora asked.

"You're the sharp one. Answer is no, but he'd find another woman to do it."

At mention of another woman, Imelda's voice descended to a bitter, knowing tone. Nora wanted to fish about and hook some small and reassuring truth that would exonerate Kennerly and release her from her guilt. "It's true Jim's always well turned out," she said. "He seems so fit! Does he exercise at all?"

"Only the golf," said Imelda. "But *exercise?* Sure, Nora, you know my Jim! He's bone-lazy, lies about waiting for me to put his dinner in his mouth, complains when it comes time to mow the grass—exercise, me arse. He doesn't even like it when he can't avoid sweating, says it ruins his shirts. No, Nora, the most rigorous activity James Kennerly engages in is the one we'll refrain from mentioning. That, and lifting a pint to his lips."

"I thought he might jog," said Nora, aware of how inane she sounded. They were entering Dublin now, passing beneath the railway overhang and maneuvering toward the chaotic City Centre where they would both debark. She hadn't much time. "I mean, not when they all could see him. I had it in mind that he might jog at night."

"*Jog?*" screamed Imelda. "My Jim? Let me tell you, Mrs. Keegan, dear, that Jim regards jogging as the work of Satan. It's an aberration so far as he's concerned, a plan cooked up by fairies in America to unsex the average European male. He would as soon jog as he would put on a dress and preside at Ladies' Night."

Nora laughed dutifully, but she felt a new chill that had nothing to do with the rain or her wet shoes. It was the story she had been telling herself—that Kennerly was one of those secret runners, the kind who don't want others to see them and so choose odd hours in which to exercise themselves. She saw now how ridiculous this was, how unbelievable, and nearly gasped aloud at how transparently foolish her little scenario had been.

As the bus drew close to the terminus in the City Centre, Imelda began to complain of the far-flung places her errands would compel her to negotiate in the driving rain, but Nora did not offer to accompany her. They were not the sort of friends who shopped together. "See you," Imelda said. "If you get back middish-afternoon, come have some coffee. I'll pour what's left of Jim's whiskey into it, and to hell with him."

Nora watched her trudge off in the direction of Capel Street. Fervently she wished she had not been looking from the window of her bedroom that night. She had a particular aversion for people who snooped and peered from curtained windows; such people were hoping to have their worst fears confirmed—against the odds, they wished to see something momentous and horrifying, and if there was nothing on the grand scale going on, well, something petty and mean would do almost as well. Missus So-and-so's delivery man outstaying his visit, or Mr. X's car driving into the Crescent in such a way as to indicate that he had taken more drink than was good for him. There had been a famous novel, Nora had never read it, about how such people could ruin whole lives in a village in rural Ireland. It had been called *The Valley of the Squinting Windows*, and she had always loved the title. She had understood, immediately, what the text of the novel must be, and purely from the title. If she had ever had an impulse, growing up in Belfast, to spy on her neighbors, it had been quashed by the words *squinting windows*, and she honored personal privacy above all things.

Why then, of all the people in the Crescent, did she have to be the one who had glanced innocently from her bedroom window at nearly midnight? On a weeknight, midnight was quiet. Even with the summer closing at the pub, which prolonged drinking hours until eleven instead of ten-thirty, midnight was a quiet hour in the Crescent. People had to work the next day. They were in bed. Who could afford to drink until eleven, except on the weekends?

She had knelt at the window, full of the new sense of tranquillity that had lately invaded her being, and watched the play of the yellowish sodium lamps on the cream stone of the opposite houses. As clouds drifted over the hard, new moon, she had heard the comforting sound of Paul's regular breathing behind her. Maureen slept in her room, Matty in his. All was right with her world. No tanks or armored cars would roar into the Crescent; no rifle butts would resound on her door in Balgriffin. No damage would be done.

And then, as if she had slid into a dream, she had seen the door of Imelda's house crack open. A shadowy figure, dressed in a dark jogging suit, had emerged, and Jim Kennerly, with a furtive and desperate look to his walk, had scurried along, heading for the Gilligan Road. There was no way out of the Crescent except by the Gilligan Road, and Nora could not say with any degree of certitude where it was Jim Kennerly was going in his jogging suit, but she thought at the time that he was on his way to the racecourse.

It had seemed odd at the time. Now it seemed an event of great importance. The jogging myth had been destroyed, and Nora wondered where her loyalty lay. One thing was certain—she could never, ever, be an Informer.

Exactly a week to the day after they had found the body, the crime still a mystery to everyone in Balgriffin, the children met to discuss their parents. They decided to meet on the seafront, directly after school, but since rain was lashing down on the estuary bed and it would have been very uncomfortable, they went instead to Janie Keane's house.

They had chosen Janie's place because they could have more privacy there. The Keanes had a corner house, and several additions and improvements had been accomplished over the years by Janie's father. He had built a large new kitchen for his wife, turned the old kitchen into the living room, and the former living room now served as a playroom. None of this would have been possible if the Keanes had been in the center houses of the Crescent, and they had had to badger the Dublin Corporation for a long time before permission had been granted. Now they were the envy of their neighbors to the left, who no longer spoke to them.

Janie ushered her cohorts into the playroom, and then went in search of refreshment.

"I wish *we* could have an enlargement," said Gervaise, glancing around the tiny room with approval. There was a xylophone in one corner, and on a low table beside it, a fleet of Match Box cars once cherished by Janie's older brother and now abandoned.

"I'd say there's no one here would benefit from an extra room like me," Terry said reprovingly. "I'm sleeping on the pull-out now, in the sitting room."

They felt stilted and unnatural with each other today, but the meeting was necessary. They waited for Janie to return, hoping a glass of orange drink might loosen them up. "How's Wolfe Tone?" Matty Keegan asked Terry.

"He's grand, thanks," said Terry.

A boy called Kevin, who had been with them that day on the racecourse, cleared his throat and said, "I hear where they've smuggled a machine for birth control into Trinity College. Some students brought it over from England on the ferry."

"A machine with *pills?*" Terry asked.

Kevin seemed to lose confidence, even interest. "I think condoms," he said, shrugging. "I'm not too sure, now. I overheard some people."

Janie came back then, carrying a tray with glasses and one large bottle of American ginger ale. She had put crisps in a bowl, and was panting slightly from her exertions. Her mother, she told them, had taken her smallest sister to Portmarnock while she visited a friend. They had the house to themselves.

Gravely, her glasses slipping down onto her nose, she poured out ginger ale and declared the meeting under way. There was an uncomfortable silence, and then they all began to speak at once. Janie went to the xylophone and sounded a deep, melodious call to order.

Terry, remembering his leaderlike qualities, took the moment. "We've convened this meeting because some of us have been noticing that our parents are, well, not acting right, you know? Ever since we found yer man on the racecourse, it's been downhill. We're here to discuss the situation and, and—"

"Find solutions," said Janie.

"Exactly right. Does anybody want to make a report?"

"I'll begin," said Janie. "I'm the only girl among you, and it's true enough I cried a bit over that man, but it wasn't desperate. Just a few tears, like, and nothin' hysterical. My mother's got it in her head that I'm so sensitive I'm havin' nightmares and all, and it's not true. She wants to take me to the doctor's surgery and get me tablets, and I don't want to go. The way I look at it, if they don't catch whoever killed that man, our lives are goin' to be miserable."

"Too effin' true," said Gervaise. "My mother used to stay home except for weekends, and now she's at the pub every night. I've got to mind my brother, he's a bold monster, and all because she thinks she'll hear about the murder if she goes to the pub every night. My da can hold his drink, but she's got a sore head every morning now."

"Mine don't drink much," said Terry. "That's not my problem. My main complaint is that we can't go out on the racecourse anymore. My cousin in Malahide was going to let me borrow his dirt bike in good weather and have a go on the stretch far out, beyond the grandstand, and now we're not allowed. Christ, my da's got this idea, you know, that it's all to do with drugs, and now he gives me a sermon every day about how I need hope, not dope."

"My da says he'll string me up by the thumbs in the toolshed if he ever finds any drugs on me," said the boy called Kevin. "He never used to talk that way. It's unfair. All I did was jump over the wall and go with youse and Wolfe Tone to the grandstand that day."

"We didn't ask to find that effin' body," said Gervaise.

"Order!" cried Janie, striking the xylophone. "Was your hand raised there, Rory?"

"Yeah," said Rory Kennerly, ducking his head and cracking his knuckles. "About two days after we found yer man, I waked in the middle of the night, needin' a pee, and when I'd finished I was about to go back to my room when I see this dark shape at the foot of the stairs. I go down real quiet, and when I'm on the last rung, I recognize that it's my mother. She's lyin' with her cheek on the carpet and singin' to herself. I tried to raise her up and get her to her bedroom, but she won't go. She's singin' 'The Boys of the Old Brigade,' real quiet, into the carpet." Rory shook his head, remembering. "I went back upstairs to get my da," he said. "I thought he'd know how to bring her back up. Thing was—he wasn't there. The bed on his side was all empty."

"Where was he?" asked Terry. "Did you find him at all?"

"No," said Rory. "He was gone."

"What did you do?" asked Janie.

"I left her there and went back to bed," said Rory. "She was happy, it seemed. Next morning, she was frying sausages."

A silence descended on the playroom. Each of the children was imagining what they would have done on discovering a mother singing into the carpet. Rory sighed and looked at his boots.

"I think Matty Keegan has yet to be heard from," said Terry. "It seems to me that Matty has important news."

"The Special Branch was at our place few days ago," Matty said. "They were questioning my mother, tryin' to make out there was some connection between the dead man and some guns that were found here just before we came?" The others were now used to his Northern habit of making everything sound like a question, but when Matty didn't continue, Terry realized that it *had* been a question. Matty wanted to know if they knew about the arms shipment in the industrial estate.

"Yeah, right," he said. "They found the stuff in crazy Denis McGuire's garage. But why should those Branchmen think your mother would know anything about it?"

"On account of them coming from Australia," said Matty. "My mam's brother, my Uncle Tommy, he lives in Australia."

Janie burst into peals of laughter. "That's the stupidest thing I ever heard!" she gasped. "Lots of Irishmen live in Australia."

"Tommy, he was in the Kesh. In prison, they said for membership, but we all knew he wasn't in the IRA. Doesn't matter, though. Most of the men and boys on our road go to prison for a while. It's just the way it's done. Important thing is—so far as *they're* concerned, my Uncle Tommy is a terrorist now operatin' from Australia."

"Why did he go there?" Gervaise asked.

"Wouldn't you?" said Terry. "If just by living in a certain neighborhood you could get scooped and put in prison anytime?"

"He'd had it with Belfast," said Matty. "He was fed up." He took a swig of ginger ale and then, looking at his shoes as Rory had done, he said, "This isn't good for my mother, now. She can't take being questioned, it's too much like home. She's worried all the time, she tries to hide it, but I can tell. Until this business is cleared up, she'll be unhappy."

"I hear where they're no closer to solving it than they were the day we found him," said Kevin.

"I'm sorry about your mother, Matty," said Terry, "but it looks like all of us are going to be unhappy until they find the killer. What are we going to do? Anybody have a plan?"

Gervaise cleared his throat as if to ready himself for an important announcement, and then was silent. Rory munched a crisp and looked solemn.

"We could *invent* a killer," said Janie excitedly. "After all, we're the ones who found the dead man. We could say we were too scared to remember, at first, and now we've had time to think it's all come back to us."

"What's all come back to us?" Terry said.

"Wait, I'm thinking," said Janie.

"If you mean pickin' some poor bastard who lives here and telling the police he did it, count me out," said Matty.

"Of course I don't mean that," said Janie. "I meant we could make up a man we had all seen—a stranger—and then they'd go off looking for him and take the pressure from us."

"I don't see how that would work," said Rory.

"She means a foreigner," said Terry. "Isn't that it, Janie? Make it something so far away it couldn't involve anyone in Balgriffin?"

"The French Connection," said Gervaise.

"No," said Janie, "that's too close. I had in mind an American. Nobody would ever catch him. Not if he doesn't exist."

For the next fifteen minutes, until the sound of Mrs. Keane's car pulling up in the driveway dissolved the meeting, the children perfected their plan. When Janie's mother poked her head into the playroom and exclaimed, "Now isn't this a grand group?" they seemed to be exemplary children of the Crescent, who had elected to come in out of the rain and pass the afternoon in quiet camaraderie.

Just before he left the Keanes' house, Matty came to Janie, laying his hand with a self-conscious and conspiratorial manner on her plump shoulder. "Stick to it about the tablets," he murmured. "They're no good at all. If she has her way and the doctor gives them to you, just flush them down the toilet."

"Right," said Janie. "I will."

SIX

Henry Connors was more than eager to talk to the police. He confessed that his Yeats scholarship was driving him up the wall, allowed as how he would rather be an honest carpenter than a professor of literature, and assured Lynch frequently that his sabbatical in Ireland had revealed worlds to him. "You're all so damned *articulate!*" he shouted at intervals. "Language *means* something here!"

"It's grand of you to say so," Lynch would reply whenever the Professor praised Irish conversational skills. It made him uncomfortable, of course, because every time Connors marveled at the Irish way with words, it made Lynch wonder what he had expected when he debarked in Dublin. A country that had produced a Yeats despite itself, by accident?

The interview was being conducted in the lobby of the National Library. All around them were depressing posters from the year of the Great Famine, mounted with consummate skill by the sort of person who knew how to do such things. Lynch could read the death toll over Professor Connors's left shoulder; beyond his right was a British *Plan for Genocide*, which involved a massive *Emigration Plot*. They were standing in the lobby because Lynch did not wish to disturb the other researchers. Connors had been at the same table for five hours, he said, and would be only too happy to stretch his legs.

"Well, sir," said Connors, "I know you didn't come over here to discuss Yeats. I suppose it's about that wallet of mine?"

Lynch shook his head, wondering why he was bothering with this open, obviously innocent American professor. He would bet his last pound that Dr. Connors had never been in trouble with the law in his life. His big forehead, made more domelike by his receding hair, was wrinkled now in honest puzzlement. He didn't look much like the dead man, but Lynch could imagine that in a poorly photographed permit picture there might seem to be a resemblance.

"I would like to ask you some routine questions, Professor," said Lynch. "Nothing for you to be alarmed about—we're simply trying to place some people at a particular time. When did you come to Ireland?"

"On March first. I have a six-month sabbatical, you see. I'll be researching here and in England, at the British Library. But look here, if you don't mind, what's this all about?"

"A man was killed in Balgriffin last week. You'll recall the event, it was shortly before your wallet was returned to you."

"But surely you don't think I had anything to do with that?" Henry Connors looked delighted at such a strange turn of events; probably, Lynch thought, it made a nice break from his Yeats scholarship.

"Of course I do not," he told him. "I am checking on a peculiar report, because I'm obliged to. In a crime of this sort, especially when the victim has not been identified, it's necessary to follow up every possible lead. Have you ever been to Balgriffin, Dr. Connors?"

"No, at least not to the place itself. I passed it once, on my way to Howth. That's as close as I ever came." He smiled at Lynch. "What's this report you're following up on? I wish I could help, by the way."

"My informant tells me that a stranger was seen in Balgriffin on the day of the crime, an American. He talked to some of the children, apparently. Their description of the man, incomplete as it was, might have been a description of you."

"Well, that's strange, Sergeant, and I see why you had to act on it, what with my wallet turning up, but lots of men would sound like me if a kid described them, don't you think?"

"I do indeed." *He was tallish-sized and goin' bald,* Terry Brannigan had said on the phone. *About the age of the man who got killed.* Lynch was not about to tell the professor that his only informants were children, and that they had sprung the mysterious American on him only that morning. Terry was their spokesman, and he had assured Lynch that all the children who found the body had seen the American the day of the murder. Nor would he tell Connors that he planned to rendezvous with the children in Balgriffin when they were released from school. The whole thing had a slightly surrealistic tinge to it.

"Thank you for your time," Lynch said. "I'm sorry to disturb you at your work—"

"Oh God," said Connors, "anytime, Sergeant. Anytime. Yeats is a remarkable poet, and I love teaching him, but scholarship just isn't my line. What I mean is, I can't seem to write about him the way he deserves to be written about. I am not lyrical, as a writer, and I only wish they'd leave me in peace and let me teach. We academics have a saying in the States: publish or perish."

"Yes," said Lynch, "I've heard of it. I wish you luck."

Connors seemed to notice the Famine material for the first time. "Hell of a thing, that famine," he said in a lowered voice. "My people came over in the wake of the famine. From Galway. I can still remember my grandfather, how much he hated the British."

"I suppose you were right here, at the library, on the day in question, Professor? It was a Tuesday, you'll recall. The twelfth." Lynch spoke as if in afterthought.

"Yes, yes, I'm sure I was," said Connors vaguely, and then he smacked his forehead and grinned and said, "No. No, I had the flu last week, a forty-eight-hour dose. I was recovering when that nice young garda brought my wallet over. Still shaky. I was in bed all Monday and Tuesday."

"I'm sorry to hear that," said Lynch. "Our changeable weather is the culprit, I'm afraid. Did you see a doctor?"

"No, I'm not much for doctors. I just gobbled aspirin and took that wonderful stuff you buy in the stores—what's it called? Something to do with lemons."

"Ah yes, it's called Lemsip," said Lynch. "My wife is very fond of it. I expect your landlady recommended it to you?"

"She couldn't very well do that," said Connors. "She'd gone to Leitrim to visit her sister. I see what you're getting at, Sergeant, and you're right. Not a soul saw me on the eleventh or twelfth. I have no alibi." He laughed. "I'm sure it hasn't come to that? I don't have to have an alibi to prove I wasn't the mysterious American haunting the streets of Balgriffin?"

"Not a'tall," said Lynch. "My curiosity comes from force of habit."

He again wished the American luck with his research, sneaking a quick look at his hands. Professor Connors had large and powerful-looking hands. Even though he was sure that the man was innocent of any crime, he had to admit that Connors's hands, if not his soul, were quite capable of garroting an enemy.

" 'Things fall apart,' " he said in farewell.

" 'The centre cannot hold,' " Connors quoted back, and then he went bounding back up the stairs, returning to his research.

"Yanks wear plaid," said Gervaise. "Did you ever notice how they're always wearin' plaid pants and such? And they have lots of cameras hanging around their necks—two or three."

"The kind of a fella we're imagining wouldn't be like a *tourist*," Terry said contemptuously. "He'd try to blend in, wouldn't you say?"

"Not if he was trying to *pass* for a tourist," Janie said. "We have to get a good picture of this man. Not too clear, or some poor man might just happen to be visiting Dublin and match up. We don't want too much detail, you know? But we have to make sure we're all making up the same man. He has to be clear in *our* eyes."

They were congregated around one of the green benches on the seafront. Wolfe Tone, as always, had followed his master and was vainly trying to interest them all in a run on the soggy estuary. This was their agreed-upon meeting place with the detective, and a last-minute panic had set in. Terry had placed the call, had described the man in the vaguest terms, had given the invented reason for coming up with vital information so late in the game. "We were scared," Terry had told the detective-garda. "Yer man said it was to be a secret. He bought us crisps at the pub, and asked about the race-course. We were afraid he'd come after us if we told." This was clearly not enough. Janie had frantically scribbled out a subtext which Terry had read into the phone.

"Our parents didn't know," Terry had read, like the most leaden of actors. "We were supposed to be home, doin' our schoolwork, and they've forbid us to talk to strangers."

"I know!" cried Rory. "Say he was sneezin'!"

"Why?" asked Janie.

"Americans always get colds when they come here. It adds the wee touch of realness."

"Reality, Rory," said Janie.

"Better agree on the cold," said Matty in his sonorous voice, "because yer man is after parkin' on the seafront. He's on his way?"

They looked up and saw the policeman, Mr. Lynch, walking toward them. He wore a belted raincoat that accentuated his portly middle, and his face was grave. The children instinctively liked him—he seemed a kind man—but today he seemed especially old. The pouches beneath his eyes seemed to have been filled with the receding water of the estuary, and appeared gray-blue.

"Are we for the cold?" Terry whispered.

They nodded their heads.

"Everything else as before?"

"Yes," hissed Janie.

Lynch stooped to pat Wolfe Tone's scraggly head in passing, and greeted them with threatening words. "Do I have the pleasure of indulging in a secret meeting with Balgriffin's Junior Mafia?"

"Oh, we're not as bad as that," Janie said, scooting down the bench to make room for him. Lynch sat heavily in the middle. He was flanked by Janie and Gervaise to the right, and Kevin on the left. Rory and Matty stood uneasily before him, and Terry, aware of his leader's role, paced along the seafront with authority.

"Would you condescend to join us at all?" Lynch called to Terry. "You were the man made the call, young Terry. I'm bound to get to the bottom of this."

Terry reacted with dignity. He came to stand with Rory and Matty and said, "I've been feelin' very guilty, no matter what you think, Mr. Lynch. I know I've been withholding information from the police, and I'm sure that's a serious offense. I take complete responsibility, because I'm the one who convinced the others."

"Better late than never, son," said Lynch. "I'd like to hear about it. Everything you remember. When did you first see him, and where?"

"Just as we were coming back from school, on the Gilligan Road," said Terry. "He was by the place where the bus stops, and I got the feeling he'd just got off the bus."

"There was a bus going by when we left Molloy's shop," said Janie. "He could have been on that one. He was just standing there, looking out over the racecourse."

"Did he speak to you, then?"

"Yes," said Gervaise. "He was friendly, like. He said 'Hi, kids,' in this broad Yank accent. He wanted to know if any of us remembered the old Balgriffin racecourse, or if we were too young."

"We told him we didn't remember," said Terry. "It was all over when I was born."

"I asked him if he was on holiday, if he was enjoyin' himself," Terry said. "That was the only time he said anything peculiar, like. He said, 'You *might* say I'm on holiday,' and he laughed."

"What was he wearing?"

"Plaid trousers," said Gervaise with conviction. The others nodded, all except Janie.

"Well, Miss Keane, you seem unsure about the plaid trousers," said Lynch. "Do you remember him differently?"

"No, they were plaid all right," said Janie. "But I wouldn't want you to get the wrong idea, now. They weren't those loud ones Americans sometimes wear. They were a dullish plaid, and old, as if he'd had them a long time. I don't remember what he wore on top. He wasn't all that noticeable, really."

"A gray cotton jacket," burst out Kevin. "I remember."

"What happened next, after you talked about the racecourse?"

"He walked along with us up the road," said Terry. "We passed the Crescent—we were all supposed to go straight home—and ended up right here, where we are now. He was asking us about our schoolwork, what it was like in school in Ireland, and it was interesting, talking to a Yank, and we just lost track of the time."

"People would have seen you, then," said Lynch. "If you were all sitting here by the estuary with a man in plaid trousers, there are bound to be lots of witnesses who noticed."

The children were silent, considering. "Why would anyone take any notice of us?" Terry said at last. "They see us every day. And there are so many kids in Balgriffin—just look."

It was true. At that very moment three girls cycled past and a host of small boys, younger than Terry and his friends, came clambering up over the seawall farther down. "They'd see us, I'd say, without really noticin'," said Terry.

"What happened next?"

"After a while he said he had to be goin', and then he walked off toward the train station. It's funny, looking back, because he never said anything about himself. Not his name, or where he was from in the States."

"You've left something out," said Lynch, opening a tube of fruit candies and offering them round. "The crisps, to be exact."

"Yeah, I remember the crisps," shouted Rory nervously. "Yer man went across to the pub and brought us crisps. Mine was cheese and onion, I remember."

"Miss Janie Keane? Did you partake of the crisps?"

"Mine were plain," said Janie, closing her eyes fastidiously.

"And you, Matty? What kind of crisps did you order from the man in the plaid trousers?"

"I told him any kind would do," said Matty Keegan stoically. "I'm not that particular."

"Well then," said Lynch, beaming at the children, "Tom Mulligan is sure to remember your benefactor. It's a rare day in Balgriffin when an American enters a pub and places an order for six packets of crisps and leaves directly. I'd like you to wait here while I saunter across and ask Mr. Mulligan if he can describe this strange man. You'll not desert me at this stage, will you?"

"Course not," said Terry. "But Tom may not remember him. He could have bought them crisps off Peter, the other barman."

"I'll bear that in mind."

As soon as Lynch had passed out of their midst, Janie leaned forward. "You think you're so clever, Terry Brannigan. You had to make up that extra bit about the crisps, and now we'll be found out! You've ruined everything."

"Go easy, Janie," said Rory.

"We're all in this together," counseled Kevin.

They sat in a morose and uneasy silence until Lynch returned. He was bearing six bags of crisps, exactly as their mythical Yank had done, and what he said as he distributed them was extremely disturbing.

"Tom remembers him, all right, clear as anything. Big, balding Yank in plaid. Now—you children eat your crisps and go home and do your homework. I thank you for your cooperation, and ask that you keep this information from your parents for a while. Understood?"

Six heads nodded.

"I'd eat quick if I were you," said Lynch. "It's going to rain."

Imelda Kennerly surveyed her washing line with deep displeasure. The things were nearly dry, given another hour they would be dry, but as sure as God had given her a heart-shaped birthmark high on the slope of her left buttock, it was about to rain. The clothes would be in that nasty state of dampness which required that they be hung out again—what good were all these miraculous new fabrics that required no ironing if they could never dry?

A pair of Jim's slim-line underpants caught her attention. They were purple, and they hung on the line at a particularly offensive angle. She sneered at her husband's Jockey shorts and spoke out loud. "You're not half the man you think you are," she said. "I've known better, though I've never told you. Before we met, of course."

This compulsive habit of proclaiming her fidelity, even when she was addressing a pair of underpants, suddenly struck her as laughable. She had a good laugh, but even as she stood bellowing at the window, alone in her kitchen, the garments on the line seemed to recall her to her many responsibilities. Next to her yellow housecoat hung Rory's football shirt, reminding her that sometime in the near future she must take him to town and buy him new shoes. Her daughter's drop-neck dress, which the girl had neglected to take when she married so early—Imelda now wore it when she was feeling confident and racy—reproached her because it was only three days until Margaret's nineteenth birthday, and Imelda had not yet chosen a gift to mail off to Athlone.

Only the purple shorts failed to move her. Why should she feel moved to responsibility in *that* quarter? Probably he had bought them, certainly she hadn't selected them, to impress the disco dolly up in Portmarnock. Or, an even worse thought, the girl had purchased them for Jim. The longer she looked at them, the angrier she became. His socks and shirts, all bought at the Dunne's chain, moved her only to contempt, but the fact that he would let some girl, scarcely older than Margaret, pick out an intimate item outraged her.

She knew she should take the clothes down, but she thought she might have time for a wee lemonade laced with vodka before the rain came. She poured a generous amount of vodka into a tumbler, and then discovered there was no more lemonade. They were likewise bereft of orange drink and Coca-Cola. The hell, why not? she thought, and simply added tap water. She drank and winced. It wasn't that she could taste anything unpleasant, it was a matter of wanting some recognizable and piquant flavor—something to cheer the old taste buds while the spirits cheered the rest of her.

She saw the first raindrops slither against her kitchen window and felt irritable. "Right," she said to her drink. "Later for you." She went out into the garden and unpinned the soggy garments, collecting them in a plastic basket and bringing them safely indoors before the deluge came. The purple underpants she left to hang forlornly on the line, as a sort of protest. When she had sorted the clothing and peeled some carrots, she returned to the unrewarding drink. She lit a cigarette and sipped at the drink again, but it was no go. Something was needed.

It was that nice barman from Sligo, Tom Mulligan, who had first introduced her to vodka and lemonade. It had been a mistake, he had misheard her order on one of the rare evenings when she had gone to the pub with the Ladies' Badminton Club, but the drink had gone down so well she'd never complained. Who would ever raise a hard word with Tom, in any case? He was a lovely man, easygoing and soft-voiced, and he had the nicest way, sort of bantering and flirty, with no real harm to it. He was also, she thought, quite handsome. She conjured Tom Mulligan up, there in her kitchen, and saw a man of her own age with a full head of dark, graying hair and tender eyes. Also, to his credit, Tom had a youthful, lean middle and a bouncing gait. Yes, a lovely man. He looked fit to play the part of a presidential candidate in an American film. The one who would be assassinated, surely.

He had seemed to favor her, that night. He had smiled at her most often, and made a little joke about Cork, and called her by her name. Flattering, that had been. Imelda wove a little fantasy about herself and Tom Mulligan. Would he not be outraged to think that she was married to a man who did not appreciate her? A man who allowed tarty girls from Portmarnock to select his underpants?

The fantasy needed a stimulant to buoy it up, and Imelda had a brainstorm. Acting quickly, drink in hand, she went through to the stairs and sped up to the bathroom. On the third shelf in the medicine cabinet she located the minty mouthwash her husband had lately begun to insert into her shopping list. She tipped a small amount into her glass, mixed the solution with her finger, and sipped.

Perfection. It was perfect. Vodka and mouthwash would be her salvation —that and the as yet unformed fantasies about the barman from Sligo.

SEVEN

Everywhere he went, Lynch seemed to see large, balding Americans in plaid. Now that it was nearly summer and the tourists had begun the annual influx, they packed Grafton and O'Connell streets, gathered in the lobby of Bloom's Hotel and the Shelbourne, queued for tickets at the Abbey and Gate theaters. Of course they weren't all balding, and not all wore plaid trousers, but there were enough Yanks who answered the children's description to make for a diabolical joke.

On the whole, Lynch liked Americans. He thought them open and friendly, decent, and rather endearingly innocent. There was no way to cast a net over Dublin and bring every visiting American in for interrogation, and he could hardly go up to one of them—that man, say, who was just crossing the cobbled courtyard of Trinity College, probably in search of the Long Room and the Book of Kells—and ask him if he had been in Balgriffin on the afternoon of . . . ? No.

Cutting through Trinity to make his way to Nassau Street, he reflected on what he *had* done, and it was all discouraging. Of the hundreds of Americans who had crossed the Customs barriers in the ten days preceding the killing, all but thirty had gone on to other foreign ports before the night of the evil on the racecourse. Of these thirty, twelve were women. Fourteen men were ruled out because they were far too young or old—the youngest had been three, and the oldest seventy-two. The remaining four were two middle-aged priests, a world-famous academic from Princeton University, and a man named Parsons whose age, forty-two, was hopeful but whose race was definitely wrong. Lynch knew Mr. Parsons was black because of his Christian names, which were Marcus and Garvey.

He swerved to avoid running into a platoon of tourists being shepherded to the Long Room. The sun was out again, and no doubt it was a glorious day, but he took no note of the blue skies or the stately gray stone of the medieval buildings surrounding him. What he did notice was that the cobbles were hurting his feet, which meant that both he, and the soles of his favorite shoes, were getting old.

A young couple, absorbed in their guidebook, brushed against him in a gentle collision. "Oh, 'scuse me," cried the woman. "I wasn't looking where I was going, was I?" She seemed inordinately concerned for his welfare, which made him feel very elderly. He thought she was from the American West. There were so many ways an American could enter Ireland undetected. You could come over from England on a ferry and never have your passport stamped, or you could take a train from Belfast. You could even be one of those Yanks who lived here on a more or less permanent basis. A writer, or a painter, taking advantage of the tax laws for artists. Some artists might wear plaid trousers, if they were very old and comfortable, as Janie Keane had suggested.

He passed into the coolness of the great overhanging inner courtyard which separated Trinity from the outside world, drawn by the far-off sound of a fiddle playing an O'Caralan lament. Here he encountered a girl in a wrap-around skirt and sandals who was selling tickets to a lunchtime concert. "Traditional Irish music," she said brightly, as if Lynch had been a tourist. "It's just begun, you've not missed much, and it's only fifty p. There's sandwiches up there, so you can have your lunch while you listen." Her voice was from Ulster, with the curious upward inflection to every sentence.

"Any pipers?" he asked the girl. She seemed no more than fifteen to him, the age of Frank's daughter.

"Och, aye," she said. "We've got Liam Barney, now. He's great on the uillean pipes."

Lynch purchased a ticket from the girl, who sported two earrings in each lobe, and climbed the stairs to a lofty, musty room where the tourists who bedeviled him munched sandwiches and watched the musicians retune their instruments. There were a fiddler, a *bodhran* drummer, an accordion player, and the piper the Northern girl had praised. He recognized the fiddler from O'Donohue's bar, and saw with a start that the drummer was a youth he had once arrested on a joyriding charge. Apparently he had become rehabilitated. "Isn't this *exciting?*" murmured a woman to his left. She wore a lime-green trouser suit and spoke to no one in particular. She was American.

The musicians burst into a rousing rendition of "Paddy Casey's Reel." Lynch felt real enjoyment, hearing the music he loved, but beneath it was the constant anxiety he always felt these days. It came of having no suspect. Henry Connors fit the bill, physically, but he could not see the Yeats scholar lurking in the gloom of the grandstand, waiting to garrote his prey. Neither could he subscribe to the rumored theory of the Branchmen—that the killing was tied in with young Matty Keegan's uncle who lived in Australia. Paul Keegan was not a suspect, and Nora's brother had not left Melbourne.

He had dutifully run a check on Tom Mulligan's supposed career in jail, and turned up one paltry period of incarceration, in Sligo Town, on drunk and disorderly. It had been fifteen years ago, and how Denis Hallelujah

McGuire knew of it was the only ominous factor. Mulligan struck Lynch as a man of acuity. He could not imagine Tom having a lapse of memory. He would, as a good barman, remember such an anomaly as a Yank, in plaid, who strode into his bar one day and demanded six packets of crisps. It was unthinkable that Tom should not remember, and yet, even as he had assured Lynch that he did remember, once his memory had been prodded, something was out of joint. Yes, plaid pants he supposed, and some crisps, he didn't remember how many, and he didn't think the man had stopped for a drink. There was no one in at the time but old Mr. Phelan and Mick, the young backup barman. Mick had been in the kitchen.

The whole time Tom Mulligan had hesitantly confirmed the children's description of the stranger, Lynch had felt that he was lying. Mr. Phelan, half-asleep in back of his pint, had been no help either. That was understandable, given his age and condition, but why should Mulligan seem to be lying?

The *bodhran* player had spotted him and looked alarmed. Lynch realized that his own expression, while ruminating, had probably seemed fierce and punitive. He gave the drummer a little wink, rose to his feet, and left the concert. As he was going down the stairs he heard the piper begin a solo run and thought the girl had been right. He was great.

Dear Da [Mulligan's daughter had written],
   Things are great here as usual. Lina is fine and sends you her love and best wishes. It's hot here, even though it's only spring, bet it's raining back home. In Illinois the sun is scorching hot and soon we'll be able to go to the beach at Lake Michigan. I hope to learn to swim. I'm after going to cheerleader practice at school today. It seems a bit foolish, but it is an honour to be chosen one. My hair has all grown back and you'll be pleased to know I don't look at all punk these days. I am sending a picture. How is Des—still bold? Hope he's staying out of trouble and doing you proud.
   Da, I hate to trouble you, but Aunt Lina's birthday is coming up in June and I would like to buy something nice for her. She is so good & also generous, but I can't ask her for money to buy her own present, see what I mean? Could you send me some money? 10 would do. I wish you would come for a visit, because I miss you. I hope Horrid Hennessy isn't making you work too hard. Don't keep on worrying about my education! The school is grand, and I don't miss the nuns at all. Not one wee bit!!!!!
   God bless, Daddy.

                                                                  Love, Nuala
P.S.—Please remember about the money for Auntie Lina's birthday.

Tom read these lines for the fourth time, standing at the end of the bar. For the tenth time he studied the enclosed snapshot. Nuala stood in the suburban back garden of his sister Lina's house in Illinois, wearing the indecently short crimson skirt of what he imagined was her cheerleader's costume. Her hands were cocked at her hips, and she was grinning at the camera. True enough, her hair was no longer eccentrically styled in the punkish Mohawk she had elected to wear before he sent her off to America. Nuala's hair, black as a crow's wing, was now short and full-looking, framing her lovely face in wholesome brackets. He imagined it would billow enticingly when she jumped about, performing her strenuous cheering activities.

He brought the photograph closer to his face, trying to study his daughter's features, wishing that she had been snapped closer up. Nuala smiled her winsome smile, and he could make out the sweet curve of her chin and cheeks, but he could not see the dark blue eyes that were his own. She was a beauty, like her late mother, but her eyes had always been those of her father. Tom's wife had possessed round, startled eyes of a pale gray hue; Tom and Nuala had deep and furtive eyes the color of 11 P.M. of a Midsummer Night's Eve.

Tom longed to show the snapshot of Nuala to someone, but no likely candidate was present. Cats were slumbering noisily beneath the TV set and a smallish party of utter strangers were drinking Harp in the saloon lounge. Mick was a possibility, but on second thought he was disqualified. Mick was only seventeen himself—he would view Nuala's legs with an inappropriate zeal and offer compliments based on lust, not paternal pride.

Tom returned the letter to his pocket and walked irritably to the front door of the pub. Ever since the policeman's unexpected visit he had experienced a peculiar physical discomfort. It seemed to gather in his spine, where it held a malicious meeting with the rest of him and proclaimed a revolution. It was guerrilla warfare, striking him where he least expected trouble. On one night it might attack his strong right arm—the one that pulled the pump and made level the pints—and leave him weakened and secretly shaking. On another, it might immobilize his neck, so that he felt a grinding ache when he turned his head and called to the one who had summoned him.

The pearly gray of the estuary, full and flowing, seemed to Tom to represent his dead wife's eyes. A few bright sails skimmed away near Ireland's Eye, but the whole of what he saw was devastating. What was the estuary but one of nature's cruel tricks? A graveyard for children, and although he was no child, he saw himself as one of them—a hapless individual who strayed onto dangerous ground in the hope of a little adventure. The tides would catch him, he was not exempt, and he would be swept out and away, far from his safe cove, into the wild and murderous sea beyond. It was beginning already. Had begun.

The vegetable man was handing a head of cabbage to a woman in a pink dress. Scobie Halloran was leaning against the wall, smiling in a secretive way. The Keegan boy was deep in earnest conversation with Halloran, and for a moment Tom thought they might be discussing him. Young Matty had been one of the children who had seen the American and reported the incident to the Garda sergeant. Tom could still feel the flush of dread that had passed over him when Lynch had so casually asked him if he remembered.

He was about to turn away from the door and the exquisitely melancholy view when someone called his name. It was a female voice, and he searched anxiously among the women lined up near the vegetable van for its source. He felt almost angry at being summoned so cheerfully from his fearful state. His daughter needed money, money which was difficult to come up with but which must be found. His wife was dead, his children parceled out to relatives. Under his loving but distracted supervision, they had not prospered; they had shorn their heads and taken to petty vandalism and in all ways seemed to be heading for tragic, tabloid endings. The police were on to him and would return.

"Jesus, you're mesmerized!" cried the voice merrily, and now he saw her. It was Mrs. Kennerly, swinging along up the road with a badminton racket slung under her arm, wearing shorts. He had not seen her in some time. It was rumored that her husband was dallying with a tart in Portmarnock, and Tom realized that it had been almost two months since he had seen them together in the pub. Jim, that was the man's name. He didn't know Mrs. Kennerly's Christian name, she was merely the missus of Jim, and now that her man had strayed, she did not, quite naturally, appear in Tom's domain.

"Hello, Mrs. K.," said Tom, forcing his professional barman's smile. He was noticing how superb the woman's legs were. Despite himself, he had to admire them. They were long and sleek and gorgeously molded—quite at odds with the rest of her. She was standing in such a way as to place them at advantage, and a momentary lust rose up in Tom to eclipse the nameless dread.

"Imelda," said Mrs. Kennerly. "That's my name, Tom."

"Well," said Tom. "*Imelda!* I never knew." He simpered a little then, shamefully, and quickly withdrew into a semblance of manly silence. He was not truly interested in Imelda Kennerly, and intended to show her so. His mistake was looking into her eyes, and detecting a wretched loneliness there which nearly matched his own. Imelda, on some level, was desperate. Her desperation appealed to that part of him which was immune to reason. He wanted to assuage her desperation as keenly, almost, as he wanted to atone to Nuala for the misfortune which had befallen her.

She was standing directly in front of the door, smiling at him with that easy flirtatiousness all women assumed with friendly barmen. He saw, now, that her unhappy eyes were fine and brown, and he suddenly felt a strong dislike for Jim Kennerly for being so public about his affair.

"Been playing badminton, I see, Mrs. K. Where's the rest of the team?"

She shrugged. "Here and there. Nora was playing, and Katie Brannigan, but Kate had to get back to the baby and Nora had something to do with Maureen's school—" She stopped suddenly, as if aware that Tom the barman was not interested in the women's chores and appointments. Probably, Tom thought, she had spoken only to other women recently and felt ill at ease. He had only to look at her to know that she was a countrywoman, originally, just as he had been a country boy.

"I think I'll come in and have a drink," she announced. This was somewhat alarming, since single women almost never came to the pub during daylight hours, but Tom nodded encouragingly. "The very thing," he said. "Just step along to the saloon bar, Mrs. K., and I'll be right with you."

He found her perched on one of the high stools, her troubling legs delicately crossed. Her racket lay on the next stool, and she was rooting around in her large, untidy purse. "I think I'll have a vodka in red lemonade, please," she said. "Oh, now, Jay, I hope I brought some money."

"No money necessary," Tom said. "This one's on me, Imelda."

"Your wife might not approve of that," she said, turning flirty again. "What do you suppose she'd say, Tom?"

"My wife is dead, love," said Tom. He tried to sound neutral. Experience had taught him that the simple words *My wife is dead* produced in women a galloping sentimentality that was cathartic for them and painful to him.

"Jesus, now, I'm sorry," Imelda said. "Me and my big, meandering mouth. I'm truly sorry, Tom."

"It's been five years," he said, and went to make her drink. The strangers had left the saloon bar, and only Cats remained in the public one. "All right, Cats?" he called, opening the small bottle of red lemonade. This was a rhetorical question, and he was surprised when Mr. Phelan bellowed, "I am *not* bloody all right and I never will be!"

When he brought Imelda her drink she gave him a genuine, sweet smile of thanks. "Was that Mr. Phelan in there?" she asked, lifting her glass to him and sipping greedily.

"It was indeed. He's here almost every day. Home away from home."

"I'd rather be away from at present. If it wasn't for young Rory, I'd join Mr. Phelan, I swear to Christ I would. Have you children, Tom?"

Eventually, the snapshot of Nuala was produced and duly admired. Tom's son, Desmond, was introduced to the conversation, and Des's current home —Kilburn, London, with Tom's older brother—held up to scrutiny. The marriage of Imelda's daughter, Margaret, was also discussed, and when they had exhausted all possible avenues in that line, she scrabbled furiously in her bag and came up with two wrinkled pound notes. "I'll have another," she said.

He hoped she wasn't the sort of a woman who turned lachrymose after a few drinks and confided her troubles. She couldn't be seriously trying to seduce him, could she? She couldn't hope to keep it a secret, not in Balgriffin, nobody living in the Crescent could. He had enough on his plate, didn't he?

"I'm puffin' like a train," she said as he returned with her vodka and red. Tom saw that she was lighting another cigarette, her third in the brief time she'd been in the bar. Her hands were shaking. Imelda Kennerly was outwardly registering what he had so far managed to conceal—panic.

As he bantered with her, trying to please her without crossing over into a potentially loverlike attitude, he was thinking grimly of how the old adage was true. You could plan a thing perfectly, and through no error of your own be caught out. He was sure he'd be seeing Lynch again, in the very near future.

EIGHT

It had been necessary to embalm Wolfe Tone's discovery, and the unknown man reposed in the Dublin morgue as a more or less permanent guest. In early June, Lynch was summoned to the Fitzgibbon Street Garda station and confronted with a very young woman who claimed that the man had been her husband.

"What did you say?" Lynch asked.

"That man who was being discovered, now three weeks ago, was my husband," the girl said. Her English was curiously stilted and foreign. He thought she might be German, but what puzzled him more than her nationality was her curious composure. She seemed unmoved. Seated in a chair, her blue-jeaned legs neatly crossed, she might have come to claim a lost pet.

Lynch crossed to the desk and sat, drawing a thick pad of paper toward him. Frank was already there, and behind the woman's head he raised his eyebrows and threw up his hands.

"Your name, Mrs. . . . ?"

"Murphy. My name is Bergit Murphy, and my husband was called Nicholas Murphy. I am Swedish, you see."

"Your husband was Irish?"

"No. He was English. His parents were born in Ireland, but Nick was born and raised in England. I have here my passport to confirm." She languidly withdrew her passport, a new, British one, and passed it over. She was undeniably Bergit Söderström Murphy.

"Mrs. Murphy, I'm sorry to have to ask you why you waited so long to contact us."

She nodded, causing her long, lank, pale hair to obscure her face. "Yes," she said flatly. "You would wonder. I was in Japan when it happened. I am traveling a great deal in my business, and I was in Japan to buy cloth."

"Cloth?" asked Frank, in tones of incredulity.

"I make art works from textiles," Bergit said. "I am an artist."

"When did you return from Japan, Mrs. Murphy?"

"Six days ago, I think, yes. I was to meet Nick in London, but he never appeared. Then, just yesterday, I am buying some fish and chips and when I have eaten them all I look down and see Nick's face. They use quite old newspapers for the wrapping of the fish and chips. I read what it said and I came straight over here."

"You lived in London?"

"No. We lived in United Arab Emirates, but I was to come from Tokyo straight to London. My husband had the flight number of my return. He was going to meet me at Heathrow, but"—she shrugged—"there is no Nick waiting. So I go to our London flat and stay for six days and hope he will be making contact."

"What did your husband do in the United Arab Emirates, Mrs. Murphy?"

"I'm not sure. I think he was an adviser to a company. He traveled around all the time. He was also retired." Her torpid light eyes stared into Lynch's with an expression of absolute honesty. "I know you are thinking how strange I know so little, but the truth is, we had only been married for six weeks. I met him in Cape Town, and we decided to get married. I had a show of my works in Cape Town, and I met him at the reception."

At the end of half an hour, Lynch had ascertained that Bergit had no idea why her husband should have been in Ireland, that he had no living family and no children, and that he had been married before, to a woman whose name Bergit had never heard pass his lips. She produced a marriage certificate, executed in Cape Town, and a photograph—a Polaroid—of the bride and groom on their wedding day. Bergit wore a shocking-pink T-shirt with her jeans, and the groom was dressed in a variation of the drabbish clothing he had been wearing when he met his death.

At the morgue, she stared dispassionately at Nicholas Murphy's face and said the man in the drawer was definitely her late husband. "I am not so emotional," she told them, "because it was a convenient marriage."

"A marriage of convenience?" Frank asked.

"He is liking me because I am so young, only twenty-two, and I am being fond of him because of the money and the freedom he promises. I need money, you see."

"Why is that, Mrs. Murphy?" Lynch's voice was carefully gentle.

"Because of my cloths," Bergit said. "It is necessary to travel, and the cloths are sometimes very dear."

"I appreciate that you did not know Mr. Murphy for any length of time," said Lynch. "But when you say he was retired—what was he retired *from?*"

"The army, I think." Bergit bit her lip. "He was in the British Army for a time, but not the regular army. The secret one that, how do you say, is like the American CIA? The intelligent?"

"Oh Christ," said Frank. "Enter the Branchmen."

"The SAS?" said Lynch. "The Special Air Service?"

"I am so sorry," said Bergit, smiling fully for the first time. "As I am telling you, I knew him for a short time, only. I regret I cannot be so helpful." The smile made her face charming.

Lynch felt at a loss, facing the young woman's bland, conversational attempts at explaining her ignorance of the details of Murphy's life. He half expected her to ask if the Dublin corporation would attend to his burial, but she surprised him there. She wanted to know the procedure for taking her husband's body back to England for cremation. "He made me promise to sprinkle his ashes from Putney Bridge," she said. "I must keep my part of the bargain."

"Bargain?" said Lynch.

"I am meaning agreement," said Bergit. "I *agreed* to do that in the event he is dying."

"And do you think he expected to die?"

Bergit shrugged. "We all do, sometimes," she said.

They parted in front of the morgue, and both men watched as Bergit strode away from them. There seemed something triumphant in the movement of her long, denim-clad legs. "Bit of a chilly creature, that. I wouldn't put it past Miss Bergit to hire someone and have him done in. After all, she'll get all his money." Frank advanced this theory in an unconvinced and unconvincing way.

"But surely, in that case, she'd put on a great show of grief," said Lynch. "If nothing else, she seemed totally honest."

All the same, they agreed to put a plainclothesman in the Gresham Hotel, where Nicholas Murphy's widow was waiting until she could take her husband's body back, across the Irish Sea.

His middle name had been Alan, his age forty-four, and his place of birth London. He had probably been in the British Army, if he was telling his wife the truth. That was all they knew about him, even now.

On the evening news he was simply described as Nicholas Alan Murphy, forty-four, an Englishman who had been a resident of Abu Dhabi for the past eighteen months. Because Intelligence in London denied any knowledge of him, no mention was made of his supposed career in the British Army, and the public was annoyed at the dearth of information coming its way.

"They don't tell you much, do they?" Kate Brannigan murmured to the shirt she was ironing.

"Poor soul," Imelda Kennerly sighed, wondering if it was too early to have a little nip. "Imagine dying, and not having a person in the world to mourn you."

"It was a Brit," said Nora Keegan to Paul when he returned from work. "The man in the grandstand was a bloody Brit."

"Are you glad he was a Brit?" Rory asked Matty Keegan outside Molloy's shop.

"Don't be stupid," said Matty. "It's not like that."

"Holy Mother," said Mrs. Keane, later that night at the pub, "what will this do for tourism, I wonder?"

"There hasn't been a tourist in Balgriffin these ten years, since the racecourse closed down," replied Scobie Halloran. "You might say we're the deserted village, and if I don't mistake myself, that's a poem by Jonathan Swift."

"Wrong for once, Scobie," said Tom Mulligan, who had come to lower the level of the television. "There was a Yank here just weeks ago. Plaid trousers and all he had, and he was buying crisps for the kids."

If Nicholas Murphy was not the original Forgotten Man, then he was very close to it. In a series of arduous and bureaucratic processes, Lynch had squared away the certificate of birth of Nicholas Murphy in London, and traced down the origins of his parents. His father, Patrick Murphy, had been born in Fermoy, Cork, his mother, Mary Agnes Flannery, in Cloghane, County Kerry. God alone knew under what circumstances they had met, courted, married, emigrated, and produced the luckless Nicholas. He had no surviving siblings, conceived either in Ireland or in England. A death certificate for a Mary Agnes Murphy survived in London. She had died at the age of eight, in Kilburn, and appeared to be the slightly younger sister of Nicholas.

As for Bergit, the surveillance had turned up a journey quite significant-seeming. On the evening after her interview with the gardai, she had left the Gresham and taken a taxi to an address in Dun Laoghaire. She had remained in the bungalow there for over an hour, and emerged, according to the report, with a haggard and furtive air. She had been clutching a large parcel under one arm.

A check of the address proved that its owner was a designer in batik cloth, a woman so well known that her name appeared regularly in *In Dublin* magazine, accompanied by the words: *By private appointment only.*

Another cul-de-sac. As everything else in this case, a genuine dead end.

The frustration of it all was capped when he returned to his house in Blackrock and found his wife, Una, in tears. "Oh, Sean," she sniffled, lurching toward him across the persimmon-colored carpet she had wanted for the lounge, "there was such a terrible phone call. A voice, young it sounded, like one of those puffed-up reporters? He was—just harassing me. He kept on blathering about police incompetence, and didn't he go on and on? I've written down the number, but I hated every last minute."

Lynch folded his arms around his weeping wife, noticing how his fingers now sunk hopelessly far into the flesh of her upper arms. Her back, too, beneath the silky material of her pale blue summer blouse, seemed to have no resilience. He could remember the time when Una's flesh pressed back along the tips of his fingers, having a life of its own. Never mind. He had changed, too, and she was still his boon companion, his wife, the woman he had chosen to share his life with—in short, she was his best friend and the receiver of all his confidences. He clasped the quaking flesh which pressed against him for comfort, and thought, with real tenderness, *Who else would shed tears at the thought of my being incompetent?*

When Una had quieted, he told her he would call the pesky fella directly, and suggested that she pour herself a glass of wine and wait for him in the garden. He went to the telephone in the little front hallway and cocked his head. He could hear Una open the fridge door, and then there was the sound of nuts being tipped into a glass bowl. Reassured, he dialed the number she had written down. The man's name was Raymond Flannery, or maybe Flannelly—he couldn't be sure which. Una's distress had made her writing wild. He saw her cross through from the kitchen and go out by the french door, and she seemed to be quite restored. Raymond whatever's phone rang twice, a third time. Una sat in her lawn chair near the radiant pink peonies she had planted, and raised her glass of wine to her lips. Four rings. He noticed that her feet were bare, which seemed odd, but then he saw a little bottle of nail varnish on one of the end tables. No doubt she had been planning to give herself a pedicure when the man had called. She had pretty feet, and was vain about them.

On the fifth ring, someone picked up. "Yes, what is it?" said a pompous voice. "This is Kennedy."

"Mr. Raymond Kennedy?"

"Yes, this is he."

"You've got Sergeant Lynch at this end, Mr. Kennedy. What can I do for you?"

There was a snide laugh. "You can start by being more honest with the public, Sergeant. That would be a good beginning."

"I wasn't aware that I was lying to the public. Maybe you would be good enough to explain yourself."

"Certainly. Notice that I did not say 'lie,' Sergeant. I don't accuse you of lying, but of withholding information. The distinction, as I'm sure you will remember from the hellish years of your boyhood—years during which you, I feel quite sure, were educated, even as I, by the Christian Brothers—is that of a sin of omission rather than commission. A sin, nevertheless."

"Mr. Kennedy, I would greatly appreciate it if you could state your grievance, clearly and simply, in a very short period of time. Three minutes, say, at the longest. Starting now."

"Police brutality has never bothered me as much as police incompetence," said Raymond Kennedy. "I have given up on hoping that you boyos can ever solve important crimes, but what I have not given up on—will *never* give up on—is the conviction that the public has the Right to Know. A very important fact was omitted from the radio and television reports of the murder in Balgriffin, as well as in the newspaper accounts today. I have called key people in the media, and been assured that the sole reason for silence on the matter was ignorance. They were not aware of the facts, because the Garda Siochana kept them in the dark."

"You have two minutes and twelve seconds left," said Lynch, "And you haven't made your point." He looked longingly at the iced bottle of Harp that Una had transported to the garden.

"My *point,* Lynch," said Raymond Kennedy with a withering contempt that was meant to be devastating, "is that the murder of the spouse of a famous artist is news! The public has a right to know that the man on Balgriffin racecourse was the husband of Bergit Söderström!"

Lynch had a sudden image of Bergit. The languid legs and lank hair and pale, unknowable eyes. "Is she so famous, then?" he asked, laughing a little at the thought of Bergit's celebrity.

"She is internationally famous," said Kennedy. "Have you never heard of *The Hanging Gardens?* Executed in raw silk and twine and leather? It's one of the seminal works, Sergeant."

"Can't say I have, I'm not up on such things, Mr. Kennedy, as I'm sure you intuit. Not my line at all."

"Precisely my point, *exactly* what I'm trying to make you understand. Because you, Sergeant, were not aware of Söderström's importance, you failed to notify the very people who were *well* aware of it—the people who would have let the public know."

"People like yourself, you mean." Christ, but he was insufferable. No wonder poor Una had been so unnerved. His schoolmasterish manner, combined with the unmistakable tone of condescension, were enough to make a more hot-tempered man see red.

"Yesss," said Mr. Kennedy grudgingly. "But you don't have to be an art critic to know of Söderström, Sergeant." There was a pause, during which Lynch gathered he was supposed to leap at the bait. When he did not, Kennedy peevishly revealed himself to be the art critic of a magazine Lynch had seen but never read. It was called *Countess Cathleen,* and he presumed it to be full of misty pieces about Yeats and Lady Gregory and that lot. Apparently it was rather more trendy then misty. He suppressed a small laugh, and Kennedy, despising a silence, said, "Do you concede my point?"

"Well now, Mr. Kennedy, I'm sure it was an annoyance for you to be unaware of Mrs. Murphy's presence in Dublin for the first twenty-four hours of her stay. How did you find out? I suppose it was her visit to the batik lady in Dun Laoghaire, wasn't it? At any rate, it's not important. My job is to find whoever it was who killed her husband. *He's* the important party so far as I'm concerned. I am not Mrs. Murphy's press agent, and I seriously doubt there can be more than fifty people in all the Republic who've heard of her, so I don't think the Public, capital *P*, have been cheated."

"Your arrogance is incredible," said Kennedy coldly.

"I rather thought it was the other way round. I am trying to bring a criminal to justice, sir, whereas you are merely striving for an interview with an artist for your magazine. The shoe, my boy, is on the other foot."

"It may interest you to know that I've already arranged for the interview you treat so lightly. It may further interest you to know that I plan to expose the ignorance of the gardai by—"

"Wait!" shouted Lynch. "It does not. I'm not at all interested, Mr. Kennedy. Write what you like, avoiding the libelous, and be sure to use the word 'seminal' no more than once. In the future, if you need to contact me for any reason, don't call here. You have apparently badgered and upset my wife, who has a lower tolerance for idiocy than myself. Good-bye, Mr. Kennedy."

He replaced the phone in its cradle and made his way to the table in the garden and the inviting Harp. "A pompous fool," he said, taking Una's hand and squeezing it briefly. "He'll not call again, Una." He poured the Harp into the tall glass and drank contentedly. The sky was strippled with blue and a peculiar shade of not quite white that reminded him almost of cream, but was too pale to be cream. Soon it would be Midsummer Night, and the light would hold until nearly eleven, changing in its miraculous solstice way from white to teal to that darkest blue that was not yet black.

"What is the color of those shoes, Una? Those sandals you like so much in the summer? The ones with the little straps you bought in Spain that time? The name of the color, I mean."

"Bone."

"That's the color of a part of the sky now."

"I believe you're right, Sean. What a strange connection."

A little while later he recollected her evening course in art. She had been quite keen on it. "Did you ever hear tell of an artist named Bergit Söderström?" he asked.

"What century? What century was this person?" She seemed to become a bit tense, angling up from her chair, like a student preparing for an arduous exam.

"Very much here and now, Una, relax yourself. She'd be a Swede, twentieth century, about Maura's age. Maybe five years younger."

"No, dear, I've never heard of her. It doesn't ring a bell at all. Is she a part of your case?"

"In a way," said Lynch, treating himself to a handful of nuts. "I'll tell you all about it later." It seemed to him to be so blissful to sit in his garden, drinking Harp and contemplating the riotous peonies, that any detailed analysis of the Balgriffin murder would constitute a profanation. Such moments of well-being were rare enough, God knew, and should be savored.

"Remember, now," said Una, "I'm no expert, Sean dear. The course ended with the French Impressionists. That's as far as we got. I remember what a trial it was for me to learn how to say yer man's name. It was fierce."

"What man was that?"

"Gauguin," said Una triumphantly, rendering the name in perfect French. "Oh, let me tell you! It was desperate."

NINE

Twice more, Nora saw Jim Kennerly leave his house in the dead of night and walk off toward the racecourse. She had a compulsion, if she glanced up and saw that it was close to midnight, to creep to the window and watch the deserted Crescent. Generally there was nothing to see, but twice she had been rewarded. It made her flesh creep, and she felt more than ever like a character from the Squinting Windows book, but Jim's midnight forays were deeply upsetting to her. At last she told Paul of what she had seen.

"Nothin' mysterious, love," Paul said. "He's off to see his girl, likely. The one up in Portmarnock."

"On *foot?* You must be joking."

"She might pick him up in a car on the main road. That'd be it. He can't go roaring off to her, not in a place where he's practically livin' in his wife's ear, so the little homebreaker picks him up by the church and they glide off to her love nest in Portmarnock."

"No, Paul, it doesn't make sense. Jim Kennerly has no need for secrecy. He's the one told Imelda, rubbing it in. He doesn't have to lie in their bed until she's asleep and then creep out like a cat. That one does as he likes."

"True. It's a shame; Imelda is a nice wee woman. Good night, love, and don't be hovering at windows. It's not our business."

Chastened, Nora had said no more, and now, only three days after that conversation, she lay beside him and pondered the strange turns the murder case had taken. That the man had been a Brit had stunned her, but further revelations were even more amazing. The papers reported that his wife, some kind of well-known artist, was Swedish, and the couple had lived in some place in the United Arab Emirates! The whole thing was getting positively international, and Balgriffin was the one place in the world where nothing of an international flavor ever happened. How did Jim Kennerly fit in?

Paul slept beside her and there was an almost preternatural silence in the Crescent. It reminded her of the suffocating quiet, back home, that preceded house raids.

The vivid remembrance forced her from the bed and brought her to the window. Kneeling, feeling guilty and absurd, she watched the door of the Kennerly house. It remained respectably closed, but some slight movement or sound made her catch her breath, and there, by God, directly below her, Jim Kennerly was walking along stealthily, silently, dressed in his dark jogging suit.

Without thinking, she pelted down the stairs in her nightgown and waited at the front door. She could not see properly from the second-floor window, but from the door she would be able to determine which direction he took. She waited until he would have been well past her house, and then cracked the door open and peered out. Jim was still walking up the Crescent, toward the racecourse. *Oh, where are ye goin', Lord Randal, my son?*

She had to advance a few steps out into the night when he came to the end of the Crescent. She crouched low against the grass, in case he should turn around, and felt the dew on the grass seep into the hem of her nightgown, chilling her ankles. She half expected him to vault over into the racecourse, but when the time came he turned smartly left on the Gilligan Road. He was headed in the opposite direction from that Paul had imagined. Not toward the main road at all.

And then, in the dark, she felt a warm and menacing presence. She could almost smell it. There was a strange noise, too, something sinister and not quite right. It grew louder, and the presence drew nearer. Something brushed against her flank, and Nora, child of Belfast, instantly rolled into the human ball prescribed for nonviolent demonstrators during the civil rights marches. She waited for the batons to strike, steeled herself against the tear gas, and said a Hail Mary. When she had done all of these things and nothing had occurred, she squinted up and saw a vast and monstrous shape on her little lawn. It was no more than a foot away, and it stretched on and on, like a tank or armored car. There were several more of them—a fleet. In the one section of the Crescent she had not thought to survey, there existed something so terrible and primeval she might have been caught in one of those American horror flicks.

She was working her lips, trying to call for help to Paul, when the noise surrounding her began to seem familiar. She had heard it before, as a child, visiting her granda in rural Antrim. It was the sound of munching jaws, large mandibles at work. It was cows.

She looked up into the face of an earnest cow who was denuding her overgrown lawn. Cows. They occasionally jumped over the wall of the old racecourse and invaded the Crescent. Imelda had told her, and Kate. It was a great problem for old Mr. Power, who kept a model garden, and wasn't there the time when Mrs. Keane, who was nearsighted, had screamed in terror when she passed a cow on her way to the pub?

Nora knew how to deal with cows. Barefoot, and in her nightgown, she bullied them back to the walls of the racecourse. At her terse command, learned from her long-dead granda, they gracelessly humped over the lowest part of the wall and vanished into the night. She giggled, a little, at the strangeness of it, and as soon as she heard the sound of her own voice she came to her senses. Here she was, dressed only in a thin nightgown, loitering near the racecourse. Swiftly she glanced up the Gilligan Road to see if the figure in the dark jogging suit were still in evidence, but she saw nothing. What if a car should go by? She ran back in the direction of her house, feeling unseen eyes peering at her from behind the lace curtains. What if some other Crescent resident, a woman probably, was as sleepless as herself, and was witnessing her mad sprint?

When she gained the safety of her own driveway, she saw that the worst had happened—a little puff of wind had made the door swing closed, and she was now locked out. Jesus, Mary, and Joseph, what next? She could lean on the doorbell and waken everybody, or she could try to waken only one. Paul slept so soundly she knew he would never hear a rain of small pebbles at the window, and Maureen was in the back, so it would have to be Matty. She stooped and scrabbled for a small stone, but it was quite some time before she located one of the appropriate size among the wallflower beds. She straightened and looked up in the direction of the trunk room, only to see her son's face, pale and perplexed, looking down.

"What're ye doing, Mam?" he whispered.

"Come down and let me in and I'll tell you," she whispered back.

When she was safely inside her sitting room, she told her story artfully, spinning it out for him. Matty found it so amusing that he began to laugh with abandon. He laughed so hard he had to stuff the edge of a sofa pillow into his mouth to muffle his glee. His cheeks grew very pink, and his eyes squeezed into little crescents of mirth.

Nora saw him as he should be: a child of twelve, and not the little man of sixty-five he had resembled ever since the terrible incident that had deprived him of his youth.

"The cows got out last night," Matty told Mr. Halloran the next day. "My mother chased them all the way back to the racecourse."

"Did she, now? And how did that come about, young Matthew?" He was bending down, alert, amused, ready for the story. There was a small group today for the vegetable man, and Matty sensed that Mr. Halloran was disappointed in the turnout.

He told his story, trying to remember the precise, brilliant narrative his mother had provided for him, and he was rewarded by the helpless shaking of Mr. Halloran's shoulders—the proof that he had succeeded. Mr. H. never laughed aloud, but when he was amused his lips curved sharply up, and he shook. It was a silent manifestation of his pleasure, and Matty found it manly and wholly admirable.

"Oh boys, oh boys!" cried Mr. Halloran in his mysterious way, still quaking. "We live in dangerous times. I often say I'd like to go to the Sea of Tranquillity for my next holidays, yes, that's the place to go, the Sea of Tranquillity."

"Where's that, then?" asked Matty.

"Oh, sure now, you'll have heard of the Sea of Tranquillity? It's a grand place, Matty. They were after discovering it a good time back. A grand spot."

Matty felt unaccountably saddened. He was a good student, in geography, and he knew that if he was unaware of the particular sea his old friend spoke of, it was bound to be some adult joke he could not fathom. "But where *is* it, now?" he pursued doggedly.

"On the moon," said Mr. Halloran, pronouncing it "meeyune."

It took Matty some time to figure out what *meeyune* (which he knew as *moo-an*) might mean. When he had made the translation, he stood mute with admiration.

"I believe that's Tom Mulligan just coming along," said Mr. Halloran, in that way he had. Matty squinted his eyes until everything was a blur, and wondered how it was that Scobie Halloran could always tell.

"Yes, sure it is," he said quickly. "And he's wearing a T-shirt, he's not dressed for work. And, wait, the shirt has something on it, something written. It says *Property of the Illi—Illinois Penitentiary*. That'd be a place in America, now." Matty knew how much Mr. Halloran appreciated being fed the little details he could no longer get on his own.

" 'Lo, Mr. Mulligan," he said as Tom approached.

"Penitentiary," said Mr. Halloran. "A fine young man like yourself, Tom? What were you inside for at all?"

Matty looked to make sure that he was joking and was relieved to see the familiar, shoulder-shaking signs of amusement. He had been afraid that Scobie didn't know about all the jokey things on T-shirts, that Scobie, for the first time in their acquaintance, had been caught out being old.

"Mass murder," said Mr. Mulligan, winking at Matty, but even as he said it, he seemed to flinch a little. He ducked into the pub, saying something unnecessary about having to change his shirt before going on duty.

"His daughter sent it to him at Christmastime," Mr. Halloran said. "She lives in Illinois at present, and I'd say he misses her greatly." He extracted a longish butt from his jacket pocket and lit it, inhaling and expelling the smoke thoughtfully. Matty knew that three of his children lived in America, and he thought Mr. Halloran was feeling sad. He had explained that he would never fly across the Atlantic, not trusting planes, and Matty had an image of the three Halloran children, stranded forever in a foreign land, separated from their father by the vast gray Atlantic. There were other children, too, in Canada and England, but of course none of them were children at all. They were grown-ups, older than his parents, and they had children of their own. The thought of all the Hallorans of various ages scattered throughout the world was dizzying. It made him uncomfortable.

Matty remained silent, out of respect for what he imagined to be Scobie's broodings on his lost children. On the seafront, he saw Gervaise and Terry waving to him, beckoning for him to join them. He was about to make his excuses when Mr. Halloran asked him a peculiar question.

"Does it strike you at all," he said in conspiratorial tones, "that Tom Mulligan is worried about something? He hasn't been in good humor lately."

"I don't see him all that frequent," said Matty. "Just the odd times, like now."

"And what would you say now, looking at his face? Is it the same as always, or has it altered a bit? You can read a person's face, same as a book."

Matty considered. It was true Tom had flinched when he had made his joke about being a mass murderer. Think, now. When he had been walking toward them, hadn't Matty noticed that Tom's easy, loping walk had changed? Hadn't Tom carried his shoulders in a high, stiff, cramped position? It was Matty's opinion that Tom, second only to his father, was the best-looking man in Balgriffin, but there had been something tense and strained in his face today. Even the comradely little wink had seemed to be a painful reflex. It was amazing how much you could see when you were trying to be someone else's eyes.

"Yeah," said Matty, "I think he *is* worried about something, now you mention it."

When he said good-bye to Mr. Halloran, who was preparing to go home for his tea, he walked across in search of Terry and Gervaise, but they were no longer playing on the seafront. He retraced his steps and turned onto the Gilligan Road, just in time to see Mrs. Kennerly, Rory's mother, glide into the saloon bar by the side entrance.

Dressed in a clean gray shirt, cuffs rolled back, Tom stood at his bar and wondered what, in the name of all the saints, had prompted him to wear Nuala's foolish T-shirt gift on the very day the gardai had surprised him at his lodgings in Tallaght? He had been frying eggs when those two bloody coppers were announced by his extra-curious landlady, Mrs. Joyce. Lynch (sympathetic, fatherly figure, despite the no more than ten years that separated him from Tom) and Browne (hard and youngish-seeming even though he was scarcely five years younger) had invaded his humble rooms with all the heavy solemnity of their profession.

"Well, Mr. Mulligan, having your breakfast? Sorry to interrupt" (Lynch). Silence (Browne).

He had turned down the flame, an act which later produced two gelid, embryo fried eggs that stared at him balefully, and tried to seem at ease in the unlovely two rooms he had inhabited ever since he'd had to send the children to relatives. He was acutely aware of the odor of cooking oil, the ugliness of the three-piece suite, which seemed to have been covered with automobile upholstery, and of Mrs. Joyce, who was slithering about in the hall, hoping to overhear.

He sat down in one of the hideous chairs and asked, sipping at his instant coffee, what it was he could do for them. At that precise moment, the bread he had set in the toaster had popped up, as if to accentuate the farce.

"Very simply," Lynch had said, "where were you between the hours of 11 P.M. and 1 A.M. on the night of May the twelfth?"

Easy, think it through. A purely innocent man would not attach the date to anything in particular. A date was just a number. "The twelfth," he said in a musing voice. "I was probably at work at the pub in Balgriffin, unless it was a Tuesday. That's my day off."

"In case you've forgotten," Lynch said, "the twelfth was the night that unfortunate man got himself abandoned in the grandstand. It was a Wednesday."

"Ah yes, of course. I was at the pub."

"Let's see, then. We hadn't moved on to summer hours yet, so you called closing at eleven, got them all out by twenty past, and took how long to clean up and close things? An hour, maybe, or would it be less?"

Clever old fox, supplying him with what, normally, would be his alibi. Tom felt sure that the detectives had checked with the pub's owner, Hennessy, and knew the truth about how long he had remained. Or Peter, the other barman, or even young Mick could have told—they had no reason to suspect him of anything and would cheerfully have provided information.

"I wasn't there to call closing, Sergeant. That week I worked two half shifts. Instead of taking the Tuesday off, I got half of Wednesday and—Friday, I think it was—off. Sometimes it goes like that, depending on when Hennessy needs me."

Browne was staring at him oddly, and he wondered if his explanation had been too lengthy. He lit a cigarette and stared back through the smoke.

"In that case," said Lynch, "when did you leave the pub?"

"Around seven, it would have been."

"What did you do then?"

Better. He'd rehearsed this bit. "I drove to the City Centre, had a drink and a sandwich at the Abbey Mooney, and then I went to that film at the Metropole, one with the two German sisters? They're called Marianne and Julianne, and one's a terrorist."

The Abbey Mooney was one of the largest bars in Dublin, no one could be expected to remember whether or not Tom Mulligan had been there or not. He had gone to *Marianne and Julianne* only a week ago, when he had begun to suspect things were getting serious. He wasn't about to tell Lynch that he had expected a film of a rather different kind.

"What time did you leave the Metropole?"

"I can't say to the minute, but it was about ten. I went back to the Abbey, had two pints, and came back here. I went to bed straight off. I was tired."

"Did your landlady see you return?"

"Mrs. Joyce? I doubt it. I try to avoid her."

"So in fact, Mr. Mulligan, there is no one you can think of who actually saw you from seven in the evening on."

Tom shrugged. "Sergeant, I didn't know a man was going to be killed. I wasn't trying to establish an alibi."

"Those your children?" Lynch asked, nodding at a framed photo of Nuala and Des. "They're fine-looking kids." Then he thanked Tom for his time and rose to go. Frank Browne spoke for the first time, at the door.

"Which one was the terrorist?" he asked.

"Which one? Ah yes, I see. It was Marianne."

When they had gone, Tom scraped his ruined eggs out of the pan and threw them into the rubbish. Then he poured himself a stiff shot of Jameson, added a dash of water, and drank it off. Drinking early in the day was something he, as a professional barman, never did, but today he needed it. He sat, looking at the photo of his son and daughter, and at length, still wearing the silly T-shirt, he rose to go to work. . . .

It was dim and cool in the public bar—the perfect place for Cats to sleep and Tom to go over and over the confrontation with the police. They couldn't pull him in just because he had no proper alibi, could they? So long as what he had told them couldn't be disproved, he thought he was safe.

Imelda Kennerly hadn't stopped long in the saloon bar. Perhaps with a woman's sensitivity she had seen that he was troubled. He was grateful to be released from the obligation of flirting with Mrs. K. and cheering her up. Women, as he had every reason to know, invariably led him straight to trouble.

TEN

Joe Scully, the Garda officer from Balgriffin who manned the lost and found offices, had left a message for Lynch to call him. Scully was an affable man, but he had a perplexed look on his face at all times, even when he was laughing. Perhaps, Lynch thought, it was because Scully wondered why, at fifty-five, he had advanced no further in the Garda Siochana. He came from Kerry—always a source of amusement to the Dubliners—and was slow in his movements. He had a long, bulletlike head of cropped gray hair, and prominent ears. When he drank his pint, he caressed it in his hands between sips. Scully also, Lynch remembered with a start, had an outstandingly beautiful wife.

He thought of Rita Scully while he dialed Joe's number. She was not even thirty, he guessed, which made her twenty-five years younger than Joe, and possessed of raven hair and the kind of figure that always seemed hampered by its clothes. She was altogether delectable—forgive me, Una—and how she had come to marry Joe was a source of endless speculation.

"Scully," said Joe at the other end in his deep, slow voice.

"Sean Lynch here, Joe. You left a message."

"I did, so. Rita's just after telling me a queer thing on the telephone. She says on the very day of the killing she saw a strange man lurking about Balgriffin. He was a Yank, she said. Even though she never heard him speak a word, she could tell by this fella's clothes. When I asked her why she never told me before, she said because she forgot until now. You know women."

"Where did Rita see him?"

"By the estuary. There were some of the kids about."

"Did she see him go into the pub?"

"Now, wait—yes. But then she went on about her business and that's all she saw of him."

"She didn't mention what he was wearing, anything else about his physical appearance?"

"Plaid trousers, that's all. I thought you would want to know."

"Right, thanks, Joe. My regards to your good wife."

Lynch hung up and groaned, audibly. Back to the Yank in plaid. He just refused to go away. And Tom Mulligan, who had now lied twice. He had not, as Lynch had thought, been lying that first time about *seeing* the man, but about the extent of his contact with or knowledge of him.

That Tom had lied in his descriptions of his activities on the evening of May 12 was certain. It was the oldest trick in the world, going to a movie, the moment you realized you had no alibi, and describing it fondly to the police. He had had to prevent men from relating the entire plots of films during interrogations, so sure were they that it would set the seal on their innocence. Some of them had not been astute enough to pick a film that had been running on the night the crime was committed, but Tom Mulligan was cleverer than that. He also knew that the chances of being recognized and remembered by a harried cashier, once a few weeks had passed, were nil, just as the chances of being remembered in the mammoth Abbey Mooney were. Even so fine-looking a man as Mulligan would pass unnoticed.

He leaned back and mentally examined the list of candidates for the role of murderer he had briefly favored. These were men in the Balgriffin area who had served in the British Army. He, Sean Lynch, would never have chosen to do so, but it was a job, and it paid. The list had been appallingly meager. Of the five men, three had done their service so long ago they were now, in the American terminology, senior citizens. He could not see a senior citizen as a powerful and efficient practitioner of the garrote. One, a Mr. Phelan, was reputedly barely able to walk. Of the two remaining, there was a man who turned out to be serving time for nonpayment to a deserted wife, in Mountjoy Prison; and a fella named Brannigan, who lived in Portmarnock and helped, with his enterprising wife, to run a bed-and-breakfast establishment. Brannigan had turned out to be the brother-in-law of Terry's mother, but that meant nothing. Half the world was married to the other half. Phil Brannigan had assured him that the night of the twelfth had been his wedding anniversary, and he had a full house of boarders to prove it.

"I was a low-level sort of a soldier," he had said. "You need to talk to one of the elites for this, Sergeant, one of the real parachute boyos. Dirty tricks, ruthless they are. Find one of them who'll talk and you're home free! The best of luck to you."

British Military Intelligence had denied from the beginning that Nicholas Murphy was one of their own. Never had been. But of what possible use was their word? They dealt in secrecy; it was their stock in trade. The "elite" men of the SAS had performed in Kenya, in Malta, in Palestine, for all he knew. They had, with the help of the American CIA, educated the secret police in Iran in the finer arts of torture. They had instructed the Shah's thugs, he thought, to bring about confessions by means the Inquisition would not have shunned. SAVAK was their creation. Idi Amin was their creation. They were the lads who had trained Qaddafi's bodyguards, and the executors of the Shoot to Kill policy in Northern Ireland.

If Nicholas Murphy had been one of them, his killer could be from Yemen or Libya or Derry City or any one of dozens of places where the SAS had cut a wide swath—about the only country that didn't make sense was America.

When he left the station for an appointment at the Four Courts it was raining lightly. The rain fell on the forbidding bulk of Mountjoy Prison, temporary home of Robert Patrick Malone. Like Nicholas Murphy (if Bergit spoke the truth), Malone was retired from the British Army, and the two men shared something else—they were both born in London, of Irish parents.

Lynch made a mental note to arrange for an interview with the imprisoned man, and then went back to the problem of Tom Mulligan.

The children convened on the following afternoon for their weekly meeting. Luckily, it was fine and warm and they were able to use the steps on the seawall for their gathering place. Gervaise was the last to arrive, looking red-faced and out of sorts.

"I had to go to the shop and get some oil for my mother," he said. "She couldn't go, on account of having a ragin' headache."

"No problem," said Kevin.

"Was it from being at the pub too much?" inquired Terry.

"No, no," said Gervaise. "Women's doings, I think."

Janie blushed.

"Right, then," said Terry. "It's been more than a month since the Thing happened. They haven't caught anybody. Nothin' has changed, so far as I can see. The important thing is—are things back to normal for *us?*"

The children stared out at Ireland's Eye, which that day assumed the look of a lump of jade. The tide was in, the sea a wholesome blue on this particular afternoon, and the gulls were darting and screaming. It was a mesmerizing view, but the children, who were used to it, stared not in admiration but in self-consciousness. Nobody had an answer.

"Is the situation normalized?" pressed Terry.

Janie cleared her throat. "That depends," she said.

"On what?"

"Well, if you mean is the pressure off at home, the answer is yes. But I don't feel normal."

"How's that?" asked Matty, never averting his morose stare from the panorama of sea and sky and rock. "How do you mean, now?"

"You'll all be laughing at me," said Janie, "but I feel guilty. I never told a really important lie before."

"A lie's a lie," said Rory rather brutally. "People tell them all the time."

"That doesn't make it right," said Janie. "I've told wee lies before, but they were always to be sparing someone else's feelings. I never lied to the gardai about a matter of life and death."

Terry rolled his eyes and snorted. "We're not doing that," he said. "It's not like we put the finger on someone *real*, Janie. Nobody is suffering because of what we told that detective."

"You don't know that," said Matty. "It's not something you can know."

"I'm feeling strange about it, too," said Gervaise. "I had a dream the other night we were all arrested for—what do they call it?"

"Being soft in the head," said Terry.

"Obstructing justice," said Janie. "That's what they call it, and it's probably a deep crime. Not to mention a sin."

"I suppose you confessed it to Father Leahy?" Terry's voice was contemptuous, withering.

"Oh, *really*, Terry. I'm not the complete fool, you know. I only said I'd told a lie. I didn't say what it was *about.*"

"Let's see a show of hands," said Terry. "How many confessed?"

Six hands shot up, including his own.

"And how many think conditions at home have improved since we made up the Yank?"

Four hands were raised with alacrity, and two others joined them seconds later. The two belated hands belonged to Matty Keegan and Rory Kennerly.

"Well then," said Terry. "It only goes to show we're a success. We did the right thing."

Robert P. Malone had the face of a saint or a jogger. It was gaunt and grooved, as if with much suffering, and the eyes were bright and furtive. There was something almost noble about that countenance, and the illusion was sustained by the melodious, upper-class voice which issued from his lean chest. Lynch had been prepared for a Cockney, and instead he was being presented with a member of the aristocracy who happened to be clothed in prison garb.

The interview room in which they sat was, he guessed, much grander than the usual Mountjoy accommodations. It was probably a room in which solicitors and barristers met with their clients, rather than the usual box. He sat at one end of a long table, Malone at the other.

Malone was, as the English said, *posh*. "I don't believe I will," were his first words to Lynch, on being offered a cigarette. "Frightfully nice of you, Inspector."

Five minutes into the interview had stripped Malone of his posh pretensions, yet the voice remained. He readily admitted that he had served time as a para, as if the memory filled him with pride. He was a man of fifty or so years who loved to recall his time of active duty.

"You know what really pisses me off? What really burns my balls? Korea. The Yanks take all the credit for Korea, and my own son won't believe that I was dropped into Korea before he was born! Vietnam! We were there! But how long? The Yanks drove us out. They own Latin America, we don't even try to get a toehold there, it's CIA territory."

"Very trying, not being appreciated," Lynch said drily, but Malone was not one for irony. He abruptly asked Lynch for the cigarette he had refused, and then began to roll his own without waiting for an answer. His lips were compressed in a kind of fury—over being usurped by the Americans in Korea?—and he began to strike Lynch as more than a little crazy.

"This nonpayment business, the reason I'm a guest of Mountjoy, is all a mistake. My wife didn't mean for them to go through with it, and I'll be out quite soon." His fingers worked nimbly at rolling the homemade cigarette, and then he seemed to lose interest. "Yes," he repeated, "quite soon, now."

"Mr. Malone, have you ever seen this man?" Lynch handed him the police photo of Nicholas Murphy.

"Yes, of course I have. He's the bloke got himself killed in Balgriffin. It was in all the papers a few weeks ago. Doesn't look a very lively chap."

Lynch didn't bother to explain that Murphy had already been dead and asked Malone to search his memory for any slightest glimpse of the man Murphy had been.

"Why should I have known him? Look, mate, I've been in here for twelve weeks, so you certainly can't think *I* bloody killed him?"

"His widow maintains that he was in the British Army before she met him. She referred to it as the 'secret' army. I assumed she was referring to the Special Air Service."

"Why not have a go at asking her, then?"

"They hadn't been married for even as long as you've been in here, Mr. Malone. She didn't seem to know him very well."

"Don't you believe it, Sergeant. These Irishwomen play it sly, believe me."

What does he think I am? thought Lynch. *Can he imagine he's back in England, giving advice to a squaddie on his way to Belfast?*

"Mrs. Murphy is Swedish," he said. "Have you ever heard of a man called Nicholas Murphy?"

Malone thought, really giving it a try, and Lynch could see a fine, rare glimpse of what he had once been. Not the para, but something earlier. There was a keen, intelligent aura to Robert Patrick Malone for a moment, and then he returned to assembling his roll-up cigarette. "Nah," he said, "the name rings no bells, mate. I've known a hell of a lot of Murphys, but none named Nicholas. Sorry."

"I'm going to leave you my card. In case anything should jog your memory, any slightest thing, I'd be grateful if you would give me a ring I'll leave word with the prison authorities."

Malone licked the paper and sealed the cigarette and then laid it down between them like a sword. "What makes you think I'll remember anything? If I tell you I don't know the bloke's face and I've never heard of his name, what makes you carry on like this?"

"Would you truly like to know?"

Malone's eyes flickered, became briefly fearful, and then narrowed in a smile. He nodded his head.

"Nicholas Murphy, like yourself—I've seen your records, remember—was born in London of parents who had emigrated from Ireland. He was the first generation, as were you, Mr. Malone. Nicholas Murphy was a bit younger than you, but not all that much. And he apparently joined the British Army at a rather youngish age, as did R. P. Malone, and then left it, perhaps to indulge in activities even more mercenary and illicit than those provided by the SAS. Finally, he ended up in a bad spot. Like yourself. It seemed reasonable to assume your paths might have crossed."

"You sound like my wife. My *estranged* wife. She's Irish."

"So was your mother."

"Oh, too true, Sergeant, too effin' true. My mother's people own the gun that shot Michael Collins, or maybe it's the other way around, I forget. She still draws a pension on my dead father from the IRA! The West Cork Flying Brigade, or something on those lines."

"It's a desperate, complicated business," said Lynch kindly. "As you well know, Major."

At the title "Major" Malone assumed an erect and alert position. Below the neck, he was all starch and indignation; above, pure struggle. Rarely had Lynch seen one human body split so neatly into Briton and Gael, Anglo-Saxon and Celt. Malone's body was ready to do unquestioning service for Queen and Country, while his face was debating rebellion. The war was heartbreaking.

"Nick the Prick," he said at last. He spoke the words so lightly Lynch doubted he had heard correctly.

"What?"

"Nick the Prick," said Malone. "I never laid eyes on him, but he was a legend, you might say. Nobody knew his right name, or nobody spoke it, but you'd hear of him now and again. He was a specialist in interrogation techniques. I first heard of him in Northern Ireland in the early seventies."

"When last?"

"Rhodesia. He'd already left, as a matter of fact. Some of the paras joined the Rhodesian Army, in case you didn't know. It was common practice."

"Do you believe that Nick the Prick is the same man who was strangled on the Balgriffin racecourse?"

"Jesus, man, how would I know? I'm only saying he might be your man. He *might*. It's a long shot."

"At least it's something," said Lynch. "Thank you, Major." He rang for the guard to let him out.

"Bob," said Malone. "Call me Bob. I'm no Major now, mate."

Lynch saw that Malone was now slumped lazily in his chair, lighting his cigarette at last. He didn't seem particularly concerned about anything, and the illusion of a man torn between the Celtic in his blood and the Anglo-Saxon of his experience had vanished. Malone was just a prisoner—the ultimate failure.

ELEVEN

"No!" cried Rita Scully, tightening her arms around him convulsively and then half pushing him away. "How can you ask me to do such a thing? Don't you care for me at all?"

"Of course I do, Rita, you know—"

"You don't! Not at all! No decent man would ever ask a woman he was fond of to submit herself to that. It would ruin me, and you know it."

She sat up impatiently, nearly rolling off the banquette and onto the plush carpet. She buried her face in her hands, and presently her shoulders could be seen to be shaking.

"Rita, love, don't carry on. I told you, likely it won't come to that at all. I meant only in the event I'm in the deepest of trouble." Tom placed his hand on her sinuous back and made gentle, soothing gestures. He knew she wasn't really crying, but it made no difference. Her distress was genuine enough.

"You only want to drag me down with you," she said. "After all I've risked for you, Tom Mulligan. I should think you'd be grateful."

He let that one go by without comment. They were in the upper lounge of the pub, a place used only for private parties by prior arrangement. It was their usual rendezvous, a bit unsettling for Tom, but utterly private. It was, in fact, Rita who had hit upon the scheme of using the upper lounge for their illicit meetings. "It's perfect, Tom," she had breathed. "You have the keys, and there's days when Hennessy doesn't come near the place. Sure, isn't he off supervising all his other bars most of the time?"

Her idea had merit. There were the tag ends of the afternoons, when Mick, or Peter, could take care of Cats and the few customers who strayed in. If he were to come regularly to Rita's bungalow, while Joe was at work, it would cause a public scandal; Rita, on the other hand, could dodge into the pub by the side entrance, whip through to the staircase, and be stripped and waiting amorously for him on one of the wide banquettes in no time at all, and without attracting attention. They had been meeting in this fashion for six months, mainly on Tuesdays and Thursdays, and no one was the wiser. The arrangement had its drawbacks—things had to be accomplished fairly rapidly—but Rita didn't seem to mind.

"I made that stupid call to Joe, telling that lie about the American," she said now, throwing back her mane of black hair and rounding on him. "Isn't that enough? Jesus, Mary, and Joseph, Tom—what are you trying to do to me?"

"I explained how it is," said Tom. "They caught me by surprise. How could I see some Yank buying crisps in the public bar when I was up here with you, love?"

"Oh, what does it matter at all?" she wailed, turning and kneeling above him, like some fierce wood sprite. She was a magnificent, healthy country girl, whose beauty had propelled her from a village in Kilkenny to seek her fortune in Dublin. Tom thought it a tragedy that she had settled for marrying Joe Scully—a tragedy for Joe, not Rita.

"Let me try to explain again, Rita," Tom said. He was glad they had already made love; otherwise the sight of Rita Scully, naked and radiant in her rage, would have proved a great impediment to his logic.

"There's a tiny, wee chance they may bring me in, on account of my seeming shifty about the Yank, and having no proper alibi. They're desperate, you see, on account of not making any arrest, and it may come to that. If, now I'm only saying *if*, Rita, if it gets to the point where I absolutely have to tell them where I was on that night—have to offer a witness to corroborate what I say—would you really let me down?"

Rita's bare breasts heaved with indignation. In one fluid, unstudied gesture she scrabbled about on the banquette for her discarded clothing. Primly she slipped into her red blouse, concealing her flesh from him in precise, punishing stages. At the first button she said, "I wish Joe had never gone off to Kerry to visit his mother." At the second she said, "Surely to Jesus, I wish I had never decided to go off with you to Bray that night." At the third she said, "Even if I didn't care about myself, Joe's a good man, and I will not see him destroyed by you. It would kill him. I believe in the sacrament of marriage." She had run out of buttons and seemed wholly satisfied that she had made her case.

"Joe will never have to know," Tom said. "It would be completely confidential. All you would do was sign an affidavit that we were together, in Bray, all the night."

"Don't be so thick!" Rita screamed. "Joe's a garda, and yer man's a garda, and how long do you think it would take for the story to circulate?"

"This Lynch is a very decent fella. I pledge he'd never say a word."

"Oh, they're *all* decent fellas," said Rita, hands on her hips. "Everyone's a decent fella, until they've a good dirty story to amuse the world with. Your Lynch would laugh himself sick over it, and within five minutes, Tom Mulligan, the whole world would know."

"Here's your knickers," said Tom, suddenly feeling weary. He handed her panties to her in much the same way he might have slid a Guinness over the counter to a customer. He felt no love for Rita Scully, despite her great beauty. He was merely a mortal man who could not resist the promise of rapture that was her chief spiritual asset.

Rita held her knickers—mauve nylon ones—in her hands like a burnt offering. On her lovely face was a look of puzzlement. His apathy had stirred her passion.

"Oh, Tom," she sighed, collapsing upon him and encompassing him in her long, strong legs, "what is happening to us?"

For the first time since they had begun to couple in the upper lounge, they made love twice. Tom's terror seemed to spur him on, and he felt twenty again. What did he care if Hennessy had chosen this day for a random visit? What did he care if Rita's cries or his own occasional grunts could be heard in the public bar below? Everything was about to come apart, his children would be orphans, himself jailed for a crime he had not committed, his dear dead wife would not be present to see it all—why not?

"Ah, Tom," Rita sighed in his ear, "that was grand."

They lay for a time on the red carpet of the upstairs lounge, where they had fallen, and then Rita briskly extricated herself and got into her white trousers. Her knickers she stuffed into her purse.

"The answer is still no," she said, foraging for her high-heeled sandals. "I won't compromise myself. Not for you, and not for anybody."

Matty's father was a hardworking man. The idea of being on the dole was, for him, so horrifying, Matty believed it to be almost as important a reason for relocating in the Free State as the Unfortunate Incident. Almost. Paul Keegan's job at the Guinness Brewery was a good one, and he never slacked or gave them less than his best effort. Matty and Maureen had been taken on the famous tour, had walked the high ramparts and seen the great foaming vats of dark porter below—had even been allowed, at the climax of the tour, to sip a bit of Guinness. To Matty it had tasted like a vitamin tablet melted down. He had not voiced this opinion; on the contrary, he had pronounced it gorgeous and looked superior while Maureen wrinkled up her nose.

Now, however, his father was laid low with some peculiar summer cold, a disease, perhaps, indigenous to the Free State. Paul Keegan lay, sweating and shivering, while Matty's mother trotted up and down the stairs, making him Lemsips laced with whiskey. Tablets were taken and strange moans heard. The doctor was summoned and the word *virus* spoken. It was a sorry state of affairs.

On the second morning of his father's illness, Matty came bounding down the stairs and stopped when he heard a bit of conversation issuing from the kitchen.

". . . on his midnight walk again," his father was saying in an unfamiliar, wheezing voice.

"Go on," his mother's voice replied. "Not truly, Paul."

"Truly, Nora. I got up to take a tablet, and then—what with one thing and another—I looked out of the window and there he was—all decked out in his jogging suit, creeping along up the road."

Matty sank quietly down on the stairs and listened intently, his fingers pretending to redo the laces of his sneakers. It was the quality of his parents' voices that prompted him to eavesdrop; they sounded worried about the man —who was he?—in the jogging suit.

"Well, now I have to admit something, Paul. That night the cows got out? I only saw them because I was after pokin' my head out the door to get a look at *him.*"

Matty's father laughed, which forced him into a coughing fit, and then he became rather stern and told Nora not to do such daft things. "After all," he said, "if the man is mixed up in that other business, he's dangerous. If he's capable of murder, what do you think he'd do if he caught you spying on him?"

Nora said it was so, but she couldn't believe he was actually behind that other business. She thought him an unpleasant man, but scarcely a cold-blooded killer. Matty fidgeted on the stairs and cursed to himself. *Who?* Would they never mention the man's name?

"For his wife's sake, I hope you're right, love."

"Poor Imelda."

They were talking about Mrs. Kennerly, then! Rory's mother. Matty felt his heart lurch a little as he recalled the first council, the time Rory had described going to get his father and finding the bed empty. He conjured up Mr. Kennerly, with his thick, black brows and mirthless smiles, and placed him in the grandstand that night. In his big hands he held a length of piano wire—no, the police had found no weapon of any kind—no, he waited in the dark, dressed in a jogging suit, clenching and unclenching his hands, preparing to kill the Yank who was coming to meet him. But no, again. The Yank had been their invention, and there was only the man in the moss-colored trousers, and the imaginary Yank had been the killer, not the victim. Matty felt confused and suddenly suffused with misery. Perhaps they had done wrong, slipping the police fake information.

While Matty ate his eggs his mind was hard at work. Maureen's constant, fluting chatter, normally so irritating to him at breakfast time, passed over him without effect. Mr. Kennerly couldn't be going out to kill someone every night, could he? Of course not. It was something else, but it was sinister. Rory's father was engaged in some terrible activity in the dead of the night, and the man in the grandstand had probably had the bad luck to catch him at it. If Mr. Kennerly had happened to see his mother, peeping out the door on the Night of the Cows, then he might have it in for her.

"Matty, would you ever pass over that butter, or do I have to eat horrid, dry toast because you've gone deaf?"

"Sorry, Maureen." There would be no enjoyment in sniping this morning. Things were too serious. It seemed clear that someone would have to find out what Mr. Kennerly was up to, and it seemed equally obvious that the some-one would have to be himself. A plan began to take shape in his head. It was vague at first, but by the time he'd drunk his tea and was headed back upstairs for his school books, it had a satisfying plethora of details. He would wear blue jeans and his black T-shirt, of course, but what on his feet? His sneakers were blue and white and wouldn't do, and his good Sunday shoes, although black, would make noise. He had to be as silent and invisible as possible. A black wool cap of his father's could be enlisted. He wished he had some of that camo cream the soldiers back home used, but what was wrong with black shoe polish? Would it come off? Oh, there were a thousand details he would have to work out.

The hardest would be staying awake long enough. If he set his alarm clock for midnight, it would wake the whole house. And what if his mother was up and saw him? He found these obstacles bracing, and when he opened the door and saw Terry and Wolfe Tone across the way, he waved and grinned and called hello as if it had been a holiday instead of a schoolday in June, when you'd rather be outdoors.

Janie came out of her house, farther down, and he thought to himself that she, of all the conspirators, was the most sensible. If he could include one of the others on his reconnaissance party, he thought he'd take Janie Keane for preference, but of course she was a girl, and you didn't involve girls in situations that could prove deadly.

It occurred to him, just before Rory and all the others came pouring out of the Crescent houses, that the person he would most like to have along was Mr. Halloran. If only he were younger, and had his sight, Scobie would have been the perfect partner.

When the last of the older children had left for school, Kathleen Branni-gan settled the baby on her hip and went out into her garden to check on the raspberry bush. It was the one secret blessing of this house, she thought, the fact that the previous owner had planted a large raspberry bush which contin-ued to flourish. The berries wouldn't be ready for some time—she thought it had been early August last year—but the very fact of their existence on her property filled her with pleasure.

It was a fine, fair morning, without so much as a hint of a rain cloud. White butterflies were skittering overhead, making the baby laugh and stretch her arms out in hopes of catching them. The sun was warm enough already, at this hour, to have evaporated the dew from the grass, which needed mowing, and from the small, unexceptional leaves of the miraculous bush. The narcissi, which had long since died during the harshest of the spring rains, reminded her of all the things she should be doing. If her life were like a film, she would be kneeling in the garden and planting asters for the autumn, her head shielded in a becoming straw hat, her hands endearing in clumsy gardening gloves.

She became aware of activity on the other side of the low wall separating her garden, to the north, from the Kennerlys'. Yes, there was Imelda, pegging out some clothes. She looked shaky and cross, as if dealing with the clothespins were a chore too complicated to master. Fascinated despite herself, Kathleen watched as her neighbor fumbled with a child's pair of jeans, the clothespin squirting out from between her fingers and falling to the ground. "She's drunk," Kate thought uncharitably. "Or she has a monster of a head from last night."

Imelda turned her head and saw Kathleen, and instantly she swerved into her comical mode, as if on cue. "Jesus, Kate," she boomed, "isn't life itself a pleasure unalloyed? Here I stand, my face red as a beacon, not able to get the wee jaws of the peg to close over the *line?*"

She had screamed the last word, and Kathleen saw that her neighbor was in a perilous state. Imelda's handsome eyes were clouded and perplexed, and she seemed on the verge of tears. Kate had always been fond of Imelda, but something about the older woman had kept her from feeling that wholehearted impulse toward friendship that Nora Keegan, for example, had inspired in her. Imelda was trouble, because she was unhappy in a way unfamiliar to Kate. Even so, her being quickened, became vigilant with sympathy. Something must be done for Imelda, if only a cup of neighborly coffee to sober her up.

"Leave those things," Kate said. "It'll not rain today, not for hours. Just come straight over to me and we'll have a drink. Coffee, Imelda. Maybe a wee drop in it, but coffee's what's needed."

Imelda regarded her with suspicion, then bent to her wash basket and withdrew a pillowcase, examining it as if she could find no earthly use for it.

"Awwwk!" screamed the baby with glee.

Kate marched back inside and plugged the kettle in. She went to the door to leave it on the latch, and Wolfe Tone slunk in, looking ashamed of himself. A few moments later, Imelda came through to the kitchen, bearing a fresh packet of cigarettes and a bottle of barley water, which proved, on closer inspection, to be vodka.

"Half-and-half," she cried gaily, while Kate was measuring the instant coffee. It struck Kate that Imelda was not a natural drunk but one whose trials had driven her to experiment with drink as an anesthetic. Surely a born alcoholic was provided with more skill than poor Imelda, who was now glancing desperately in all directions, possessed. Real drinkers, thought Kate, remembering with distaste her Uncle Barry, were tough and untouchable, hardened by their apprenticeship in the Secret Society, and unapproachable as well. Imelda was not one of these—she suffered too openly, and not of her own volition. Not, so to speak, by choice.

"Imelda?"

But Imelda, before she had even touched the coffee, had allowed her head to droop on Kate's table, and was even now weeping mute tears into the sugar bowl.

TWELVE

When the new issue of *Countess Cathleen* came out, Lynch was not at all surprised to find a large spread on Bergit Söderström, accompanied by a picture of her taken in her room at the Gresham Hotel. The article had been authored, of course, by Raymond Kennedy, and was written, to Lynch's somewhat prejudiced eye, quite badly. He read it straight through, looking for any scrap of information that might have passed him by, and came up with nothing.

Instead, he found an unpleasant reference to himself, in the concluding paragraphs. "Söderström is the widow of Nicholas Murphy," he read, "the man who was found murdered on the disused racecourse in Balgriffin. She has returned with his body to place him in his final resting place, in his native England. The death of this greatly gifted artist's husband should have been a matter of public knowledge, but due to the arrogance and anti-intellectualism of this country's police force, the fact was swept under the carpet. Detective-Garda Sergeant Sean Michael Lynch admitted to me that he did not find the matter sufficiently important to inform the public. Since no arrests have been made in connection with Murphy's murder, perhaps Sergeant Lynch finds *it* unimportant, too."

Visions of being called up before Internal Affairs and reprimanded for placing the Garda Siochana in a position open to criticism appeared. Of course, no one read *Countess Cathleen* that he knew of, but there was bound to be the odd call, and the newspapers would surely carry the story. He was still quite sure that the killing had nothing to do with Bergit and her textured-fabric art, but the jibe about no arrests had flown straight home.

Reluctantly, he acknowledged that it was time to apply some pressure to that likable fella Tom Mulligan—the only man he had interviewed who seemed even remotely suspicious in his movements on the night of the murder.

He summoned Frank, and together they drove to Mulligan's lodgings in Tallaght. The landlady, Mrs. Joyce, received them with breathless excitement and offered tea, which was politely declined. In her spotless little parlor, sitting beneath an oleograph of the Sacred Heart, Mrs. Joyce cocked her head and folded her hands and asked how she might be of service.

Lynch remembered that Mulligan had said he tried to avoid his landlady whenever possible, and this was a completely reasonable statement. Mrs. Joyce reminded him of a ferret. She was furtive and vicious by temperament, he guessed, and these qualities had been exacerbated by the long boredom of her widowhood, the necessity of having to take in lodgers, and her general descent in the world. He noticed that Frank could hardly bear to look at her —later, Frank would tell him that she reminded him of his terrifying and venomous Aunt Bridget—and Lynch found her an ordeal was well. It was her desire to do another person damage he found so unattractive. He had encountered it, on this case, only in Denis McGuire, the born-again character assassin.

"That Mulligan never came here at all on that night," Mrs. Joyce asserted, in answer to their question. "If he says he was home and in his bed, he's lying. I never saw him until he came slinking in, quite a late hour it was, the next night."

"How can you be sure, Mrs. Joyce?" Lynch asked. "You had no reason to remember that particular evening, had you?"

"Oh, hadn't I now? I was up the night long with a stomach disorder, I hadn't a wink from dark to dawn, and that Mulligan never came near the place. I don't even want to *think* what he might have been up to; Mr. Joyce, God rest him, protected me from that class of a thought."

"How can you be sure it was *that* night, though?" Frank asked, addressing his question to the Sacred Heart.

"I can be sure because of the linen," said Mrs. Joyce triumphantly. "I change the linen on the beds on given days, and I keep a wee book to make sure I'm on target. I had a peek in at that Mulligan's room, even though I knew he hadn't slept in the bed, just to be sure. The bed was as neat as a pin, it hadn't been slept in, now, and so I left the linen on for another day. It disturbed my schedule, but I try to be fair. Fair is fair, they say, and isn't it the truth?"

She went scuttling off to locate her linen logbook, and returned with it clutched in her trembling right hand. "There!" she cried triumphantly, stabbing at the date in question. "Just *there's* the proof."

Flats 1, 3, and 4 bore the caption: *changed.* Flat 2, which was Tom Mulligan's, was ominously labeled *missing—postpone linen.* The date was one day after the body of Nicholas Murphy had been discovered in Balgriffin.

"There's no question he was out all night long," Mrs. Joyce told them. "God alone knows doing what. That Mulligan."

"If I didn't know better, I would think you didn't like Mr. Mulligan. I've always found him a pleasant man, Mrs. Joyce."

The landlady's small eyes blinked rapidly, in confusion. If he's so pleasant, what do the police want with him? she seemed to say. "Why, I don't dislike Mr. Mulligan," was what she did say. "Hasn't he the best quarters in the house—sitting room, bedroom, and kitchenette? And he does pay promtly, I'll give him that. It's only a feeling I have, a feeling that he isn't always as truthful as he might be. And he's one for the ladies, too. Many's the evening I've seen that Mulligan go out wearing fancy shirts and smelling like a flower garden, and not to the pub, either. I don't object to a widower having a lady friend, providing his intentions are honorable, but there's more than one female voice that calls him up—I know, because he has to use the phone in the hallway, and don't I answer it often, and don't I hear a *variety* of them—"

"Thank you, Mrs. Joyce," said Lynch, leaping in when she was forced to take a breath. "We'll be leaving now."

"When Mr. Joyce was alive he used to say I was too hard on people, but I do have a talent for seeing beneath the surface. One of my first lodgers, I'll not say her name, was a lovely, innocent thing to look at, but—"

"I'm sorry, madam," said Frank, "but we will be late for a very important appointment if we don't leave."

"I thought so," he muttered as they were getting in the car. "I would have staked my life on it. She's peering out at us, from behind the curtains."

"Poor Mr. Joyce," said Lynch. "He's earned his rest in peace."

On the fifth night of his vigil, Matty felt sure Mr. Kennerly would appear. He had perfected his plan of action, and felt like a well-oiled machine waiting for someone to throw the switch.

Things hadn't gone at all well on the first night. He had fallen asleep around ten-thirty and wakened the next morning. On the second night he remained awake, but there had been nothing to see, and he had almost dropped off in history class the next day. On the third night he had crept into Maureen's room and borrowed her wristwatch, the one you could set and a peeping noise would go off, a noise loud enough to awaken the sleeper, but not the whole house. He set it for midnight, and returned the watch to Maureen's room when it became apparent there was to be no action.

He knelt at the window, dressed in the dark clothing he had put on before going to sleep. He had even slept in his sneakers, or rather Gervaise's sneakers, which were black. They wore the same size, and Gervaise had agreed to trade for a while without suspecting anything.

There was nothing going on in the dark Crescent below. It was eerily silent tonight, and suddenly Matty remembered what it was like, back home, in the small hours, just before morning. That was when the soldiers came on their raids, or to lift people and take them off for interrogation. One moment it would be silent and peaceful, the little streets pitch-dark, and the next thing you knew the air was full of the sounds of armored cars—pigs, they'd called them—and rifle butts smashing on doors, and angry, screaming voices. Matty had always felt the purest dread in the moments before the raids, but now, kneeling at his window in Balgriffin, he thought of them almost nostalgically. At least, back home, you knew who your enemies were.

Mrs. Naughton's big, bushy-tailed cat went streaking over three front gardens, seeking some unseen prey. A curlew called from the racecourse. The Kennerlys' door cracked open and Mr. Kennerly appeared, just as Matty had known he would.

It was 12:42 by Maureen's watch. Matty swung into action, setting his plan in motion. Without taking his eyes from Jim Kennerly, he reached for the two lumps of coal he had nicked from the shed and began to blacken his face. He had experimented with the shoe polish, rubbing some on his stomach, where no one would see, and the black patch was still visible. Jim Kennerly crossed the Crescent to Matty's side, which seemed odd until you realized that the only dog likely to bark in the night was Seamus, Gervaise's spaniel. Mr. Kennerly was making a wide berth around Seamus. Now he was passing below Matty's window. Matty let him get about twenty feet past the house, and then he crammed the black skullcap on, left his room quietly, shutting the door, and sped lightly down the stairs. He put the door on the latch, counted to ten, and then inched it open and peered out. His quarry was approaching the end of the Crescent and making to turn left onto the Gilligan Road. As soon as Kennerly had rounded the corner, Matty ran noiselessly after him. He didn't want to tailgate, but there was always the possibility that someone was waiting, in a car, on the Gilligan.

But there was no one, nothing but Mr. Kennerly walking along only a little ahead of him. There were plenty of trees on the Gilligan, and Matty hugged them, or people's hedges, as he went along. His blackout outfit was pretty good, but there was a high little half-moon sailing over the racecourse, opposite, and it cast a surprising amount of light.

Kennerly stopped momentarily at the point where the road forked by Molloy's shop. He lit a cigarette, tossed the match away, and took the left fork. Matty waited for a good while before he followed after, because this section of the road was treeless and afforded little protection. His hands were sweating in the black wool gloves, but that couldn't be helped. He kept hoping Kennerly would turn off into one of the side lanes, but he continued straight along, past the community hall where Maureen had briefly taken step-dancing lessons, past the new, white estates that were not nearly so nice, in Matty's opinion, as the Crescent houses. He followed cautiously after. Once a car went by, heading for Donahide, and he simply turned his back and hoped to be taken for a tree stump. He looked ahead to see what Kennerly was doing. The answer was nothing. He was walking in an unconcerned manner, hands in the pockets of his jogging pants.

They were coming to the bare fields near the industrial estate, were, in fact, nearly out of Balgriffin, and Matty was beginning to feel nervous. The bloody old moon seemed to fairly blaze down. He was hoping it would go behind a cloud, when Kennerly turned into the rutted dirt road that was the first entrance of the industrial estate. Matty had to run to catch up—he imagined the estate as a complicated warren of mazelike roads in which his prey could easily disappear. But when he reached the dirt road he saw Kennerly trudging along purposefully.

Matty felt more protected here. There were piles of junk, sheds, and the carcasses of old trucks to hide behind. The only thing that worried him was the animals of the Traveling People. They kept a few dispirited-looking horses, knacker's ponies, his da called them, and dogs. Mightn't the dogs summon up enough indignation in their starved bodies to produce a warning barking?

Kennerly turned left, and when Matty did the same he found himself in a rubbly road, full of pitted gullies, which seemed to consist of dingy warehouses. His foot dislodged a stone and sent it thudding into a hole, and he pressed against the side of one of the warehouses, willing himself to melt into it. He thought Kennerly broke stride a little, and saw him glance back over his shoulder. He had the unreasonable idea that the man could hear his breathing. Then there was another thud, a louder one this time, and Matty could see, tethered at the end of the road, on a small shoulder of grass, one of the knacker's ponies. He was stamping one hoof in a fretful manner, thud, thud, like the stone, and Matty wanted to laugh. Kennerly shrugged and walked on, passing the pony and heading into another road.

Here was the garage and warehouse of Denis McGuire, the man who had sold his father the Renault that was now the Keegan family car. The warehouse was the place where the arms from Australia had been found. Matty had seen Mr. McGuire's business card. The words *Praise Jesus!* had been printed in the lower right-hand corner.

Kennerly went straight in by the front door of the garage, as if he were expected, and disappeared from sight. Matty crept up to the door and laid his head against it. He could hear the rumbling of the two male voices, but the words were indistinguishable. Mr. Kennerly and Mr. McGuire sounded pleased with themselves. He even heard them laughing.

The moon seemed to be even brighter now, and Matty imagined it as a kind of sun that would melt the coal dust on his face and make him visible. It took him some time to realize that the light came from a window in the garage, a window in the connecting part that led to the warehouse. Carefully, soundlessly, he inched his way to the window, crouching beneath it. He pulled the black cap lower, to just above his eyes, and peered in. Jesus! Denis McGuire's head was about a foot away. He was gesticulating, a bottle of lemonade in his hand. Matty crouched down in great haste. He hadn't seen Kennerly at all.

When he heard McGuire's voice receding, he dared another look. The room was empty, and the door stood open. Matty clung at the window, like a bat, and tried to focus on what he could see in the dim recesses of the warehouse. The two men passed in and out of his line of vision, but he was no longer worried about them. He was focusing on a number of television sets stacked up near McGuire, and some crates, or large packages, which bore the familiar logo of a brand of whiskey, he wasn't sure which one it was. Strangest of all, something was hanging—he could glimpse it behind Mr. Kennerly's head—which didn't make sense. Matty squinted. Yes. Even though the Balgriffin industrial estate was an unlikely site for them, he knew that he was looking at—sides of beef!

He half felt in a dream. What was there in tellies and whiskey and beef that drew Mr. Kennerly out at night? Information culled from movies he had seen on television tossed the phrase *black market* into the forefront of his mind, but the black market had been during times of war. The Free State, so far as he knew, was not at war. He was suddenly tremendously sleepy, a dangerous state.

Even now Kennerly and McGuire were heading in his direction, striding quickly back to the office. Matty dropped back out of sight, but not before he had seen the pile of money, pounds and pounds of it, McGuire was extracting from some secret place.

He ran back home, speeding over the earth in Gervaise's sneakers, choosing alternate routes to avoid Kennerly. When he arrived in the Crescent the door was still on the latch, and he entered his house without trouble. He remained at the bottom of the stairs, trying to still his ragged breathing, and when he was sure he was able, climbed up to his room and looked out the window. Kennerly was just returning home, his step bouncing and triumphant.

Matty returned his sister's watch, scrubbed the coal dust from his face, and fell into an exhausted sleep, still fully clothed. For the first time since he had left Belfast, he dreamed of the time when he had been shot. The plastic bullet that slammed into him had miraculous powers, turning him, at the moment of impact, from a boy to a side of beef. *Praise Jesus!* cried the voice of Denis McGuire.

On the following day, he was sent to Brother Ignatius, the guidance counselor. "Is there something troubling ye, Matthew?" Brother Ignatius asked.

"No," said Matty, who had a hard time understanding the counselor's Galway accent. "Not a'*tall*."

THIRTEEN

They quite understood his desire to preserve the lady's anonymity, and they even commended him for his chivalrous attitude, but surely Mr. Mulligan could see they couldn't accept his alibi without a shred of evidence to back it up? If Mr. Mulligan could tell them the name of the hotel where he and the lady had stayed, perhaps they could authenticate his allegations through the desk clerk?

Mr. Mulligan, who was now sterilizing some glasses in the machine, relived every moment of his interview with the Gardai detectives. The one who had always struck him as being sympathetic, Lynch, was helpful as could be, offering Tom every conceivable loophole through which he might escape suspicion. Even Browne, whom Tom had not thought particularly sympathetic, had seemed to be on his side this time around. "Possibly you used an assumed name," Browne had said. "If you'll give us the name, we can verify at the hotel."

The trouble was that there had been no hotel. He had taken Rita to the bungalow of an old friend who lived in Bray, and who was off fishing in Cork. The detectives assured him that they would hold the entire matter in the strictest confidence. No one but Lynch and Brown would know the identity of the woman, but he had been up that particular street with Rita, and it was no go. He told them so, told them the woman in question would rather perjure herself than admit to her sins, and would see him imprisoned for life rather than admit to the naughty night in Bray. That was just the sort of a female she happened to be, he told them, picturing their reaction if he let it slip that his lover was Scully's wife.

"Tom!" implored Cats Phelan, who was trying to make his way to the men's room without notable success. Poor Phelan's feet weren't up to it. They rose and fell, chopping at the air, without propelling him in any special direction. Tom came from under the hatch and went to Cats, slipping his arm beneath the arm of the old man, and conducted him to the place where he could relieve himself. Waiting, shepherdlike, outside the gents', he heard the voice of Imelda Kennerly in the saloon bar. She was ordering a vodka and red from Mick. She would be perched on the high stool, twiddling her badminton racket against her bare thighs, waiting for him to appear.

Mightn't Imelda, unlike Rita, quicken to his plight? Wasn't she a natural ally?

Cats hurtled from the door, like a bull from its pen, and Tom caught him in his arms, half carrying him back to his bench. Then he removed the sterilized glasses, smoothed his hair, and went through into the other bar. His tentative plan was outrageous, but so was his predicament. Imelda would either grasp the situation at once, or she would take offense. In either case, he had to act. Lynch had made it very clear that Tom was between a rock and a hard place. The next time he was summoned for questioning, Lynch had implied, might be the last. Tom must be prepared to offer up some concrete facts.

"How're you doing, then, Tom?" She greeted him.

"Poorly," said Tom, "and that's the truth. I'm doing poorly, Imelda."

Her nice red face reddened further, with concern, and her eyes became positively misty when he described the horns of his dilemma. He never mentioned Rita's name, but he played heavily on the fact of her callous nature.

"The bitch," she said. "The class of a *bitch*, not to care!"

"She hasn't your finer sensibilities, love."

"Oh, but, Tom, this is very serious, isn't it? Can they really arrest you and all, just because you can't prove where you were that night?"

This was a delicate matter. Tom, although afraid, did not really see how the police could arrest him without evidence, but they could make his life miserable. And there was always the chance that some fantastic coincidence could crop up, something that would appear to link him with the crime. It suited his purpose that Imelda be made to fear the worst, and so he said, a little guiltily, "You know how it is, Mrs. K. Or you can imagine, Imelda, what it's like for the boyos in the gardai. Put yourself in their shoes. What does it look like to the public, a fella murdered and weeks goin' by without any arrest? They get desperate, after a while, and then they'll collar anyone they can. Right now I'm the only likely suspect. They might even plant evidence."

"Jesus, the beasts!"

He could see he'd gone too far. "Well, this Lynch, he seems a decent, good man. He's no Heavy Gang garda, Imelda. He guaranteed everything would be confidential. My lady friend wouldn't have been subjected to anything *improper*, you know. But even Lynch . . ." He let the sentence trail off meaningfully.

Imelda was gulping her vodka and red and shaking her head in disgust. Suddenly she froze and regarded him with crafty eyes. "I wouldn't know this lady friend, would I? Is she local?"

"Ah no, no. She's someone I used to know in Sligo, when we were kids."

He went to replenish her drink. He considered making it a double, which would have the effect of making her twice as sentimentally sympathetic, but he couldn't justify it. Imelda was on the verge of having a "problem" and he did not wish to contribute to it.

"I've been thinking," she said when he returned. "You know who might be able to help?"

"Who's that, Imelda?" he asked softly, hoping she was being coy.

"Joe Scully. He's a garda, after all, even if he only works the lost and found. He could tell the detectives what a good man you are, how ridiculous it is to even suspect you of murder, and maybe—coming from one of their own—they'd believe him."

' "No! Sorry, didn't mean to shout, Imelda. No, Joe wouldn't be yer man, love. Not at all. In fact, Joe Scully is the very last person to approach."

"Why's that, Tom?"

Why? "Joe Scully," Tom improvised, "thinks adultery is ten times worse than murder. He'd want to bring back hanging in my case. Did you never hear him go on about how all this random sex is ruining our society?"

"No," said Imelda. "I didn't think he was a moralizer. And with that wife of his, that stuck-up Rita, I should think Joe got more than his share. Of, you know, sex. But maybe you're right. Maybe it's because of Rita, her being so much younger and all, that he's down on adultery."

They were both silent then. Imelda splashed a bit more lemonade into her drink and stared into the reddish liquid moodily. "Well," she said at last. "What *would* help, Tom? Do you have a clue at all?"

"The only thing that would save my neck is something I can't see happening. Not in a million years. No, it's not even worth mentioning, Imelda, because it'll never be."

"Go on, Tom. Never say never, as James Bond would tell you. The way I look at it, you've got to grasp at every available straw."

"If a lady, a lady who was a friend of mine and wanted to be helpful, if this lady would present herself at the garda station and swear—*in confidence*—that she had been with me all that night, the pressure would be off."

Deliberately Imelda extracted a cigarette from her packet and lit it, declining his proffered match, with an orange butane lighter. The cool manner of her inhalation intimidated him, and he laughed. "You see how impossible the situation is," he said.

"Oh, shut yerself up, Tom Mulligan," Imelda said. She continued to smoke, with a wise and canny air, and Tom didn't know where to look. A loud, crashing noise was heard in the public bar, and he darted in, expecting to find Cats lying in the aisle. Instead he encountered a local fisherman who had upset a barstool. He served the stout and passed a few matey words, all the time fearing that Imelda Kennerly had used this God-given opportunity to desert him. Yet when he returned to the saloon bar she was still there, sedate and contemplative.

"All right," she said. "I'll do it, Tom. I'm yer woman, only what do I wear?"

"Wear?" he asked, weak with gratitude.

"Do you want me to look tarty? Or just regular?"

"Regular would be grand, Imelda. No need to overdo it."

He squeezed her hand in an inarticulate, powerful gesture of thanks. He felt love for her at that moment, or, at the very least, a true and boundless affection. It was more than he had ever felt for Rita.

A smallish shape was approaching. One of the children. A boy. Something about the walk . . . "Would that be young Matty Keegan?" Andy Halloran said to himself.

"Mr. Halloran," Matty said, stopping right in his path. "Are you going home for your tea now?"

"That was my plan, yes."

"Do you mind if I walk along with you? There was something I wanted to discuss with you."

"Of course," Andy said, smiling at the boy's serious manner. He was aware that Matty had to adjust his pace to walk by his side, and felt sorry. One of the joys of childhood was in the capacity for speed. He remembered himself, a boy of Matty's age, seeming to cross St. Stephen's Green in a few leaps, bounding up the six flights of steps to his family's flat, without feeling it at all. And later, when he was a messenger boy, pedaling the heavy old bicycle, moving like the wind . . .

"Just supposing it was true," Matty was saying. "It's not, but just if it was?"

Scobie understood that the boy was proposing to tell him a story—he had heard part of what Matty had said, through his reverie—and that he was supposed to regard what he heard as fiction. The boy wasn't old enough to realize how common a ploy was his technique of confession, and confession was exactly what he had been receiving from Matty. Some small transgression, probably. *What if a boy waited and waited at Molloy's, to pay for some sweets, and nobody came, and he finally walked out with them in his hand? Would that be stealing?*

Instead, Matty was laying the groundwork for a more intricate tale. It had to do with roving about the town in the dead of night and seeing something peculiar. Two men, known to the fictive narrator, had amassed many goods in a warehouse, and money was exchanged. Large amounts of money.

"Just imagine, if there was whiskey and tellies and big sides of meat," Matty said. "What would you make of it?"

They had reached the end of the back lane leading from the pub. To stall for time, Scobie searched out a longish butt and lit it. "People shouldn't go gallivantin' about in the night," he said. "It could be dangerous."

"Yeah," said Matty fervently, "but what do you make of the other? The stuff in the warehouse?"

He could feel the boy's desperate desire for enlightenment, and he had no doubt that Matty, or one of his friends, had witnessed just such a scene. A warehouse meant the industrial estate, for there were no other warehouses in Balgriffin. Mother of God, what was a child the age of Matty Keegan doing, prowling about the industrial estate in the middle of the night? Why was he there, and what was the world coming to?

It appeared he had spoken the last words out loud, because Matty now said, "What were you doing in the Customs House when the Black and Tans lobbed that bomb in, and afterward you had a drink and all, and you weren't much older than I am now?"

Matty had spoken with asperity, and Scobie had to laugh. His shoulders shook with laughter, and he permitted himself to say, "Oh boys, oh boys."

"See," Matty said, "I saw it on the television, but my mother made me go to bed before it was over. I never found out what the two men were doing."

"Why not ask your mother? Or your da?"

Matty's silence was pitiable. Clever as he was, he could not sort out the truth from the reality. Scobie didn't wish to bait him, but he did believe that parental authority was needed. Someone must see that Matty stayed in his bed at night, and that someone could not be half-blind Andy Halloran, who, much as he liked the boy, was not up to the task of supervising him.

"They wouldn't know," said Matty at last. "They weren't watching. It was an American crime show."

"Well," said Scobie, relenting, "I wouldn't know about America, but I'll tell you what they were doing here, in Ireland. All those things in the warehouse—they're much cheaper over the border, in the North. You lived in Belfast, Matty, but a body doesn't have to go so far as Belfast. Ah no, right over the border, in Newry Town, a man can buy whiskey for a third less than it would cost him here. And television sets. And joints of beef. It's the British pound and our poor Irish punt, Matty."

"The black market."

"Similar," said Scobie. "A fella knows a lorry driver who makes the regular run up North, and there you have it. The lorry driver makes a bit of extra, the fella who's arranged it makes another bit, and the one who sells it makes the most of all."

"In the show, the man who owned the warehouse was payin' off the other man," Matty said thoughtfully. "It's against the law, isn't it?"

"You can bet on it. If it was legal, Matty, sure, the men wouldn't have to off-load it at night." They began to walk on, turning into his road. He smelled the perfume of roses from a neighbor's garden, and regretted that all he could see of them was a dull smudge of red. When they reached his house, Scobie idled a bit, finishing his cigarette, trying to think what would be best for Matty.

"Do you think the boy should have done something?" Matty asked. "Told the police?"

"No, I don't. He wasn't sure what he was seeing, and it *could* have been something legal—I'm only after telling you what I think they were doing. And if it was the illegal business, there's no need to tell the gardai."

"How's that, then?"

"They'll find out soon enough, on their own."

"But our gardai never found who killed the man on the racecourse," said Matty stubbornly.

"Ah, now we're talking about real life again, young Matt. Now, if both these events, the ones from the film and the killing, if both had occurred in real life—I'd say there would be no connection between the two."

"That's good, then." Matty's voice seemed, to Scobie's ear, to reverberate with relief.

"It's too bad you couldn't see the ending of it," he said, unlatching his garden gate. "I'd be interested in knowing if the boy learned his lesson."

"Which lesson would that be?"

"That when he goes to bed, he should stay there until the morning comes. Even the cleverest boy could come to grief alone, in the night."

"That's so, Mr. Halloran. Thank you for talking to me."

"All the best, Matty."

As he walked up the path, Scobie pondered the identities of the men in the warehouse. He was fairly sure that one was Denis McGuire, the odd lad who had been so prompt to notify the authorities about the arms from Australia. Denis McGuire had acted with such alacrity because he wanted to be above suspicion. He planned on using the warehouse to receive goods smuggled over the border, and it wouldn't do to be less than an exemplary citizen. But who was the other man?

He remembered the peculiar Englishman who used to come to the pub of an evening. Bob, his name had been. There had been something very wrong with Bob, some subtle spring in his head that had come undone and prompted him to behave in a dangerous manner. Surrounded by Irishmen, Bob would deliberately boast of his time in the British Army. Sometimes what he said was plausible, but at other times he seemed to be weaving grotesque fantasies. Once he had leaned over in an intimate manner and whispered, "I have the gun that murdered Michael Collins. It's been in my wife's family's possession for years."

Bob seemed to want, when he had drunk more than was good for him, to inflame the passions of his fellow drinkers, to turn them against him. He seemed to be asking to be punished, but it never worked out that way. People were elaborately polite and courteous to Bob, as they would have been to a madman. He seemed a likely candidate for mischief until Scobie remembered—at the exact moment his wife opened the door and inquired what had kept him so long—that Bob had gone off to serve time in Mountjoy Prison.

Imelda had taken pains with her appearance, and she thought she looked both attractive and respectable. The yellow dress brought out the amber in her dark eyes, and the hem was just short enough to draw attention to her legs without making her seem a tart. Daintily she recrossed her legs and looked back at Lynch unflinchingly.

"Yes, that's right, sir, we spent the entire night together. I didn't get back until the next morning, in time to make breakfast for my son. He's still in school, you see. He's only eleven."

She was passing with flying colors. Tom had rehearsed her, in the saloon bar, and she had given Lynch the address of the bungalow in Bray, together with the information that nobody had seen them.

"Didn't your husband wonder where you'd gone?" Lynch asked.

Imelda permitted herself a dramatic laugh, a real film-star laugh. "Oh dear," she said. "My husband. My husband is involved with a disco dolly from Portmarnock, sad to say. He wouldn't notice whether I was there or not, Sergeant."

"I'm sorry to hear it, Mrs. Kennerly."

"Sure, Sergeant Lynch, do you think I would have strayed without provocation?"

Lynch dipped his head in an embarrassed manner and waved his hands about. "There is one thing I'd like to ask you," he said. "Mr. Mulligan gave me to understand that you would never consent to do what you are doing now. What made you change your mind?"

Oh, this was great stuff! She was being asked to philosophize. Exhilarating, it was. She, Imelda, was needed not only as an alibi, but as a human agent, capable of thought and feeling.

"It's like this," she told Lynch. "You notice when a marriage begins to go sour, but there's always meals to be made, kids to worry over, the washing to do, and, what with one thing and another, you pretend *not* to notice. Sweep it under the rug. But at the end of the day, when it's too late, you wish you hadn't. You're sorry.

"When Tom first asked me would I help him, I was feeling sorry for myself. I mean, there's my husband carrying on with a girl barely older than our daughter, and here's *me*, being unfaithful for the first time in my life—Tom is the only other man I've been with, Sergeant—and what happens? I get involved in a murder case. Oh no. I told him I couldn't put up with that sort of a humiliation. I was imagining headlines and public snickering—oh, the lot. But Tom told me that you were an extremely nice fella and everything would be confidential, and then I got to thinking.

"What if Tom got put in prison because I was back sweepin' things under the rug again? I lost my husband for ignoring reality, Sergeant Lynch. I didn't want to lose Tom his freedom, too. I couldn't have lived with meself."

"You have my heartfelt thanks, Mrs. Kennerly. And Tom was right about the confidentiality—your name will never pass my lips."

The gallant little phrase remained with her as she waited in the bus queue. She did not feel at all guilty about lying. In fact, she felt exalted. *Your name will never pass my lips.* She had got Tom off the hook and had a secret adventure. And there was another, meaner, consolation. She had struck back at Jim. Even if there was only one man in Dublin who believed it, it was sweet to think she had put the horns on James Kennerly.

FOURTEEN

Robert Malone's appearance at the pub in Balgriffin caused a stir. It had nothing to do with his long absence—most of the patrons knew he had been in Mountjoy—but rather with his physical condition. His left temple was bruised and discolored, and clotted blood darkened one whole side of his face.

"Here's trouble back," Cats Phelan wheezed in Andy Halloran's ear. "Someone's fetched him a tremendjous clout."

"Oh Jesus," breathed Mrs. Higgins (who was the grandmother of Gervaise). "Ice is what's needed. Someone get him some lumps of ice." Her husband obediently went to the bar and got some ice from Tom Mulligan. Mrs. Higgins was fumbling in her bag for a hankie, but Malone had dropped down on the bench near Scobie Halloran.

"What the hell ran into *you?*" asked Neal, the gravedigger and football coach. Margaret Corcoran passed through and averted her eyes. The young girls knew not to come too close to Malone.

"If I'm not mistaken," said Scobie Halloran, "Bob is in our midst again."

And then Malone, accepting ice and hankie without thanks, began to speak. "Oh, bloody hell," he said in a dramatic voice. "I took the shortcut, over the fields, and I was set upon by a gang of boys. Teenagers, they were, seventeen or eighteen. Big lads, spoiling for trouble." He had taken out a roll-up and was making a cigarette. The ice was melting in the ashtray, but Mrs. Higgins's handkerchief remained plastered to the side of his face. He was wearing a laborer's flat cap and looked pale.

"Were they Balgriffin boys?" cried old Mrs. McGreavy.

"Don't know, but they had lead pipes. They were shouting at me. 'Get out, you bloody Brit. *Brit! Brit!* Bloody *Brit!*' "

"Oh, the shame of it," clucked Mrs. Higgins, "the terrible shame."

"I can tell you," said Malone, bending in close to Scobie, "I'll be armed next time. I intend to make a full report of this."

"Oh, by all means," Scobie replied. "That's a very wise move, Bob." His shoulders were shaking.

While Malone was at the bar, ordering a Guinness, Cats said the man was full of shite. Scobie nodded in agreement. "There's something wrong there," was what he said.

"Aye," said Cats. "He's an eejit."

"A troubled soul," said Scobie. "He needs to go to the Sea of Tranquillity."

"Balls," said Cats.

When Malone returned from the bar, bearing his pint, he sank onto the bench with a depressing, an artificial, familiarity.

"Here now," he said to Scobie, unmistakably, as if he had singled him out for special favor. "Did I ever tell you that my wife's family owns the gun that murdered Michael Collins?"

"Oh boys, oh boys," said Scobie gleefully. "Many's the time you've told me, Bob. Michael Collins was a fine lump of a man, wasn't he?"

"It didn't prevent his getting killed, you'd admit?"

"It did not."

"They all die, in the end," said Malone. "Everyone dies."

"Sooner or later," said Scobie. "Sooner or later."

"This isn't my first drink, you know," Malone announced. "I called in at the pub up on the sea road, about a mile from Balgriffin."

"Who cares?" screamed Cats, who was the only one present who was habitually rude to Robert Malone. "We can see it's not your first, man. Christ."

Malone ignored Cats and homed in on Scobie, as he had so often in the past. It seemed strange that he should seek the company, the approval, almost, of a man so much older than himself. "I'll be armed, next time," he repeated. "What do you say to that, Mr. Halloran?"

"With the gun that shot Michael Collins," Mr. Higgins whispered to his wife in a sarcastic manner.

Scobie, it seemed, could scarcely control his mirth. "If you want to report the incident, there's a garda just down the bench, Joe Scully. Of course, he's not on duty now, but he'd be delighted to hear your complaint."

They were all having to control laughter now. The very idea of Joe Scully coping with Robert Malone! Very few of them believed Malone's story about the vicious youths with lead pipes; even those who had thought it true initially had been persuaded, by the man's general looniness, to doubt. He had been injured, that was surely true, but not in the manner he had told of.

To everyone's discomfort, Malone stayed on until closing. By ten he was going on about parachuting into Korea, when everyone gave the Yanks all the credit on *that* operation, and by half-past he was touching on the dangerous topic of tours of duty in the North of Ireland, which he called "Ulster." During most of the final hour he retreated to the far end of the bar, where he surveyed the room with an expression both grandiose and melancholy. His face was drawn and pale, like that of a man who had been in prison, but it had always been like that, for as long as any of them had known him.

Just before closing, he came back to Scobie's table. "I'll be making a full report," he said, as if to take up the conversation started two hours earlier. "Higher circles are called for. Top secret. Do you understand what I'm saying?"

"Oh, to be sure I do, Bob. Safe home, now, all the best."

Malone blinked at the words of farewell. He seemed confused, a man who had not planned to leave but who would now have to do so. He pulled his cloth cap down and left without another word.

"Why does a man like that come into a place like this at all?" Gerry O'Hara said.

"His time inside has driven him over the edge," said Neal. "He's become a lunatic."

A fisherman who rarely spoke looked up at Gerry in amazement. "Sure, he's always been like that," he said.

"Come along lads, *please!*" bellowed Tom Mulligan, beginning his first plea for closing. He could hardly bear to look at Joe Scully because, pressing against his chest, in the pocket of his own shirt, was the small and costly bottle of scent he had bought as a thank-you present for Imelda Kennerly. He had forgotten to remove it before going on duty, and all night long it had seemed to be singing from his pocket: *Sinner!*

"The Malone fella's out of Mountjoy," Frank told Lynch.

They had just returned from the Four Courts, where the case they were due to give evidence for had been postponed yet again. Lynch's face had an ominous, thundery look to it. He went on two-fingering his report, seeming oblivious to Frank. Just when Frank was about to leave the room, though, Lynch looked up and sighed.

"Would you like to know how he spent his first evening as a free man?" he said.

"Malone, you mean?"

"The same. He brought his oldest son with him to that wee pub up Donahide way, on the sea road. They had a few jars together, and then they proceeded to get into a violent quarrel in the car park. Quarrel turned into a fistfight. Nice carry-on, right Frank? Malone, Sr., was the loser—he is not, as they say, a spring chicken, and the lad is twenty-two. Malone just went reeling off and turned up in the Balgriffin pub sometime later."

"How do you know this, Sean?"

"I thought it best to have a man tail him for the first few days of his return to society. I thought it possible he might do something of a revealing nature, something to do with his less than pristine past."

"You mean to say you connect him with the Balgriffin business?"

Lynch opened a desk drawer and withdrew an ancient packet of Player's. It had been there for as long as Frank could remember, and he had only seen Sean take a smoke from it once before, on the day Una had called to say their daughter had gone into labor up North. He had given up smoking before Frank had known him, but the packet of Player's remained for emergencies. How this moment qualified as an emergency, Frank could not imagine. It made him uneasy.

Lynch didn't even inhale deeply, as a true, deprived addict might have done. He smoked in the manner of an inexperienced young girl, lightly puffing and exhaling. It was the mechanism which seemed to comfort him. The old ritual.

"Supposing Malone is still half-sane," he said, speaking through a cloud of smoke, "he has provided us with the only conceivable identity for the dead man. You'll recall Nick the Prick? Sure, I know you remember everything, Frank, no need to glower. The city of Abu Dhabi draws a blank on Mr. Murphy. M15 and M16 draws a blank on Mr. Murphy. *Everyone* draws a blank on Mr.—"

"Bergit could have been lying," Frank pointed out.

"I don't think so. Our Lady of the Sculptured Textiles, or whatever the hell they are, is quite capable of lying, but I don't think she had the need to lie. She'd only been married a few weeks, Frank, and she wasn't very particular. I think she was as confused about him as we are, only she didn't give a damn. What difference did it make *what* he was, so long as he paid the bills?"

"The Brits could be lying, too. If he was involved in some ugly operations, something bad and covert, like deep interrogation techniques, say, they'd deny him. He might be an embarrassment to them."

"Oh, no doubt a'tall on that, Frank. It's the two things together, though, that make me suspicious. Even a retired SAS man is bound to leave a record in the United Arab Emirates, especially if he's an 'adviser' to a company or corporation there." Lynch scrubbed at his head irritably and then extinguished his cigarette with a furious plunge into a small tin ashtray.

"Your best bet," he continued, "is that Murphy was a mercenary. He may have started out in the SAS and then opted out. You heard what Malone said —a lot of them joined the Rhodesian Army for a while. At the time of his death, he was a bit advanced in age to do the dirty, and taking up a career as an adviser wouldn't really line his nest, would it now?"

"Not enough to draw Bergit in," said Frank.

"But becoming an arms dealer would," said Lynch. "Very profitable business, I've been told."

Frank sat on the edge of the desk. Lynch's theories, like the brightly plumaged birds in the zoo at Phoenix Park, were attractive and interesting, but somehow implausible. Too exotic. They did not belong in Dublin, no more than did the birds.

"What's Malone to do with this?" he asked. "A man on the dole who couldn't afford to pay the child support to his estranged wife? A fella was in jail when the deed occurred?"

"Oh, all he did was provide a connection," said Lynch impatiently. "It's the Yank that figures here, Frank, the Yank the kids saw. Isn't it possible the Yank and Murphy were both mercenaries who crossed paths in Rhodesia or Vietnam or whatever Christ-forsaken place in the world you can call up? Mightn't Murphy have 'burned' the Yank, as the Americans say about drugs, and got his comeuppance on the racecourse?"

"You mean," said Frank, aware of how slow he sounded, "that Murphy promised arms and failed to deliver?"

"You could put it that way."

"But what were they both doing in Dublin?"

For answer, Lynch tipped the tin ashtray with its one butt into his wastebasket, and closed the drawer viciously.

"What were they fighting about—Malone and his son?"

"Best as O'Keefe could tell, about Mrs. Malone. The lad was defending his mother."

"Where's she, then?"

"In County Cork, son. Deep in Michael Collins country, and very ill. In the bosom of Mother Ireland, where there's no divorce."

The calm in Balgriffin was a superficial one. The children were merely biding their time until school would be over, and could scarcely bear to go to bed during the long, white nights of early summer. Midsummer Eve came and went, and it was nearly eleven when the last light faded from the sky. The weather held, and people remarked on it, but superstitiously, always careful to add that it could break at any moment. Rhubarb in the Crescent gardens grew strong and tall, nearly ready for pies, and Mrs. O'Rourke's mauve hydrangeas looked good enough to eat.

Imelda Kennerly was able to wear her shorts quite a lot, and she surprised Kate and Nora by her seemingly miraculous recovery from despair. They no longer had to keep an uneasy watch over her, dragging her off to play badminton, or forcing her to drink coffee and eat biscuits in their kitchens.

Imelda, if not happy, was at least no longer wretched and never, to the best of Kate's knowledge, paralytic at nine in the morning.

Humble holidays were planned. A week in Wexford for the Brannigans, a visit to Belfast, which was comparatively quiet at the moment, for the Keegans, who wished to see their families. Gervaise Doherty's parents announced plans to go to Tramore, while Janie Keane would actually be taking the ferry to England, where the Keanes would visit relatives in Sheffield. But all these bold plans were in the future, July or August, and in the present there was only a sense of anticipation, and the artificial calm.

In spite of the sunny skies and droning bees and the promise of rhubarb pies, Nora Keegan knew that Jim Kennerly did something ominous by night. Her son knew what it was, although she didn't know he knew, and he was burdened by the knowledge. There was a vague, unvoiced fear in the pub that Malone might return one day with the promised gun and run amok. One read of such things. And, also unvoiced, there was a common edginess in Balgriffin which had not been there before the man had been discovered in the grandstand. They had all agreed that the murder had nothing to do with them or their village and that the murderer—whoever he was—was many miles away and would never return. Nevertheless, the people of Balgriffin, and especially those of the Crescent, were careful to lock doors that had formerly been left on the latch. Some of the older residents, like Mrs. Higgins, crossed themselves hastily whenever they went by the low wall of the racecourse.

It was the children of the Conspiracy who suffered most. As day after day went by without an arrest, they began to feel they had done something dreadfully, monumentally wrong. Because they were different in character and temperament, they reached this conclusion at different stages. Matty and Janie Keane were the first to acknowledge it, if only to themselves. Gervaise, Kevin, and Rory began to suffer from guilt at a slightly later date.

Terry Brannigan was the last to be smitten, but this was not because he was thick-skinned or stupid. He had been praised at school so often for his initiative—what he called his "leadership qualities"—that it had never occurred to him to doubt that what he proposed was correct and righteous. Now monstrous doubt entered his heart and tormented him. He had been the leader. Even if Janie had been the one to suggest an imaginary Yank, the idea of the Council had been his. If the murderer lived among them, undetected, he would never be discovered because of their lie to the detective. And if he killed again, it would be Terry's fault.

"Oh, Wolfe Tone," he whispered, catching the dog by its paws and executing a melancholy jig in the garden, "what have we done?"

FIFTEEN

On the map, the peninsula was a thin finger pointing into the Atlantic, small and accessible. In reality, there seemed no end to it. Lynch felt as if he had been driving for hours, jouncing over rutted, unpaved roads, in an immensity of gorse, seeing no human figure. Occasionally he came to small farmhouses, but there was never any sign of life within.

He had been in County Cork many times—in Cork City, and once, on a holiday, fishing on the Blackwater at Fermoy. The part of the county in which he was now floundering was unknown to him, although the names of some of the towns were familiar, having played their tragic parts in Irish history. Skibbereen, Clonakilty, the Bay of Kinsale . . . Jesus, but it was a lonely place, this peninsula!

The road turned sharply left and upward, and there appeared a dizzying view of the sea, blue and disorienting to look at. A little ahead of him he saw what seemed to be a stone cottage, but when he came nearer it proved to be a ruin. The roof had long since fallen, and a tree now grew in what had been someone's home. The sea disappeared, as if by magic, and the road ended abruptly. He got out of the car and immediately heard the hollow booming of waves on rocks. He was on the brow of a cliff, then.

Cautiously he walked in the direction of the sea sounds. The ground was rocky, covered with the pale gray vegetation that grows only in sight of the ocean. He could hear gulls screaming and thought of how frightened Una would be. She disliked heights, and had nearly fainted at the Cliffs of Moher. This, he acknowledged, was a different matter. In elusive West Cork, the sea played games with you. It appeared and vanished, reappeared on a different side of the car than it ought to be, and finally dared you to come out of your car and hunt it down.

"I am supposed to be a detective," he said aloud, the wind snatching the words from his mouth. "Killers may elude me, but if I can't even find the Atlantic, I'd better chuck it in."

A few more steps, and he had his reward. He seemed to be standing at the top of the world, at the apex of two jutting heads of land. The cliffs were of a peculiar, terra-cotta color, and the long swells bashing away at the rocks below were green, not blue. Behind him he could see the road he had taken, a deceptive road that looped back on itself in its steady climb upward. At one point it dipped down to a sort of cove, and then it forked in two directions. He had obviously taken the wrong fork.

There seemed to be a sort of lesson in this wrong decision of his. He had taken the wrong road because it looked like the more likely of the two. Imperceptibly, it seemed the more well traveled—although that phrase in this place was a joke—and it also had seemed to be an extension of the road he had come down, while the other meandered off to the devil knew where. What could he learn from this simple driver's mistake? How could the impulse that had propelled him in the wrong direction be put to any practical use, even supposing he understood it?

Gulls were flapping away beneath him. Far beneath. A few seemed to hover motionlessly, like helicopters. He felt a brief spell of vertigo pass over him: a sign of the aging process.

He went back to the car, reversed down the steepest part of the road, and turned, heading for the cove.

Robert Malone's wife looked, like her estranged husband, as if she had recently emerged from prison. Her face was drawn and wan and revealed much of the bone structure beneath the flesh. It was fine molding, and he guessed that she had once been very pretty. Her reddish hair, brittle now from the effects of her illness, was cut short and neatly combed. She wore a white smock, festive, inappropriate red jeans, and thong sandals. Like Una, she had slender and aristocratic feet. Her toenails were painted palest pink, and Lynch wondered who had performed this service for her. Her name was Maeve.

The woman who had answered the door he took to be her mother.

"Good afternoon," he had said politely, wanting to allay her natural suspicion, that of a countrywoman, at any unexpected happening. "I've come down from Dublin in the hopes of a few words with Mrs. Malone." He could see Mrs. Malone, seated in a chair, raise her head in alarm at his words. There was a long silence, during which he had had time to observe her, before anyone spoke.

"Ye'd best come in, then," said the older woman, standing away from the door. "Will I bring you some tea?"

"Please, Mam," said Maeve Malone. Her voice was low and melodious. Lynch knew her name from reading the reports on Malone's nonpayment charge. He knew that she was ill because the reports had included the fact that the wife in the case was incapacitated and unable to work. What a difference to be confronted by the woman who had existed only as a name in police files; how real she was, putting away the Sunday supplement she had been reading and indicating to him that he should sit. Maeve.

"Run along now and play for a bit," she said.

He had trouble with this, until a tall, freckled girl of perhaps twelve rose from the depths of a battered sofa that faced away from him. She left without a word. She would be the younger of the two dependent children. The oldest Malone child, a man, really, had recently battered his father over some matter pertaining to his mother. It all seemed unutterably sad, and Lynch wondered how the woman from this lonely Cork peninsula had ever met the man he had interviewed in prison.

Mrs. Malone took up the poker and stirred at the little turf fire burning beside her. Even in summer, it was chilly inside the old stone house. "You've come about Bobbie?" she said. "And are y'from the gardai?"

"I am, Mrs. Malone. Detective-sergeant, but I've not come in my professional capacity."

She dropped the poker with a clatter. "Not come?" she asked. "But surely . . . Is he dead, then? Is Bobbie dead?"

"No, no, Mrs. Malone, dear. I'm very sorry to have alarmed you so." Lynch spoke in desperation, out of his own alarm. The poor, frail creature had showed him a face of resigned dread. For years, he felt, she had been waiting for the moment when some official personage would appear to tell her that Malone had died.

"He's out of prison?"

Lynch nodded.

"Has he done something so soon?"

"No. I've come about something else, something I thought you might be able to help me sort out."

The mother came in with two cups of tea, which she deposited on a rolling tea trolley he had not noticed. She disappeared again and returned with a half loaf of warm soda bread and a crock of sweet butter. "I'll just go to the byre," she said to her daughter.

"It was a mistake, his going to prison," Maeve Malone said, staring into her tea. "I never intended it. Only I thought he was still working for the Forestry—I never knew they gave him the sack. I've got the two young ones, Mr. Lynch, and it's hard, and I went to this solicitor in Skibbereen. If only I was after knowing he'd been sacked."

"He told me it was a mistake, Mrs. Malone. When I interviewed him, *visited* him, in Mountjoy. He knows."

"What call had you to visit him in Mountjoy? What has he done now?" Mrs. Malone attempted to sip from her cup of tea, but her motor coordination was failing her suddenly. Her lips fell shy of the cup, and her hands trembled badly. A degenerative nerve disease? Lynch thought of Malone's hands, in prison, trembling as they tried to roll a homemade, and was sickened by the irony of it. She set the cup down with a clash, defeated.

He told her about the death on the racecourse, describing the events in as neutral and professional a manner as he could. He included periodic reassurances—Robert Malone, having been in Mountjoy at the time of the murder, was not under suspicion. She listened with intelligence, was even able, at one point, to sip tea with a steady hand. He reconstructed his vain attempts to link the dead man with the SAS and reiterated his feeling that Nicholas Murphy, in some way as yet unknown to him, had been killed for mercenary activities. At last, when the story lay unfolded before her, he broached the topic of her husband's hints about the victim's possible, only *possible*, identity.

"Nicholas," said Maeve Malone. "Nick, for short. They had a rhyme about him, you're after guessing it, I know. Are you not?"

"Nick the—next word begins with a *P?*"

"It does," said Maeve saucily. "Five letters. The word with the *P* doesn't begin to sum him up, Sergeant. It's far too innocent to describe yer man."

Lynch heard the far-off bellowing of cattle and smelled the warm odor—cow breath sweetened on clover, and cow dung, rich and offensive—through the half-opened window. *The gun that shot Michael Collins.*

"How would you describe him?" he asked.

"Sure, I've never met him. I've never laid eyes on him, and I'd say neither did Bobbie. He was a legend, though, for a while, and ye'd hear various things about what Murphy was up to. Bobbie would, I mean, and sometimes he'd tell me."

"What sorts of things? Can you recall any?"

Maeve Malone looked away from him. "Why not ask Bob?"

"Your husband—forgive me, but I must be truthful—is somewhat given to exaggeration, Mrs. Malone. I would rather hear it from you."

She smiled, and it seemed genuine, if rueful. "Aye, he is, Mr. Lynch, but in that case I'm no better as a source of information than he is. I got the stories from him, did I not?"

He spread a slice of soda bread with butter, fairly troweling it on and ignoring his diet. Una would be horrified at the amount of cholesterol he was preparing to consume. He would mark it down to occupational hazard; he was doing the business with the bread to make Maeve Malone think he was embarrassed at having been bested. That way, when he answered her, she would be caught off her guard, and inclined, because of the personal nature of what he was going to say, to speak the truth.

"How I see it," he said, leaving the bread untouched, "is that your husband wasn't always the way he is now. I don't think you married a compulsive liar, Mrs. Malone. I see all that as coming later, after he'd left the British Army and joined the private sector. A problem of learning to adjust, in his case." He bit into the bread and chewed slowly, with pleasure, giving her time to react to what he had said.

"Ye seem to know him very well," she replied wearily. "From the age of eighteen he was in the army, and he should never have been in at all. He wasn't that class of a man should have been a soldier to begin with! Bob could have done grand, fine things, Mr. Lynch, for he had the true intellect. It was the intelligence did him in. Didn't the British Government decide to award one scholarship a year to the poor but deserving? Didn't they pluck some ragged Paddy from the heart of Kilburn, or wherever, and send him off, all free, to some posh Brit school where all the sons of the landed gentry could make sport of him?"

She was speaking in a low, rapid voice, as if imparting the greatest secret of all. She glanced nervously in the direction of the door, as if she feared that her mother might overhear.

"Bobbie went to *Eton*," she whispered. "From the time he was fifteen. That's how he got that upper-class voice, Mr. Lynch, and his mam and da was just like mine—culchies from the southwest of Ireland, only mine stayed and his emigrated to England. Just you try and imagine, man, what it was like for a Kilburn Paddy to find himself at Eton?"

Lynch tried, and could not. He heard a cow bellowing from the byre and, suddenly, the sound of the little girl's laughter quite close. "It must have been atrocious," he said at last. "I can well imagine, Mrs. Malone. What I don't understand is—why did he join the army at such a young age?"

"Who else would have him?" cried Maeve Malone. "He wasn't one thing nor the other, was he? To the boys at Eton he was only a human joke sent in for their amusement; to the lads back in his home turf he was a renegade—a traitor. Poor wee Bobbie, they threw stones at him, Mr. Lynch, and let me tell you something worse. His own family, his parents and his sister? They hadn't a clue what to do with him. When he came home on holiday from school, they treated him like he was a lodger at a bed-and-breakfast! Oh Christ, man, the *pity* of it!"

Maeve Malone was breathing heavily, and Lynch wanted to comfort her. He was afraid, on account of her unspecified illness, that he had agitated her to a dangerous degree. "Are you all right, Mrs. Malone?" he asked. "Can I do anything? . . . Tablets? . . . Anything you need?"

"It's good you came," she said, ignoring him. "That needed saying, it did. I've never spoken it. I tried to explain to my eldest boy, one who's up in Dublin, but he never took it in."

A calico cat came stalking in from the kitchen and leaped to the arm of her chair. Carelessly she dragged the cat into her arms and began to stroke him. Her trembling hands became steady as they made the journey from ear to flank. She seemed, in her attentions to the cat, to be gathering courage.

"This Murphy," she said, "was supposed to be clever about interrogating people. He enjoyed it, they said. I'm not referring to the sort of interrogation a man like yourself would conduct, you understand. Murphy was a torturer, a kind of a psychological torturer. Sure, I suppose he had a go at the physical stuff as well, but his specialty was the other. It was Murphy who helped to mastermind the scheme where a man's sense of time was taken away. He said it was borrowed from the KGB, but I don't know if that's true." She continued to stroke the calico cat mechanically; its thrumming sounds of satisfaction provided a background to her muted voice. "They'd not feed a fella for a long stretch, ten hours, say, and then they'd bring him a meal every two hours, and so on. It drove them crazy, especially back in the days when they were allowed to keep them standing and hooded, with the noise machines going. They had to pack that in when the Amnesty people stepped in, but for a short while it was most effective."

"You're talking about Northern Ireland, now?"

"Not only. Murphy got around, Mr. Lynch. He also was big on using pictures during interrogation, pictures of dead people. At the right moment, the interrogator would whip out a police photograph of some poor soul who'd been shot—you must have seen a bold few of those photos in your line of work—all in perfect close-up, blood dripping from the open mouth, or the face all caved in and smashed, or sometimes it might be one with a jaw shot off or the eyes gone. . . ."

"And then," Lynch guessed, "the interrogator would insinuate that the same fate awaited the suspect if he didn't talk?"

"Ah, worse. Far worse. The photo would be of someone the suspect had known and loved. A father, or son, or sister, or fiancée. It was Murphy who hit on the idea of using the computer system, so that available photos could be matched up with incoming suspects. You're well able to imagine the demoralizing effect such a photo could have on a man, Mr. Lynch. And the whole thing had other benefits. The plan could be used in all sorts of countries. A photo speaks every language, whether you're in Uganda or Cyprus or County Antrim."

He thought she had finished. Her voice had a sort of finality about it, and he was glad. He had always known that a form of "deep interrogation" was practiced in the North, and he had acknowledged that the tactics used in such operations were unacceptable to him, and morally repellent. The idea of using computers to maximize the pain and terror of a man under interrogation bewildered and sickened him.

"There's worse," Maeve Malone said. "But likely ye've heard enough?" She seemed to be mocking him now. Her confessions had made her angry, and she turned on him a hard and bitter smile.

"Give me your worst," said Lynch.

"Ye'll have heard of black propaganda?" she asked, confident that he had not.

Black propaganda was part of the dirty tricks. It was news items planted, by the British or Irish pro-British press, to make the other side look bad. It was mainly used when the other side was looking good. If the Americans worked themselves up to a lather over some outrage, the British press retaliated by planting an item, for immediate, international release, stating that the IRA had tarred and feathered a young mother of twins, or raped a grandmother. By the time the story had been proved untrue, it no longer mattered. Everyone had forgotten, and the whole matter was swept under the carpet.

"Is something wrong, Mr. Lynch?"

"I was thinking of my daughter. She lives in Fermanagh and kindly educates me from time to time about life up there. Yes, I know about black propaganda, Mrs. Malone. I imagine our Murphy took to it like a duck to water."

"More like a fly to dung," Maeve Malone said. "What I'm about to tell you is bad, it's so bad I found it hard to believe at the time, but I assure you it's the truth." She paused, glanced again toward the door, and clasped her hands over her knees. As if to refute the notion of evil, the girl's laughter and the joyous yapping of a small dog could be heard from outside, together with the wholesome jingling of milk cans from the byre.

"Well then," she said. "D'ye remember when the Brits were wanting to renew the Prevention of Terrorism Act, and there was a hue and cry about how thousands of innocent Irish people would be harassed? The IRA was bein' quiet at the time, and it seemed an overly harsh measure. There were protests, and a lot of foreign interest?"

"I do," said Lynch. "And then there was a bomb, and the act was renewed almost overnight."

"The bomb was needed to push that act through," said Maeve Malone, "and not up in Belfast or even in Dublin itself, but in England. Ordinary, decent English people had to be made to think they could be blown apart in their own cities without it."

"There was a considerable loss of life, as I remember," said Lynch, who suddenly felt the taste of iodine in his mouth.

"Eleven people died in that pub in Nottingham," said Maeve Malone. "Seventeen were injured, some maimed for life. There was no warning, you see, none at all. Just your ordinary, everyday, mindless, vicious, brutal, murderous terrorist operation."

"Carried out by?"

"Yer man."

The taste in his mouth was unbearably unpleasant. He sipped at the dregs of his tea, hoping to alter it, and struggled with a new conviction—that the killer of Nicholas Murphy had done the world a favor and should not be hunted down.

"Are you actually telling me that the British Secret Service authorized such a monstrosity?" he asked.

"It's yes and no," said Maeve Malone. "Yes, they did, and they'd do the same tomorrow, but no, they didn't mean for all those people to die. There was supposed to be a warning."

"What happened?"

"I'm not entirely sure, now," said Maeve quietly, "but I've always reckoned Murphy thought it would be more *effective* his way. That's why your secret service doesn't know his name—they cashiered him after that little job, and he struck out on his own. Christ knows what he's been up to ever since. Sure, I don't want to."

They sat on in awkward silence then, until her mother came back. Maeve Malone seemed to draw inward, invalid that she was, and content herself with the nursing of old wounds. Lynch rose to go, and she seemed scarcely aware of him. He thought he had lost her, but she rallied and cried, "Wait!" The mother had gone once more to the kitchen, and Lynch hovered above the chair where Mrs. Malone sat, obeying her plea.

"Bob knew how wrong it was," she said. "At least he knew right from wrong, Mr. Lynch, grant him that. After the business in Nottingham, he stayed drunk for three days. It was the beginning of the end, for me."

He dropped a hand on her shoulder, feeling awkward. "I'm sorry, Mrs. Malone," he said and then, because she made no move to rise, he let himself out the door.

The little girl waved at his departing car, as if she had nothing better to do.

SIXTEEN

In the week before the end of the school term, Matty once more donned his black costume, or as much of it as he had time to leap into, gave his face a quick scrubbing with coal, and went out into the night in pursuit of Jim Kennerly. He did so by impulse, and quite against his own instincts and the advice of Mr. Halloran.

It had happened by accident this time. Matty had eaten a quantity of salted peanuts before retiring and awakened burning with thirst. He had passed by the window, on his way to the bathroom, just in time to see Mr. Kennerly slicking along up the Crescent. It had seemed an omen, such a perfect coincidence it could not be without meaning.

That was how he came to be speeding along the Gilligan Road in his bare feet. The jeans had been easy to put on over his pyjama bottoms, and he'd found a dark T-shirt easily enough, but his father's wool cap had long been returned to its place, and he and Gervaise had traded back their original sneakers. It couldn't be helped. His hair, at least, was dark, but he thought of his pale bare feet as twinkling like beacons.

There, just ahead, was Kennerly. Matty decelerated, deciding to make a detour through the fields. It would be safer, and he wouldn't be tempted to groan when some mean little pebble bit into the tender soles of his feet. Jesus! There was another one, felt like glass. He hopped away into the field, running low and trying just where to calculate his exit to coincide with the industrial estate. No moon to speak of tonight.

He slowed his pace, picking his way. The grass was kinder to his feet, but there were rocks mixed in, and the odd aluminum can, and who knew what? He became aware that he was still clutching a lump of coal in his hand. He chucked it away, laughing to himself, and suddenly felt very confident. He would be able to navigate, even in the gloom, and he would find the warehouse with its odd treasures, and there would be something else. Some new knowledge, he felt sure. Otherwise, why had he awakened *just* as Kennerly was setting out?

He began to run again, cautiously at first, and then headlong. Something told him he had lost control, should rein himself in, but the exhilaration was too great. Timidly he groped toward a fantasy: he was the Secret Protector of

Balgriffin, out risking all while the good citizens slept on, unperturbed. Scobie and poor Imelda Kennerly, his mam and da and Maureen, the girls from Molloy's shop and the boys of the Conspiracy—even Wolfe Tone— were preserved in their innocence because Matthew Keegan went loping through the night, taking all their troubles on his shoulders.

Janie, too, was able to sleep in tranquillity because of him. He was wondering if she slept in her glasses when his right foot flew into something large and hard, and he felt his balance going—he flailed and threw himself backward, but it was no good. He went down, tumbling across the large obstacle and flying prostrate into the field, his face grazing the grass.

No damage done, he told himself. He was wondering if he had tripped over a log, when the tingling sensation began at the nape of his neck and sped down his spine. The information was being transmitted from the region of his bare ankles. His feet were resting, not on the rough bark of a log, but on cloth. The cloth of a man's trousers and, beneath it, legs. He had tripped over the body of a man.

Unaware of the whimpering sound he had made, Matty slithered away from the thing, his mind full of the man in the grandstand. *His moss-colored trousers. Oh Jesus, not again.*

He sat for what seemed ages in the field, not moving. When he forced himself to look at the corpse he found that it, unlike the first one, was lying on its back. It was too dark to make out much, but Matty could see that this new dead man was lying, arms akimbo, in a remarkably relaxed position.

He tried to rise, but in his confusion and panic, Matty stumbled against one of the outflung arms and fell sprawling over the chest of the dead body. He found his head pressed to the dead man's chest, squashed to his pullover, and he smelled the combined odors of sweat, tobacco, drink, and dirt. Oh, Holy Mother, roll away in a clean, neat, dexterous ball and be rid of this horror. He had managed to distance himself a little way from the body when it became horribly active.

Strange grunts filled the air, and a hand clamped over Matty's wrist with awesome strength—something from the grave had caught him. He smelled the foul breath of the creature and felt its strength. He was being pinned to the earth, examined by the creature, and the pain in his shoulders was as nothing compared to the extremity of his fear.

"What's your name?" inquired a posh, Brit voice. "What are you doing here?"

"Matty Keegan, and this is where I live and all," replied Matty, by rote.

"The Ardoyne?" asked the hated voice.

"No, Falls Road."

"Falls Road, is it? Lots of little Fenians running about on the Falls Road, Master Keegan."

"Don't shoot, mister," implored Matty. "I've already been shot once. Oh, please don't shoot." He hated the abject sound of his voice, but it was all for his mother. She couldn't survive another plastic bullet, it would drive her straight round the bend. He tried to explain it to the soldier, but he found himself appealing to her, instead. The moment he heard his voice calling for his mother, lucidity returned. For those few instants, what with the British voice questioning him, he had believed he was back home. He was lying in a field in Balgriffin, and he was still in danger, oh, very great danger. He twisted frantically, but the strong hands continued to pin him firmly to the ground. He kicked, but his bare feet found no target. "Let me go," he shouted.

The man's hand withdrew and there was a great silence. Matty heard the scrape of the wooden match, and then he was being subjected to a close scrutiny in the flaring, phosphorous light. The match burned out, and a new one was ignited. By its light he could see the gaunt face of the man who hovered over him. He was neither soldier nor corpse, but a real and seemingly perplexed man, a man who had taken too much to drink, and gone lurching home across the fields.

"Christ," said the man, "you're just a little kid. What the hell are you doing out here at this hour?"

Matty had no answer, so he remained silent.

"You're afraid of me, aren't you?"

The second match had also burned out, and the question was terrifying. Matty's thirst, the original thirst that had awakened him and never been slaked, was desperate now.

"Don't be afraid," said the man. "I have a little girl your age, down in Cork. I'm not going to hurt you."

"I think I'll be on my way," said Matty, but he did not get to his feet.

"What's your hurry? I was sleeping off the drink, getting myself sober, and you just came plowing into me, mate. You gave me quite a start, and now you're just going to bloody walk away?"

"I'm thirsty. I'm perishin' for a drink, mister."

"At your age? Jesus, kid, at this rate you won't live past forty."

Matty knew the man was trying to joke with him, but his thirst now seemed to threaten his life. "I really am," he said.

The man seemed to consider. "There's no freshwater pond in this field, so far as I know," he said. "You have an odd way of looking for water, Master Keegan. I'd say you're a long way from home, judging by your accent."

"And so are you," said Matty boldly.

A sibilant chuckle punctuated the dark conversation. "Point taken," said the man. "We're about equally removed from our true origins, Matty, but I don't expect you to understand that. It is a complicated equation which requires more years than you have lived to understand. By the by, why did you ask me not to shoot you?"

"I thought you was a soldier, mister." Matty's entire thinking process had been short-circuited, and he could only answer honestly.

"Retired," said the man. He fumbled in his jacket pocket and produced something that he held to his lips. "This is better than nothing, I suppose," he said, handing the bottle to Matty. "It won't satisfy your thirst, but it'll wet your whistle, mate."

Matty drank some of the foul-tasting stuff and instantly felt as if he had swallowed a hornet. "What is it? Whiskey?"

"Paddy's." The man laughed. "Appropriately."

His captor didn't seem drunk at all, now, and Matty wondered if it was really possible that he had slept himself into sobriety. "What time is it?" he asked, just to keep the conversation going.

By the light of another match, the man studied his watch. "Quarter to two," he said. "Past your bedtime. Christ, but your face is dirty, kid. What'd you do—fall in the coal pile?"

"Something like that. Where do you live, mister?"

"Up the Donahide Road."

"How'll you get home?"

"Never mind about me. Are you living in Balgriffin?"

"That's right. I'd better get home, now." Matty got to his feet, and the man made no move to prevent him. From a little distance away he heard the sound of a large vehicle, a lorry, probably, and wondered if it was slipping out of the industrial estate, laden with whiskey and tellies and beef. There was the problem of avoiding Mr. Kennerly on the return journey. Matty felt shaken and confused. The man was rising to his feet, too, brushing at his trousers.

"Balgriffin's a nice place," he said. "I use the pub there sometimes."

"Do you know Mr. Halloran?" Matty asked. "He often drinks there in the evenings."

"Mr. Halloran," said the man wonderingly. "Now, why would you mention him? Are you related to him?"

"No, but I like him. I like to talk to him."

"I'll tell you a secret, then. Just between the two of us, Mr. Halloran reminds me of my father. When I talk to him, it's like having my old da resurrected from the grave, and that's the truth." Matty didn't know what to say, and his companion, as if embarrassed by his sentimentality, said, "Right, then. I'm off to bed. You nip off home, mate. And don't fall over me again. I might not be so pleasant another time."

They parted in the field, and Matty groped along in the dark, his knees shaking. Not until he got to the road did he fully understand how terrified he had been. He was trembling violently now, and the taste of the whiskey in his mouth made him sick. He forgot all about looking for Mr. Kennerly, who was secondary, in any case. His coincidental awakening, his being drawn out into the night, his decision to detour by way of the fields, all culminated in the discovery of the man with the posh voice. *He* was what Matty had been intended to discover, and he was almost surely the killer of the man in the grandstand. Matty didn't even know the man's name. There was no one to turn to, no one to tell. He couldn't call another Council, on account of Rory. How would he justify being out at that hour without revealing the business in the industrial estate? His mother would go daft with worry, and his father would have his hide. He could hardly go to Mr. Halloran and make up another crime drama he had not been able to see to the end.

He wished he had never eaten all those peanuts.

"What a sad and dreadful story," Una said, pulling the heavy quilt from the bed and folding it neatly. It was a warm night, too warm for quilts, and she was retiring it for the moment.

"Yes," said her husband, who had found himself relating Mrs. Malone's tale, for reasons he could not fathom, nearly a week after his journey down to Cork.

Una got between the sheets and, as was her habit, stretched her arms and sighed. "I can't help but feel sorry for the Malone man," she said. "He was a victim of extraordinary circumstances, was he not? It would make you weep."

"Better think than weep, dear," said Lynch.

"If I were you, pet," said Una, "I would try to make a list of all the people who had a loved one done in by the Nottingham bombing. You'd have a perfect pool of suspects, people who wanted that Murphy dead."

"How's that, Una?"

She thought, burrowing into the pillows in an irritable manner. "Ah yes, I see," she said at last. "Everyone still believes it was an IRA bomb. Forgive me, Sean. Back to square one, we are."

Her voice had a thin, strained quality which let him know that she was genuinely tired. She sometimes suffered from insomnia, and he did not wish to provoke her and force her into a state of artificial wakefulness.

She snapped her table light off and turned toward him, on her side. "It's taking too much out of you, this case," she said. "I don't like it, Sean." She became very still, as if sleep had overtaken her, and then she trumpeted, against his chest, "I haven't a speaker. Oh dear, I haven't a special guest for the club!"

Una belonged to a high-minded group of ladies who met and discussed Works of Literature. The group met twice a month and was held in the homes of the members, taking turns. Four times a year a speaker seemed to be required. He never knew how such matters were decided, but the club had Byzantine rules, and Una, who hated to break rules she had voluntarily agreed to keep, seemed distraught.

"I'm so forgetful these days, Sean," she wailed. "It makes me so angry with myself. How will I ever get anyone at all on such short notice?"

"How much time d'you have?"

"We meet the day after tomorrow. It's hopeless. It takes weeks of negotiating to get a proper speaker, like the nice young poet from Trinity Madge Byrne scared up for us last March. Oh, there's no way out, no way out." Una spoke like the heroine of a dramatic play, but he knew she was not exaggerating her distress. A friendly, open face swam into his consciousness.

"There may be a way out, love," he said. "Would an American Yeats scholar do? A professor fella?"

She looked up in bewilderment and nodded. "Oh, that'd be the very thing," she said. "Do you know one?"

He explained about how he had met Henry J. Connors at the National Library. At the business of the stolen wallet, Una clucked and said what a shame, and what would he think of Irish people, under the circumstances?

"I can't promise," he told her soothingly, "but I'll try to hunt him up tomorrow."

Una soon fell into a deep sleep, as if her relief at the prospect of turning up a speaker had felled her. She was still asleep when Lynch woke up in the morning, and he left her in peace. He shaved and dressed silently, made himself toast and tea, using a tea bag rather than brewing a pot, and listened to a very low-volume version of *Bright Love of My Heart* as performed by Paddy Twomey, before he drove into Dublin. It was an intoxicating day, and the brief glimpses he had of the sea along the Blackrock Road were bracing, like a tonic. The sea here was orderly and blue, not greenish and murderous, as it had appeared at the lonely promontory in Cork.

He presented himself at the National Library at a little after ten-thirty— an hour he judged appropriate for cornering an American scholar.

"Dr. Connors has been over in England," the librarian told him, with a shifty smile. "You know how it is, sir—these American scholars shuttle about, don't they? Never stay put for long. Sure, Dr. Connors crosses the water with a regularity. It's two weeks here, a few days at the British Library, then back again. It's in the nature of the research, you see."

Lynch thanked the librarian and was descending the marble stairs when a small, bearded man came hurtling from the inner sanctum and called to him. "Sir!" cried the man. "May I help you?" He made his way down the stairs until he was standing one step above Lynch. "I couldn't help but overhear your conversation," he said. "You wanted to speak with Hank, didn't you?"

"Hank?"

"Dr. Connors. Well," said the short man, beaming, "he's due back today. He's taking the ferry from Holyhead to Dun Laoghaire. I know, because we're supposed to have dinner together tonight. Could I give him a message? Would that be helpful?"

"It would indeed," said Lynch, marveling yet again at the straightforward friendliness of Americans. An Irishman might have tried to be as helpful, with just as good a will, but he would have approached the thing in a far more complex and obscure fashion. An Irishman would be at the stage of establishing contact when the American had already laid the whole subject open.

"I'm Bill Gleason," said the American, seizing Lynch's hand and giving it a muscular pump. "I'm over here on a sabbatical, like Hank."

"Are you a Yeats scholar as well?"

"No, no," said Bill Gleason with a little laugh, "I'm a Joyce man, mainly, although I'm looking into Beckett."

Lynch gave him the numbers where he could be reached, and said that the matter was one of importance to him personally. It had nothing to do, he stressed, with his line of work. Since Bill Gleason was about to ask about his line of work, he said that he was a policeman.

"This matter," he said, feeling suddenly foolish, "is something quite out of my line. A speaking engagement, as a matter of fact."

The energetic American stroked his beard briefly, then nodded. A strange expression flickered in his eyes and then was gone. Lynch wondered if he was witnessing the manifestations of professional jealousy. He felt himself a fraud. Doubtless Dr. Gleason was picturing a lecture of high prestige, conducted in a soaring Georgian hall, and concluding with a pleasant honorarium. He wondered, if Connors should prove unavailable, if Una would find a Joyce man, who was looking into Beckett, acceptable.

SEVENTEEN

The boat that took day trippers out to the island known as Ireland's Eye left from the port at Howth. It was an ancient boat, overpacked and tending to ride low in the water, but it made the journey hourly. It departed from the enclosed waters of Howth Harbor, labored briefly through a sometimes choppy sea beyond, and put in at the sheltered shore of Ireland's Eye in less than twenty minutes. It was a summer voyage, only operating in July and August, and most of the passengers were local to the area. They came to experience the transcendent oddness of having a picnic on a rock they saw— day in, day out throughout the rest of the year—as a shifting shape in their sea.

Ireland's Eye loomed in the mind as a constant, but differently, depending on where you lived. For those who saw it from the Balgriffin estuary, the Eye was shaped like a gravy boat, with the definite imprint of a round tower rising from its northerly extremity. On fine days it had the clarity of an etching; on misty ones it was partially obscured or altogether vanished.

There were children living in the vicinity of those waters whose first, most urgent, thoughts had been prompted by the mysteriously changing shape of Ireland's Eye. Since they had been unable to articulate these startling thoughts when they first appeared, in the shady area of life when speech was not commensurate to feeling and emotion, the metaphysical properties of Ireland's Eye were never mentioned. It remained an uninhabited rock in the Irish Sea—a place where one might venture to picnic in fine weather.

From the hill he had climbed to, Matty could see his family, small, at this distance, on the blue blanket they had spread out. His mother was restoring some of the uneaten sandwiches to the picnic basket, while his da sprawled near her, his chin propped in his hands. Maureen appeared to be doing nothing, but he knew she was mooning over a boy called Fergus Flanagan, whom he considered a great fool. She had not wanted to accompany him on a survey of the island, preferring to think sticky thoughts of Fergus and cram her face with shortbreads.

There were swarms of children investigating the round tower, but he didn't know any of them, and he wasn't interested in the tower, anyway. The sheltered side of the island, where the boat had docked, was unimpressive, but Matty knew that the side that faced the open sea would be smashing. He could see the vast sweep of the ocean from his hill, and he counted three white sails and a trawler. "All right, then?" a voice said, quite close. A young father had been shielding his little daughter, a girl of four or five. The child had been urinating, squatting on a large rock, and Matty averted his eyes. Ireland's Eye had no lavs, of course.

He stared down on his family again, hoping that one of them would look up and wave. He felt vaguely embarrassed—a big lad like himself wanting to wave from the mountain at the people who signaled him. They appeared to take no notice and then, amazingly, the tiny figure that was Maureen plucked at his mam's arm, pointing, and three heads turned to observe him while three arms shot up. Matty waved back, and then, invigorated, sprang off onto a path that wound close to the island's edge.

The path dipped down, then up again, and ended in an outcropping of gray rock. Matty edged out along the rock and found himself in an alien world. He had once seen a film about North American Indians who had been cave dwellers. The caves were stacked on top of each other, like high-rise flats, and the Indians ascended to them by ladders. Here there were no ladders, but this seaward coast of Ireland's Eye was honeycombed with natural indentations, little ledges enclosed by rock. He guessed that the indentations carried on all the way to the bottom, because he could now hear the hollow booming of surf in an underwater cave, far below.

He crawled into the nearest cliff dwelling and scanned the horizon. The water seemed calm enough, but the trawler, far out to sea, was wallowing. It made him quite queasy to watch it, so he looked instead at the wheeling gulls beneath him. Odd to look down on birds. Then he became aware of movement directly below. He inched forward, hands firmly clutching the lichen-studded rock, and looked down to see a balding head in the chamber underneath him.

The man raised his arms. He was holding a powerful piece of equipment, and—in that new and disconcerting way that Matty had developed lately, the business of seeing something everyday and normal as sinister—appeared to be aiming a gun at the impersonal sea. Binoculars! It was only binoculars, and the man was probably a bird-watcher. Matty eased himself back into his crevice, breathing easier. A second later, the stone his sneakered foot had dislodged fell with a plonking sound into the man's chamber, and Matty heard him say, "What the hell?" The accent seemed to be American. Thinking to apologize, Matty inched to the edge again, looking down.

"Well, hello there," said the man.

" 'Lo," said Matty. "I'm sorry about the stone, mister. I kicked it down by accident, now."

"No harm done," said the stranger. "Isn't this a splendid place?"

"Yeah," said Matty. "Smashing."

"You're not all on your own, are you?"

"No. The folks are down below, having a picnic." Matty felt he had entered a new dimension of being, because the man, whose face he could now see clearly, seemed to be the very Yank he and the others had invented. He did not seem to be wearing plaid trousers, but in all other particulars he filled the bill. He was the right age, he was losing his hair, and he was kindly. He seemed the very man to saunter across the road and buy crisps at the pub, if they had been in Balgriffin and not on the seaward coast of Ireland's Eye. Even the costly-looking binoculars he wore on a leather strap around his neck were somehow right.

Distressingly, the man offered his hand, stretching his arm up to Matty's haven. "Delighted to meet you," he said. "My name is Henry, or Hank, if you'd prefer."

"I'm Matt Keegan," said Matty, slurring the words and joining his hand to that of the stranger.

"You're from Scotland? That's my guess."

"Northern Ireland. Belfast."

"Aha! I should have known." He was again scanning the sea with his binoculars. "Fantastic," he said. "Unless I miss my guess, that's a cormorant down there. She's foraging with the gulls."

"Could be," said Matty, gathering himself for departure. "So long, then, mister."

But the Yank was offering the binoculars, passing them up in a casual, matey gesture. "Have a look," he urged. "It's fascinating. There's so much going on that you can't see with the naked eye. Nature is secretive, Matt. Everything goes on in secret."

Matty had never looked through binoculars before, and he felt his body grow taut with surprise when he saw how close everything became. The name of the tossing trawler was *St. Brigid*, and he could make out moving shapes on one of the sailboats. The cruel beaks and inhuman, beady eyes of the gulls were impressive, but nowhere did he see any secrets. He couldn't even see the cormorant the man had mentioned, but it didn't matter. He swept the binoculars over the horizon, but there was nothing but sea. He wished he was in a position to be able to look down on his parents and his sister. They seemed so far away, and with these high-powered binoculars he would be able to bring them close; he would be able to see the smallest details, right down to the plastic-bubble barrettes that held Maureen's hair in two bunches.

"Thanks," he said, feeling dazed and handing the binoculars back. The American seemed far closer than he had been.

"Sure," said the Yank that he and the others had imagined on the seafront. "Anytime, pal."

Matty felt a strange reluctance to leave. It was partly to do with the fact that not one of the other children would believe how uncanny was the resemblance between this real man and their imagined one, and partly because he felt sorry for him. Hank. *Hank the Yank*, he thought, and wanted to laugh. Hank was all alone, and Matty had never seen an American tourist who appeared to be solitary. They always traveled in groups, or at the very least with their husbands or wives.

"All on your own, are ye?" he asked.

"How do you mean, Matt?" The man's eyes clouded with concentration. He honestly seemed to consider the banal question, as if there might be more to it than met the eye.

"Well," said Matty, "are you here in Ireland by yourself, solo? Or are the wife and kids with you?"

"Oh, I see what you mean," said the man. "No, I'm on my own, Matt. But I'm never lonely, not in this country. I feel alive here, really alive, and I'll be sorry to leave it."

"Why have you to leave? If you like it so much, you could stay."

"I wish it were that simple." He sighed, turning away and surveying the sea. "Yes," he repeated, "I wish it were that simple." He bent and opened a rucksack, from whose interior he extracted two speckled pears. "Have one," he said, in the same offhand manner in which he had offered the binoculars. "Guaranteed delicious."

Matty accepted the pear, wishing he had something to offer in return. "I have to be on my way," he said. "Me mam will be sure I've fallen into the sea."

"Eat it on the way," said the Yank. "It's a long climb down, Matt."

"Good-bye, then, and thanks. Good luck, mister."

"The same to you," said the stranger, smiling. "Good luck."

Grasping the pear, Matty climbed out along the rock ledge and regained the path through the gorse. He looked back, but the man was no longer visible. Matty imagined him, secure within his cliffside chamber, pressing the binoculars to his eyes, joyfully searching out secrets in the foreign Irish Sea.

Imelda's husband vanished, did a bunk. Overnight, it was. One day Jim Kennerly was a familiar figure in the Crescent, the next he was a Missing Person. It was characteristic of Imelda that she did not know he was missing until, on her way to Molloy's shop, she encountered Mrs. O'Rourke.

"Well, dear, your good man's away on a business trip, is he?" said Mrs. O'Rourke. She was not speaking out of malice, but out of high spirits. It was rare for her to find something to mention to the younger women, apart from the weather, of course.

"Not if I know it," Imelda said. "He doesn't travel in his line. Who told you that at all, pet?"

Mrs. O'Rourke looked stricken. "Nobody," she said. "Only I saw him getting into the car, quite early it was, and he had the two cases. He was dressed so smartly—oh Jesus, now, I hope I haven't said—"

"Never mind," said Imelda, patting the old lady's arm. "It's no secret Jim and I have had our differences. Just try to remember what time it was you saw him, would you?"

"Well before six, long before he usually goes to his work. I'm awake so early these days, it's like that when you grow old, and I was just looking out to see if that Wolfe Tone was on the loose—it's collection day for the rubbish—and, well, I hope I haven't spoken out of turn."

Imelda assured Mrs. O'Rourke that all was well, and then, instead of proceeding to the shop, turned and walked back to her house with dignity. Once inside, she charged up the stairs and flung open the closet in their bedroom. Her furious fingers scrabbled among the hangers, determining what was missing. His best suits, some casual trousers, and nearly all of his shirts were gone. "Bastard!" she cried. "Bloody, whoring, no-good *bastard!*"

This was no dirty weekend Jim had embarked on—even supposing a dirty weekend could commence on a Tuesday. Jim had left for good, and in the most cowardly and disgustingly furtive manner she could imagine. He had gone off with his disco dolly, without so much as a thought for his wife and his young son. What sort of work did Jim think she could find that would pay enough to feed and clothe Rory, let alone herself? Perhaps he just didn't care, and the thought made her so angry she kicked viciously at the old dresser, hurting her toe. She had slept innocently beside him, a little surprised that he had stayed at home that night, and while she slept, Jim, the class of a bastard, had gone sneaking away like a thief in the dawn. She wondered if he had already packed the cases, anticipating his escape, before he retired.

"Right, we'll just have a look," Imelda snarled, going downstairs on a current of adrenaline so strong her feet barely seemed to touch the wood. It had occurred to her that Jim would be quite capable of stealing her little supply of housekeeping money. It was an irrational thought, because Jim had in fact been remarkably generous lately. She had put it down to guilt, because never before had he been so easy with his money.

In the kitchen, she reached to a shelf that contained an old Christmas cake box. It was scarlet and silver and had a pretty design of angels blowing trumpets on its cover. In this box, for many years, she had deposited whatever was left over from the housekeeping money Jim gave her each week. Sometimes she had nothing to put in at week's end; the greatest amount she could ever remember depositing was two pounds and twenty-six p. Still, it mounted up, and the little fund came in handy for emergencies.

Her hands trembled as she lifted the box from its shelf, and she ripped a fingernail in prying the lid up. Her eyes squeezed shut against what she might see, she felt inside the tin, expecting it to be bare. Her fingertips encountered paper and silver, quite a good pile of it, and she breathed a little easier. With luck, if they lived on fish fingers and baked beans, she could feed Rory for a few weeks. She would have to apply for a deserted wife's allowance; count on the government to give the damned thing the most humiliating title they could find.

She opened her eyes and saw, among the notes and coins, a scrap of white paper. She didn't remember putting it there, and when she bent closer, she saw that it had been torn from one of Rory's school notebooks. *Imelda*, she read. *Sorry for this, love. I'll be in touch after a bit. No time to explain so you tell Rory whatever you think best. It's nothing at all to do with Miss X in Portmarnock. In the meantime, have a look in the fridge, bottom shelf, above the veg crisper. Keep it to yourself. Your Jim.*

Miss X, indeed. Did he really think she didn't know the identity of his fancy piece? Her name was Florrie Devine, and a little sleuthing had even provided Imelda with Miss Devine's telephone number, although she'd never lowered herself enough to make a call.

She opened the refrigerator, not for the first time that day, and addressed herself to the bottom shelf. She hadn't given it much attention when she'd been making Rory's breakfast. Something alien was indeed reposing above the veg crisper. It was shoved far back, and when Imelda brought it out it was nothing but an old cigar box. She closed the fridge door with a gentle tap and carried the cigar box, which was unpleasantly cold, back to the kitchen table. She laid it in the center of the table and looked at it as she would at a time bomb. In her earlier mood, she would have assumed the box's contents to reveal some final, taunting object of Jim Kennerly's contempt for her—a pair of Florrie Devine's knickers, say—but the odd note had sobered her. She regarded the cigar box with the dread she reserved for the mysterious and unexpected.

At last she forced herself to open it and saw stacks of notes neatly piled inside. Good, then, Jim had thought to leave her some money. Relieved, she pulled the box toward her and began to count the pound notes methodically. She had reached twenty before she realized that the notes were not ones, but twenties, and occasionally fifties. She dropped them, losing count, and tried to make some sense of what she was seeing. The cigar box contained more money than she had ever seen at one time in her entire life. It was altogether possible that Jim had left over three thousand pounds on top of the veg crisper, and where had it come from?

Logic told her that Jim's abrupt departure had to do with the money, and not Florrie Devine. He was in trouble, and she'd had no inkling. How could things come to such a head without her knowledge? She stuffed the notes back into the box and pushed it violently away across the table. It was tainted money, surely, and not hers to spend. Oh, life was a confusing and shameful stint! She, who had hated Jim Kennerly with a white-hot rage moments earlier, was now anxious for him. She had been softened by the money, not for itself, but because it meant he had not utterly abandoned her and Rory. He had provided for them, in what she had to regard as a felon's way, and now she was obliged to worry about him. The gardai would no doubt pay a call before the day was over, and she could only hope they would not appear in the forms of Lynch and Browne.

Imelda sat on at the table, her mind whirring with possible courses of action. She thought of burying the money in her garden, of giving it to Nora Keegan to keep, of telling Rory that his da had been called to the bedside of a sick relation.

She even thought of taking the money to Tom Mulligan and asking him to hold it for her, but this seemed too preposterous. In the end, she put the cigar box into the vegetable crisper, secreting it beneath a head of cabbage and a pile of Common Market carrots. It seemed best so.

By the end of the day, everyone in the Crescent knew of Jim Kennerly's dramatic departure. For one thing, the detectives who had been in charge of the murder investigation visited Imelda in the afternoon. For another, Imelda's conversation with Mrs. O'Rourke had been repeated by the latter lady, who really could not hold herself back after the police had been seen. It seemed impossible not to link Kennerly with the unsolved murder—why else would he flee, just hours before the detectives arrived? Mrs. Naughton repeated to everyone who would listen that, in her opinion, poor Imelda's husband had always seemed sinister.

Nora Keegan felt stunned, as if something that had occurred in a nightmare were being repeated in the sunlight. She wanted to comfort Imelda, but couldn't bring herself to walk the short distance across the Crescent. Imelda might think she was prying. She telephoned, instead, and asked if there was anything she could do to help. "Perhaps a bit later, love," said Imelda, sounding much more strong and confident than Nora had possibly imagined she might be.

Nora watched for the children to come home for their tea. Maureen had been playing tennis with a school friend, and Matty had gone off on his own, as he so often did these days. The once close-knit group—Matty and Rory and Terry and Gervaise, and even little Janie Keane—seemed to be avoiding one another lately.

When Matty came home, Maureen was already full of the story. Sitting at the table, eating tomato and cheese sandwiches, she told them both that Jim Kennerly had run away. "The gardai are after him," she said. "They're after grillin' Mrs. Kennerly for *hours,*" she fairly shouted. She had had the story from Teresa, who worked behind the counter at Molloy's.

"Don't repeat everything you hear, daughter," said Nora sharply. She had noticed that Matty, who had sat at the table in evident keen anticipation of his food, was now listlessly studying a bottle of chutney. His face was pale and unhealthy-looking—how long had it been like that, and why hadn't she noticed? He seemed to regard the chutney bottle with longing, as if he wished he could lose himself within it, or was that her imagination?

"Matty?" she asked. "Are you feeling yourself? Is there something troubles you?"

"No, Mam," said Matty, pushing his plate away and leaving the room. She heard his feet on the treads of the stairs.

When the phone went, she ran to it, expecting Imelda, but it was Kate Brannigan, Kate who had always come straight to the door. "Have you heard?" Kate demanded breathlessly. "Are you watching the news? They've arrested Denis McGuire, the odd one who sold your Paul the Renault. Jim Kennerly's mixed up in it, too, and they've found his car abandoned at Dun Laoghaire, where the ferries go to England."

"Dear God," said Nora, "whatever next?" She listened to Kate's explanation of the sordid affair, but all the while she was wondering about the discolored patches beneath her son's eyes. Out of the frying pan, into the fire.

EIGHTEEN

Imelda had told no one of the money, not even Rory, although she did tell him that his da had left plenty of money to care for them in a special bank account. He was young enough not to pay much notice to such things—and, she hoped, to believe that Jim had gone off for an extended period of time to investigate work situations in England.

"Yeah," he had said. "So long's yer not anxious, Mam." His eyes had been curiously flat.

To the police she had been equally untruthful. Oh, fair enough, she had not known of any relationship between her husband and Denis McGuire, but the moment Lynch introduced the subject, Imelda understood where the money had come from. No, she told them, she'd had no inkling that Jim was flusher than usual. *She* had not seen any of the money. Even as the words were leaving her mouth, she remembered a fragment from some fairy story, a tale in which inanimate objects had suddenly proclaimed a villain's guilt. What if the pound notes should sing out, from beneath the cabbage and carrots? If Denis McGuire had said that he was thick with Jim, she told them, that didn't mean it was so. Everyone knew McGuire was a bit off, and he was a vicious gossip into the bargain.

She was hoping the police would assume that Jim had run off with Florrie. It would put them off his track for a while. Not long—Portmarnock was a small place with very few resident disco dollies, and they were bound to find Florrie soon—but long enough to give Jim a head start in his flight.

It made her feel queer to think that the money was her sole reason for lying to protect Jim, but she told herself again that it was not the money but the fact that he had not, after all, utterly forgotten her.

It was the evening news, with the bit about the car abandoned in Dun Laoghaire, that upset her most. Luckily, Rory and the Brannigan boy were playing on the seafront when the news came on, but Rory would be bound to hear. There were no secrets in Balgriffin.

She lay in bed, on the second night after Jim's scarper, thinking how stupid it had been of him to leave the car like that. He must have been in a terrible frame of mind. Any reasonably clever person would have crossed to England with the car and abandoned it in some out-of-the-way corner of

Wales. "Ah, Jim," she whispered, in their darkened bedroom. "What happened?" The bed felt very large to her, despite the fact that Jim had often been absent from it. This was a new emptiness, a permanent one, and for the first time Imelda knew what it would be like to be a widow. Beneath, in the kitchen, there was a nearly full bottle of vodka. She knew that an hour's dalliance with that bottle would bring forgetfulness and allow her to sleep, but the drink had no allure for her now. The drink had been to relieve her of the misery of humiliation, and the new pain was of a different order. It came to her differently, and seemed to require sobriety.

One good thing, anyway, Imelda told herself, the police had thought she'd be desperate about the car, had explained that the car could not be returned to her for some time. Something to do with complex procedures they had for finding evidence. She didn't give a damn about the car because, as she told them, she had never learned to drive.

Imelda had always taken buses.

"Sorry for yer troubles," Matty blurted out. He had been on his way to the vegetable man's van, both to purchase some cucumbers for his mother and— two birds with one stone—to seek out Mr. Halloran. Rory had loomed up, climbing over the racecourse wall on the Gilligan Road. At Matty's words of sympathy, he seemed to become paralyzed. With one leg over the wall and one inside, his pale face frozen and immobile, Rory said, barely moving his lips, "Thanks. My mother must think I'm mental, you know?"

"How's that?"

"She gave me the long speech about how he went to England to get a better job. Everyone knows he ran off with that tart in Portmarnock." Rory dropped over onto the pavement with a supple, listless movement. His eyes were fierce, and he approached Matty in what seemed to be a fighting mood. "Don't you go pretending you didn't know," he said. "I even told you, all of you, when we had the Council. The second one, when we told how our parents were comin' unglued. You think you're such an effin' hero because you got shot up North!"

"I don't."

"You effin' do."

"I *never* talk about it," cried Matty, stung by the injustice of Rory's words. It seemed that Rory was spoiling for a fight; his fists were balled and he was breathing heavily. Matty tried to remember how to fight, but it was useless. He would have to rely on instinct.

"That's a part of it," said Rory. "You never talk about it because it's better like a secret. You get more power that way."

"That's a load of bloody old shite," screamed Matty.

Then Rory was all over him. He knocked him to the pavement in a flying leap, and Matty felt the power of his rage. Rory was pummeling him with his fists, striking ineffectual blows at his chest and shoulders, swiping at his face with an open palm. The greatest discomfort he felt was the pressure of pebbles beneath his back.

They rolled about on the Gilligan Road, simulating a bloodthirsty fight. Matty could sense that Rory's heart wasn't really in it. Rory was in a rage, all right, but it had nothing to do with him. Rory struck blindly, and he appeared to be in tears. Snot or tears covered his face. His face was all liquid and melting.

Oh Jesus, thought Matty, hooking his ankle around Rory's thigh and assuming the superior position, *this is a sad state of affairs. Better to get shot than have your da run off. Better to nearly die than have your mother so upset, like his must be.*

"Rory," he panted, his knee on the boy's chest. "I'll tell ye all about it if you'll only stop."

"Who cares," Rory muttered, the fight gone out of him. And then, again, "She must think I'm mental. Everyone knows."

Matty rolled away and Rory rose to his feet, dusting himself off with elaborate care. None too soon, either, for Mrs. Naughton was approaching from the direction of the shop, carrying two old-fashioned string bags. "No offense," said Rory, and then he went back over the wall, returning to the racecourse. Matty saw him go loping off, running low, as if the racecourse were now his natural habitat.

"Having a bit of a donnybrook?" Mrs. Naughton called, shaking her head to indicate mild disapproval.

Matty continued to watch the retreating figure of Rory Kennerly. Something about the movement of the smallish figure on the vast grounds of the wild racecourse chilled him. He was not sure what constituted grief, even though he had seen it many times, back home. He had seen it in his own mother, and—to a lesser extent—in his father. He didn't think he had felt it yet, himself, although it had begun to pull at him in the days when his mother had been so queer and unreachable.

It was an odd feeling, that grief. Matty was the one who'd been shot, but since he could not remember the incident, and since, by the time he'd been conscious again, life was a pleasant matter consisting of nurses who coddled you and saw to it you were comfortable, he could not claim any real knowledge of grief. He likened it to certain experiments demonstrated by the Brother who was in charge of science at school.

If two elements were brought together, a certain result was bound to follow—an egg, say, dropping through the mouth of a bottle which was ordinarily too narrow to permit the passage of something as large as the egg. Grief was like that. If certain elements combined, in life, grief would surely result. His mother had known it, on account of his being so badly hurt, coupled with her lack of power to prevent it or do anything about it in the aftermath. He, in his turn, had been snagged by it because his injury had been the vent that had nearly deprived her of her senses. Long after he was out of danger, his mother had been wounded, and he had been left to bear the guilt. It had been dreadful, that conviction, that guilt. He had felt that his mother was slipping away, forever, all because he had left the house when she had forbidden him.

Matty shook himself, like a dog who had been swimming in the estuary, and climbed over the wall. It seemed important to him to find Rory and explain to him the nature of guilt and grief. His feet hit the earth with a painful thud, but his night running had accustomed him to pain. Expertly he zigzagged his way across the racecourse, avoiding the deeper gullies and making good time. The gold and white flowers were trampled beneath his feet, and also the condoms, the glass, the plastic bottles and cans and pocket combs that lay in the long grass. He could not see Rory now, but he ran toward a little grove of trees that provided a natural cover. It was warm but sunless, the sky whitish and sullen-looking. The sight of the trees refreshed him.

"Rory!" he shouted, but there was no answer. One of the big black-and-white cows was plodding in his direction, cut off from the herd. He called Rory's name again.

In the grove there was a narrow avenue of tangled grass, as if whoever had planted the trees wanted to provide a footpath. It curved and meandered, and around each turn Matty expected to encounter Rory. It was unnaturally silent, and he had stopped calling Rory's name. All he could hear was the odd lament from the estranged cow.

When he emerged from the grove he was bewildered. The racecourse, vast and unpopulated, had swallowed Rory up. He retraced his steps and ran to within twenty feet of the black grandstand, calling Rory's name again. He could not bring himself to actually enter the wreck, and he didn't think Rory could either. The entry place, a black, gaping mouth, reminded him of a burned-out bakery on the street where he had lived in Belfast.

By the time he got home, sweaty and dirty, it was nearly time for his tea. He washed his face and hands and presented himself in the kitchen, where his mother was doing chips and listening to a radio drama. She smiled at him, and Matty smiled back sickly. What he dreaded, more than anything, was the moment when Mrs. Kennerly was sure to appear at their door.

Andy Halloran came back to the pub on the night when the big rain hit and the lines came down for an hour. There were candles lit, which many of the women present said provided a nice touch, but to him it was a source of embarrassment. He needed the brighter light to identify people by the ways their blurred shapes moved.

"You've been missed," said the voice of Mrs. Keane in his ear. "Where were you, then, these last two nights?"

"I was at the disco in Howth, Mrs. Keane, with two blondes," said Scobie, who had been suffering from stomach trouble.

She laughed and said he was a wicked man, if only in his imagination. "Not many here tonight," he said, venturing a guess, and hoping she would provide him with an answer.

"A hell of a thing, that young lad missing," said the voice of Tom Mulligan, quite close. He was collecting empty pints at a nearby table.

"Yes, surely," said Mrs. Keane. "I wonder if Balgriffin isn't cursed, Tom? First that terrible murder, and then the business with Denis McGuire, and now there's poor little Rory gone missing? I expect it's the shame over his father has driven him away."

"Mrs. K. is desperate," said Tom, and Scobie could hear the sympathy in his voice.

Scobie thought of the amazing visit and quivered with impatience. It had been yesterday, the first day the Kennerly boy had been pronounced missing. He had been sitting in the garden, listening to the wireless through the open kitchen window, when his wife's voice announced, "There's a boy, Andy, says he must talk with you. I'm after telling him you're not well, but he looks in a terrible state."

Soon enough, young Matty Keegan had been in the garden, stammering apologies and behaving as if he had been granted an audience with the Queen of England. Normally, Scobie would have put him at his ease by saying "the very thing" or "oh boys, oh boys," but Matty's distress had seemed so great he had said, instead, "Is there something troubling you, Matt?"

It seemed too harsh, but he could no longer remember how he had dealt with the miseries and problems of his children when they were small. He wanted to be helpful to his young friend, but the disparity between their ages was too great. If he had been allowed more contact with his grandchildren, he might have been able to cope more ably, but emigration had deprived him of that privilege. He was meditating, bitterly, for him, on the fact that Ireland's young were driven away, when the importance of what Matty was telling him intruded dramatically.

There had been a hasty, halfhearted fight. An escape to the racecourse.

The boy, like his father, was now missing. But wait! What was this? The children had apparently lied to the gardai, manufactured a Yank, and now young Matt was saying he was sure the murderer was an Englishman whom Scobie immediately recognized as Bob Malone. He had been able to set the lad's mind to rest about Malone, explaining that he had been in Mountjoy when the murder on the racecourse had occurred, but about the runaway Rory he could only repeat meaningless platitudes about how runaway boys had a habit of turning up.

"We lied about the Yank," Matty'd said. "That was wrong, Mr. Halloran. We only wanted to take the pressure off."

The lights came back on in the pub, and Scobie was jerked from his remembrance of Matty's visit into a world where dim shapes were discernible as living people. The wiry, efficiently moving shape before him was surely that of Tom Mulligan, emptying the ashtrays.

"How's Scobie?" cried the jovial voice of Tom.

But for once he had no ready witticism for a reply. The light had prompted a memory, and the memory was significant. It was important for him to retain it, because it might so easily go slipping away. How could he be sure that the voice he had heard, from over half a century ago, would still be with him in the morning? It was the voice of his second son, Paddy, who had gone to live in Canada.

Mrs. Keane was trying to involve him in some badinage about the blondes up in Howth, but he shook his head irritably. For the first time in the memory of anyone in the pub, Andy Halloran seemed to be in bad humor. He rose from his seat and made for the door, leaving well before Tom called closing.

The men on the special number line transferred the call to Lynch. They dutifully heard the caller's advice about the missing child, although—as they later admitted—they thought it was useless, the ravings of some old-age pensioner who had nothing to do but ring the gardai whenever possible. The only reason they bothered Sergeant Lynch was because the caller claimed to have information about the Balgriffin killing.

Lynch identified himself and waited courteously for the caller to gather his thoughts. When the man began to speak, it was in the voice of a very old Dubliner, but it was a strong voice still, and authoritative in its own way.

"I told the other lads, but now I think I should tell you, because I have the feeling they didn't take notice. If I was you, Inspector, I would get myself up to Howth and take a boat to Ireland's Eye. Yes, that's what I'd do."

"Do you have any information leading you to believe young Kennerly is on Ireland's Eye?" Lynch asked. The idea was not nearly so preposterous as it might have seemed. A man had called the special line earlier, after they'd first broadcast a description of Rory, to say that he'd picked up a young hitchhiker on the afternoon of the disappearance. The hitchhiker was on the Portmarnock–Balgriffin road, and he answered to Rory's description. The man had dropped him off in Howth, where the boy claimed to live.

"Information," said Lynch's caller. "No, I haven't information, Inspector, but a strong feeling. My own son, a few years back, once made the threat of running away from home. He was only coddin' us, really, because we were a happy family. 'And where would ye run to?' the missus asked. 'Ireland's Eye,' sez he, 'it's perfect for a hiding place.' 'And how would ye get there—swim, is it?' the wife said. That silenced him for a bit, and then he said, 'I'd stow away on one of the trawlers.' "

"That wouldn't be necessary today, would it?" said Lynch.

"Indeed it would not. Haven't they boats leaving every hour in the fine weather? All the lad would need would be a few bob in his pocket. The whole country could be looking for him, and there he'd be, just a few miles from his home, on a rock in the sea." The voice halted, began again, as if the caller needed strength to continue. "The rock would not have been very hospitable last night, in the lashin' rain. He'll want off, Inspector, but he may be wet and perished and afraid to come home all the same."

"Thank you for your advice, Mr. . . . ?"

"Swift."

"Mr. Swift. I intend to make a check of Ireland's Eye, and I have you to thank. It may interest you to know that a boy answering Rory Kennerly's description thumbed a ride to Howth."

Frank had come into the room, carrying two cups of weak-looking coffee. Lynch passed a note to him, asking him to find out if the boats to Ireland's Eye were running. It was technically the "fine weather" Mr. Swift had mentioned, but in the wake of last night's summer storm the sea might be choppy and unpredictable. He was wondering how long it might take to requisition a police launch, when the caller's voice shifted into another kind of urgency. It reminded him of the drone of the pipes—an atmospheric interval designed to prepare you for a new melodic turn.

"Inspector," said the drone. "Another thing, if I was you, and still involved in that other business—"

"What business is that, Mr. Swift?"

"Murder. What happened last May on the racecourse."

"I am very much involved," said Lynch, waiting for the melody.

"Forget the Yank."

"I beg your pardon?"

"The American. I'd forget all about him, if I was you. Sure, he doesn't exist at all."

"Do you refer to the American the Balgriffin children saw on the day of the crime?" Lynch asked, feeling that the obscure and aged caller had seized the upper hand.

The line was dead. Mr. Swift had gone. Yet, in the moments it had taken him to replace the phone in its cradle, words had been spoken. *They meant no harm*, the old man had said. He had been speaking to himself.

NINETEEN

"How was your holiday?" Matty asked Janie Keane, meeting her on the Gilligan Road.

"Oh, it was gorgeous," Janie said. "There was a leisure center in Sheffield as big as all Balgriffin. My Aunt Rose took me swimming every day."

"Would you consider livin' over there?"

Janie paused, looked out at the racecourse, swimming in a haze of heat on this day, and then shook her head briskly. "I don't belong there," she said, "but it's good for a holiday."

They resumed walking. Janie suddenly, and without looking at him, said, "I heard about Rory. Will he be all right, do you think? My mother said he was lucky not to have pneumonia, staying out on Ireland's Eye like that."

"Sure, he's only a cold. It was lashin' rain that night." Matty felt uncomfortable, not knowing how much Janie knew of the situation. The cat, as his granda would say, was well and truly out of the bag. Rory, confined to his room after a visit to the doctor's surgery, had conveyed the news to Terry Brannigan, who had passed it along to Matty. The way Terry told it, he had been playing with Wolfe Tone in the garden, when a window next door had come cranking open and Rory, pale and wheezing, had beckoned him closer.

"The detective fella knows we lied," Rory had whispered in sepulchral tones. "Somebody called the garda number and informed."

"You admitted it?" Terry had asked.

"Yeah. Comin' back over on the boat."

According to his calculations, the informer must surely be Mr. Halloran. Terry was too confident to feel the need to set matters straight, and Kevin too shy. Janie had been in England, and Gervaise was still away.

Matty felt a certain relief that the falsehood had been exposed, but he also felt a pervasive anxiety. At any time he expected Lynch to arrive at his front door, demanding an explanation. Even now, strolling up the Gilligan Road toward Molloy's, he cast a look over his shoulder to see if he wasn't being tailed. He, and all the others, could be formally charged for inventing a murder suspect. What would the charge be? Not accessories—that would imply that they had helped to kill the man on the racecourse. Conspiracy?

They had conspired, surely, but not to commit a crime. They had conspired to—

"Obstruct justice!" he cried, so pleased at having hit on the right term that he spoke out loud.

"What?" Janie whispered. "What did you say?"

She had been the architect of the plan; it had been Janie who had invented the Yank to begin with. He did not wish to add to the crushing burden of what he thought of as her guilt, and so he said, "Nothing."

"Balls," said Janie, shocking him. "You said *obstruct justice*. Just precisely what did you mean, Matt?"

She spoke in the sharp, schoolmistressy tones of a nun, and he looked into her small, plump face with dread. Janie Keane seemed suddenly to have gained years on him. Her mouth was set in determined lines, and behind her spectacles he could see that her blue eyes had contracted to show absolute moral authority.

Miserably, he told her what he knew.

"Mothera God," said Janie, reverting to the small girl he recognized and respected.

"Sure, it'll be all right at the end of the day," Matty said, wondering if it would be the appropriate thing for him to offer to carry her mother's shopping bag.

"Oh Jesus," said Janie.

They were saved by Mrs. O'Rourke, who came toiling toward them lugging a wheeled cart full of frozen pancake packets. Mrs. O'Rourke's face split into a vast smile at sight of them, and she called out, inquiring whether the heat wave wasn't the grandest thing, the very thing they all needed after the unseasonable storm?

"Sure, it's great, missus," Matty replied recklessly.

"It's *gray-yut*, missus," Janie mocked, imitating him, when Mrs. O'Rourke had safely passed.

Matty balled his fist, pretending to menace her, and when they entered the shop, they were taken by a fit of laughter.

"Sean dear, would you be good enough to boil a Lemsip up for me?" Una's voice was fogged and indistinct, because she had a summer cold. She lay in a lawn chair, pretending to read *The Irish Times* and tutting at the amount of ink that made its way from the paper to her fingers. Occasionally she wiped her hands on the grass, something she would never do in good health.

Lynch went obediently to the kitchen and put the kettle on. The evening was heavy and warm, and Una's magenta roses swam magically in the haze. He could see them from the kitchen, and also a crescent of white sky. Visible, also, was the cross-weave plastic of his wife's chair, and her gray head above it. The little sliver of a scene put him in mind of one of those modern, realistic paintings, the kind where a common sight—a bathtub being filled, say, or a table still burdened with the remains of breakfast—was faithfully recorded by the artist.

He slit open the packet of Lemsip and was immediately, and pleasantly, rewarded by the aroma of lemons. The kettle came to the boil, and he poured the water over the pale powder and stirred it.

He carried it out to Una and presented it with a comical flourish.

"Thank you, dear," she said. "I'm sure it does no good at all, but it makes me *feel* better."

"Professor Connors is with you there," Lynch said. "He's fond of the odd dram of Lemsip himself."

"Is he indeed?" Una scrunched herself about in the lawn chair, looking interested. Ever since Connors had appeared to lecture her club on Yeats, he had been a sort of hero to her. "Such a grand man, Sean," she said fondly. "So unaffected and natural. May Brennan herself, the great intellectual who's after reading all of Beckett, said he was the finest speaker we had ever had."

"I'm glad I could help out in the crisis," Lynch said.

The lurid light in the garden fascinated him. The sky was nearly the color of pale lettuce, and Una seemed to glow like an extraterrestrial creature.

"It's a bad night," she said, "but it's lovely in a ghastly way. Will it storm, do you think? It's so thundery, it might, but I don't smell rain. Not that I can smell anything at all. Was it like this for that poor wee boy on Ireland's Eye?"

"No," said Lynch, squatting on his heels near a bed of spinach. "It was a proper storm, Una. The boy slept in the tower."

He remembered finding the child, Rory, on a high hummock above the seaward side of the island. Rory had looked at him with wild eyes at first, but he was filthy and shivering and frightened, and he had grasped the proffered hand with alacrity. Small wonder, then, that Rory had lain against his breast, on the boat, and confessed that yes, the Yank had been a confection made up to pacify the gardai. There had never been a Yank in plaid pants, and never would be. He was a figment of the children's collective imagination and did not exist.

The odd light shifted yet again, and seemed to send the spinach beds into a kind of dull phosphorescence. Was this what Bergit Söderström saw that compelled her to render her visions into tapestries and wall hangings?

Bergit was on his mind because, while he had been out on Ireland's Eye rescuing the Kennerly lad, a call had come through from her. She had said she would talk with Mr. Lynch or Mr. Browne and, neither of them being available, declined to leave a message. She had left a number where she could be reached, in London, but Lynch had tried it five times without success. He had had the number traced, and it was registered to N. Murphy, so he had no doubt that it was correct. He excused himself, leaving Una with her Lemsip and her inky *Times*, and went to try again.

This time the phone was picked up on the second ring. "Haloo?" said a very Scandinavian, female voice, and Lynch felt his luck begin to turn. He identified himself and asked Bergit what she had wanted to discuss with him.

Peals of laughter greeted this reasonable question. He thought that Bergit was either quite drunk or on some sort of drug.

"But I am not Mrs. Murphy," the voice said, still gasping with laughter. "You are the policeman? About Bergit's husband?"

"Yes."

"I am her sister, Maj. Maj is my name. Bergit is not here at present." She giggled again, and Lynch realized that she was very young. He asked when Bergit would return.

"Oh, very late perhaps. I will meet her at a club and we will return quite late. I am visiting, you see, and she is going to show me the sights. I have never been to London."

He gave Maj his number in Blackrock, and instructed her to have Bergit call him, no matter how late they returned from the club. Maj disappeared for quite a long time, locating a pencil, and copied the number down. "Yes, good, fine," she said, suddenly sober and efficient, "I will tell her."

"Enjoy your night out," he said, and she giggled again.

It was, in fact, nearly five in the morning when the shrill of the telephone awakened him. Una slept on peacefully, wheezing slightly, and he ran down the stairs as quickly as possible, hoping she would not be disturbed. The opal light of dawn was seeping in around the drawn curtains, and birds were already singing in the garden.

"Hello, Sergeant," said the cool voice of Bergit Söderström, and Lynch wondered how he could ever have confused Maj's voice for her sister's. Bergit's was the voice of utter control; even if she had danced the night away in some Mayfair disco, she was perfectly capable of conducting business. "I am sorry to call so late, but you did say I was to call at any time?"

"Yes," said Lynch. "I've been unable to reach you."

"I took my little sister to Wales for two days." There was a pause, and he could hear the metallic snap of a cigarette lighter, and then her indrawn breath. "The reason I have called is this," she said. "I have been here and there, traveling about, and my neighbor in these flats is good enough to receive my mail for me. Some few little days ago, she is not sure exactly when, a small package arrives. When I open it, it is a pair of topaz earrings. Very nice. The address on the package is typed on a label, to B. Murphy, with my address in London. There is no note, no return address. The post-mark is from London, but the date is—how do you call it?"

"Blurred?"

"Exactly so. But the really strange thing is, the earrings are from Nick. They are a present from him."

"You'll have to explain, Mrs. Murphy. How can they be a gift from your dead husband?"

"Oh, no doubt at all. He knew I wanted a pair of topaz earrings. We discussed the setting, and these are exactly what we agreed on, Sergeant. They are a present from Nicholas. No one else could have known."

Lynch was silent, making connections. The package, already wrapped and addressed, must have been taken from Nicholas Murphy's dead body and sent on to Bergit. Nobody but the murderer could have been responsible. The man who had murdered Nick Murphy had waited for some time, and then courteously posted the package to its intended recipient.

"Have you the original wrappings?" he asked, dreading the answer.

"Oh no," said Bergit. "It was a cool day, and I had a fire. I threw the wraps in before I knew what was inside. The package has no marking—it could come from anywhere—and I burned it, too. I detest clutter, you know."

"I didn't know," said Lynch, "but I might have guessed."

"Was it right for me to call you?" Bergit asked. "Is it of some importance?"

Lynch ignored this disingenuous plea. "I would like to have a look at the earrings," he said. "It might be possible to trace them to a private jeweler in Dublin, or abroad."

His worst fears were confirmed when Bergit inhaled and exhaled audibly and said, "I know what you think of me, Sergeant. I can imagine. You are thinking that Bergit sold the earrings, but you're dead wrong. I threw them off of Putney Bridge, the same as Nick's ashes. It seemed the right thing to do. It was, you call it, *spooky*. I don't wish to wear a dead man's gifts. It's bad luck."

"In fact, then," said Lynch, "no evidence survives to prove that the earrings existed. I have only your word."

"No," said Bergit, with a touch of malice. "My neighbor, Mrs. Plant, will testify about the package, and my sister, Maj, saw the earrings. I shall give you Mrs. Plant's telephone number, if you please."

"That won't be necessary," said Lynch, who believed the story in any case. "Is there anything else I should know?"

"I can't think of anything," she said, sounding bored and tired. "I only know whoever killed Nick is in London now, or was. *Somebody* mailed those earrings to me."

"Indeed," said Lynch, and rang off.

Waiting for the kettle to boil at the non-hour of 5:12 in the morning, he thought of Jim Kennerly, still at large somewhere in England, and wondered if Imelda's husband had dropped the topaz earrings into a letterbox. And if he had, why? Given the man's character, it made no sense.

Late the next day, Imelda Kennerly appeared at the Garda station, requesting to see Lynch. Frank showed her in, his face elaborately free of expression. Frank found the romance between Mrs. Kennerly and Tom Mulligan exceptionally amusing. Lynch asked himself if he would have found it funny at Frank's age, but the answer was no.

Mrs. Kennerly was wearing jeans and a faded green blouse today; unlike the time she had come to confess to her sins, she had taken few pains with her appearance. Her face reflected the terrible events of the past week—a husband missing, and wanted by the police, and the overnight disappearance of her small son.

"How is Rory?" Lynch asked, rising to greet her.

"Much better, thank you. It was only a cold. Now he knows the truth about his father, things are looking up for him. He thinks it's better to be a felon than a man gone off with a girl his sister's age." Her voice was not bitter or sardonic. She was simply reporting things as she saw them. She sat in the proffered chair and looked uneasy. Her hands kept fiddling with the large plastic bag from Dunne's stores that lay on her lap; she smoothed and patted the bag as if it were a carrier with a cat inside.

"Let me get this in order," she said awkwardly. "Denis McGuire received the stolen goods, and my husband sold them. The lorry driver just went up North to fetch them, but he got a cut. Who's the most guilty of the lot?"

"Technicalities aside, Mrs. Kennerly, they're all equally guilty. They acted in collusion to transport goods over the border and sell them at a profit here, in the Republic."

"Then why did my Jim disappear while the others stayed put?"

Lynch selected a ball-point and rolled it in his palms. "That's hard to say, but I could make a guess. The lorry driver was probably off on some legitimate haul when the tip-off came, and couldn't be reached. Your husband realized the gravity of the situation and put as many miles between himself and Ireland as a man without a passport could do."

"And McGuire?"

"Mr. McGuire is an odd case, Mrs. Kennerly. It's quite possible that he sees himself in distorted, grandiose terms—as someone protected from the law. Above it."

"A real nutter," said Imelda.

Lynch smiled, for it was the precise word he had privately thought of in connection with Denis McGuire. Aloud he said, "Certainly a distorted personality. A bit of a fanatic."

Imelda prodded her carrier bag, frowning. "Really," she said, "I came to ask you a wee question. It's to do with Jim, of course."

"Of course."

"He's not such a bad man as you think. He has his faults, and plenty of them, but he's not the complete villain. He was a good father to our girl, and he was good to Rory, too, until Florrie Devine got hold of him. Even then he wasn't bad, or a brute. He was just, how will I put it . . . absent. Jim didn't seem quite *there* anymore."

Lynch nodded sympathetically. It was the old story of the wronged wife, who would gladly string her husband up with her own hands, until the wretched man came to grief. Then some impulse of loyalty impelled her to tell anyone who would listen that he hadn't been such a scoundrel after all. He had heard it from battered and abused wives, wives whose children had been brutally attacked, once, even, from a wife who had been slashed with the carving knife at Sunday dinner.

He realized that he believed Imelda Kennerly's assertion of Jim's essential decency because of his own prejudices. He was a man with a married daughter, and he would rather have her betrayed and deserted than beaten or stabbed. He would prefer, if she were to be hurt, that the hurt not be physical.

"I was reading about that mid-life crisis business," Imelda was saying. "At first I thought it was a bloody old load of you-know-what—I mean, a woman has a mid-life crisis all her life long—and then I thought, well, maybe there's something to it? Maybe the men are so sheltered they don't realize what's happening until it's down their throat? Could that be the way of it, Sergeant?"

Lynch rolled his ball-point fervidly. "Sure it could, Mrs. Kennerly," he said, "it could at that. I'm too old for mid-life crisis, I believe, but I take your meaning."

"Well then, if a man was basically a decent sort, and then he went and behaved like a criminal after years of being straight, couldn't there be a special dispensation for him?"

"That's in the hands of the courts," Lynch said.

"But if he could pay back the money he had stolen, or part of it? Would that not help?"

She sat rigidly upright in her chair, her eyes desperate and pleading. Her hair was less tidy than he remembered, but it was the only aspect of her being not concentrated toward a pronouncement of clemency for her runaway husband.

"Are we speaking of Mr. Kennerly now?" he asked gently.

She blinked once. It was a nod, meaning yes.

He was so weary. It seemed to him that women and children—those members of society he had always loved best—were willfully pulling him apart. Children misled him with their fanciful Yanks, or ran off and required dramatic rescues. Women called at dawn to report gifts from the dead, or appeared to try to bribe him with the promise of reparations. At least men behaved in straightforward ways. They came to his attention as corpses, or populated his imagination as garroters. They killed, or were killed.

"At the end of the day," Mrs. Kennerly said, "would Jim get a lighter sentence if he returned the money?"

"That is possible," said Lynch.

"Right." She opened the neck of the Dunne's bag and withdrew a cigar box. She placed the cigar box on the desk, squarely in front of him. He looked into her crusading eyes and saw nothing but the determination that had brought her to him.

"Open it," she commanded.

He saw the notes and realized that the operation had been greater and more professional than he could have dreamed of.

"I had it in my veg tray," she said proudly. "I didn't know where it came from, but he left it, the day he went across. Jim left it for me and Rory. You see? He was a good father after all."

He stared at her, and then back at the money. Finally he sighed rather more loudly than he had intended and said, "All right, Mrs. Kennerly. Shall we begin at the beginning?"

TWENTY

TERROR NET YIELDS UP A WANTED FISH! screamed the headline on the English tabloid available in Molloy's shop. In the wake of a rumored IRA bomb-campaign scare, the British had cast their nets and come up with Jim Kennerly, who was, it turned out, not a terrorist but what they called an ordinary, decent criminal. He had been trying to get to the Isle of Man, but his Irish accent did him in. He was detained under the Prevention of Terrorism Act, and sometime during his detention his resemblance to the man called James Kennerly, who was wanted in Ireland, was noticed.

He had, of course, denied that he was Kennerly, had insisted that he was called Jack McGirr, even producing a badly forged driver's permit to prove it, but he was not believed. Finally, realizing how much better he would be treated as a black marketeer than as a suspected terrorist, he had ruefully confessed his identity. Ten days after his scarper from Balgriffin, Imelda's husband was back in Ireland, on remand in Mountjoy Prison, awaiting trial.

Everyone in the Crescent was very kind to Imelda. Mrs. Naughton baked her a rhubarb pie. Mrs. O'Rourke brought a huge pot of lasagna, a dish she concocted with large additions of cabbage. Kate Brannigan and Nora Keegan came to her house and performed the humbler household tasks Imelda might find unendurable just at present. Nobody—not even Janie's mother—mentioned Jim's troubles. They made it seem as if they were the grateful ones—"Oh, I baked more of this than I can possibly eat, missus dear. Ye'd be doin' me a favor to take this cake off me, and that's the truth."

Rory, too, became the recipient of much kindness from the other children. They, unlike their elders, did not need to result to subterfuge, and the topic of Rory's father's imprisonment was discussed endlessly.

"I used to go visit my uncle in Long Kesh," Matty said. "It was grim, like, but here? I heard the Free State prisons are like country clubs."

"Anyone could go to prison," said Janie. "It's no disgrace. People forget."

"I heard where it's all that bloody Denis McGuire's fault," Kevin confided. "He'll bear the brunt of it, not yer da."

"Hallelujah!" shouted Terry. "Praise Jesus!" He was always able to make Rory laugh.

When Gervaise returned from his holidays, he casually presented Rory with the skeleton of a sea horse he had discovered on the beaches of Tramore. All of them pooled their pocket money to make sure that Rory—whose mother was a bit short of cash these days—never had to do without his favorite brand of crisps, cheese and onion.

In Mountjoy, Jim Kennerly continued to express amazement that anyone could associate him with the crime of murder.

"Look, Sergeant," he told Lynch, "I couldn't kill a cat, could I? I never mailed no bloody package of earrings to anybody, nor why should I? If I'd killed yer man down on the racecourse and found that package on his body, I would have opened it and sold the effers. Or I would have thrown them in the estuary more likely."

"Or presented them to Miss Florrie Devine?"

"Her," snorted Kennerly. "Bloody little gouger."

"In any case, she's left County Dublin."

"Good," said Jim. "No loss."

"You'll have to admit that it is a queer coincidence that Mrs. Murphy's earrings were returned during the period when you were in England?"

"No more than the bomb scare, Sergeant, and I had bloody eff-all to do with that. Lots of things can happen, and it doesn't mean a thing. You're an educated fella—don't you know that nothing is connected?"

"On the contrary, Mr. Kennerly, *everything* is connected."

"You're barkin' up the wrong tree here." He accepted a cigarette and inhaled with pleasure, luxuriously. "I'm no killer," he said at length. "I'm greedy, but I'm not a killer. If I was a killer, I'd of done it long before this."

When asked about his whereabouts on the night of the murder, Kennerly merely rolled his eyes and said he wasn't a bloody woman, was he, and he didn't keep a diary of his comings and goings. He allowed as how he had probably been in bed, beside his wife, and admitted that his nocturnal prowlings, whether to the arms of Florrie or to the industrial estate, made his alibi impossible to check. He repeated, again and again, that he was a man incapable of murder.

The odd thing was that Lynch believed him. He did not think Jim Kennerly had garroted Nicholas Murphy on the racecourse, any more than he thought Tom Mulligan had done so. The only people he saw as possible culprits were in the clear. Denis McGuire, who seemed a likely suspect, had been, incontestably, at a Charismatic Prayer Circle. There were a dozen witnesses prepared to swear that McGuire had remained until the small hours, drinking coffee and quoting scripture.

The other man Lynch saw as a possible killer had been in Mountjoy during the entire month of May. The lorry driver in the black market setup—an unknown quantity—could prove that he was in Athlone on the night in question.

Someone had killed Nicholas Murphy on the racecourse, but Lynch now despaired of ever finding out who that someone had been. He was beginning to see the entire event as a no-win situation. Murphy had been an evil, a worthless man. Some unknown person had terminated his life, for a reason Lynch would never know, and some instinct in him argued that there was an end to it. Poetic justice had been done, that night in Balgriffin, and Lynch was not meant to tamper with it. The event was complete, had been accomplished. These thoughts came from the side of himself Una called the renegade, the side that was at odds with his usual self—the one that loved law, worshipped justice.

He had felt that side jarred for the first time when their daughter married and moved up North. Within a few months of her relocation, there had been a murder not far from where she lived. A farmer had been shot dead in his fields in Tyrone, seated on his tractor, tending to his business. The farmer, the papers had said, was a part-time policeman, a member of the Protestant Ulster Defence Regiment, the UDR.

"Now there's a tragedy," he had shouted down the phone at her, beside himself with anxiety on her behalf. "An innocent farmer shot down in his own fields."

There had been an embarrassed little pause at her end, and then she had said, "Yes, it's awful, Daddy." Something in her voice struck him as unconvinced, halfhearted.

"It's always awful when someone is murdered," she had gone on. "Death is terrible. I agree with you there."

"And is there something you don't agree with?"

Again the embarrassed pause. "Well, Daddy, you called him an innocent man. He wasn't really innocent, you know. He was a member of the UDR, after all."

He had felt as chilled as if he had been an American father in the sixties, hearing his well-loved daughter calling the police the "pigs." He, a detective, had to listen to his daughter excuse a murder because the victim had been a member of the part-time police force in Ulster.

"You don't understand," she had almost wailed over the phone. "They're sectarian killers, the UDR. It's not what you think, Da. That poor, innocent farmer shot an unarmed boy last week. He shot him in front of his father, and he shot the father, too. The boy was seventeen, and he died. The father, he lived, but that family will never be the same."

"There was some reason, surely?"

"Reason?" she had said on a sharp, inward breath like a gasp. *"Reason?* Sure, Daddy, there doesn't need to be a reason here."

"That can't be true," Lynch had said, feeling his alarm grow. "You're saying it's total anarchy up there, pet, and I can't believe it."

"All right, Daddy," she replied, sounding cool and weary. "There's a reason, and here it is. He felt like killin' somebody. He had the power, and he knew nobody'd ever hold him to account if he plugged a Taig. One of us. That's all in the world it was—he was in the mood to kill."

She had hung up then, and Lynch had felt himself becoming what Una called a renegade. Maura was not an emotional girl, not given to fanciful passions, and if she said that men in the North with the authority to kill did so when the mood struck them, then it must be true. He had not told Una of that conversation, but that evening he had drunk more Bushmill's than was good for his health, listening to tapes of Paddy Moloney, and found himself mumbling "Terrible, terrible," as he swayed up to bed.

Looking, now, at the beetling and distressed brows of Jim Kennerly, he reminded himself that he was not in the North. He would never be called upon to exercise his judgment in that tragic province. He was a senior detective in the Republic, and it was still his duty—no matter how difficult—to find the killer of Nicholas Murphy. There was nothing remotely political about it. It was his job.

"How's my wife?" Kennerly was asking. "How's Imelda?"

"Well enough," Lynch said. "Considering."

"And the boy? My son, Rory?"

"Grand," said Lynch.

He had remembered someone else who was in England during the time of the posting of the earrings, and although the connection seemed so fantastic as to be fruitless, something told him it was worth following up. As he had just told Kennerly, everything is connected, sooner or later.

The weather being fine, the children decided to hold their last Council on the racecourse. There had never been a lifting of the ban that prohibited them from climbing over the wall, but, by tacit consent, the people of Balgriffin had decided that the police didn't care anymore. Dirt bikes and kites reappeared, as well as the occasional solitary figure making a study of wildflowers or grasses.

"How're you going to call us to order without your xylophone?" Terry asked Janie.

Janie giggled. "The meeting is called to order!" she shouted.

They were sitting in a circle, in the shadow of the secretive grove of trees.

A tube of Polo mints was their sole refreshment on this occasion; it was passed along in a grave and ritualistic manner.

"It's bloody hot," complained Gervaise, swatting at an insect too small to see properly.

"You think this is hot?" Kevin asked. "I read where it's so hot in America this summer they're droppin' like flies. It's over a hundred in some places. Poor Yanks."

"Order!" cried Janie again, but the mention of the Yanks had already accomplished her purpose. Yanks, or one Yank in particular, was why they had assembled, and they fell silent.

"We're here on account of what Rory told me, when he was laid up," Terry explained. "We're not putting any blame on him, isn't that so?"

"Right!" replied the others.

"Hear, hear," cried Matty, and then instantly felt embarrassed.

Rory then told, at some length, of how he had confessed the truth to that Lynch, when the two of them were on the boat coming back from Ireland's Eye. While he spoke, he pulled little tussocks of grass from the earth, fiddling them in his fingers. "I wasn't meself," he explained. "I was feverish, like, and I wanted to tell the truth."

"It wasn't you, though, not to begin with," said Terry. "Somebody phoned them up. Who could have known?"

The sonorous voice of Matty Keegan cut in like the tolling of a bell. "I'm to blame," he said. "I told Scobie Halloran. He must be the one who phoned."

"Old Mr. Halloran lives up the lane?" Janie asked.

"Blind Scobie?" Kevin's voice was full of wonder. "Why him?"

"I wanted to tell the truth," said Matty. "Just like Rory. Mr. H. is a grand fella, and I'm the one to blame."

"Oh no," said Janie, hastily swallowing the remaining crunchy bits of her Polo mint and pushing her glasses upward. "I'm the one at fault. I was the one suggested we make up a Yank—remember? It was all my idea."

"It was Wolfe Tone's fault," said Terry. "If not for him, none of us would be involved here."

"Where is he?" asked Gervaise. "Where is Wolfe Tone? He ought to be here, seein' as how he was here at the beginning."

"At the vet's," said Terry. "Mange, they say."

"Order!" screamed Janie. "Please now."

"Let's just say it's nobody's fault. We were all in it together, and when Rory told, it wasn't like informin'. He was under pressure. The point is—has anybody heard from the cops?" From the silence it was obvious that no one had, but Terry seemed to want to stretch the matter out. "You sure?" he asked again, looking hard at each of them. "Because if my da ever heard I'd been mixed up in this—"

"You and me both," said Gervaise. "I wonder why that Lynch didn't tell our families?"

"We're not that important, you know," said Janie rather sarcastically.

"He seemed a decent fella," said Matty. "Maybe he just didn't want to get us in trouble?"

It all seemed a bit anticlimactic. Each of them, when the word had been passed round about a council, had secretly suspected some momentous revelation to be unveiled, but nothing had happened, and they were off the hook. They felt relieved and a little disappointed as they dispersed and straggled back over the racecourse.

"When can you see your da?" Matty asked Rory.

"Next week. Mam says he's fine, she seen him yesterday. He wanted magazines and a deck of cards."

Kevin was calling back that he had found a pair of girl's knickers in a gully. Terry and Gervaise rushed over, keen for a glimpse, and Janie walked away quickly.

Matty didn't bother. He trudged on, with Rory, wondering why Rory seemed so quietly happy. He supposed it had something to do with knowing where his da was—safe and sound, locked up in Mountjoy Prison, where he couldn't get into any more trouble.

It was in these hours of the late afternoon that Tom Mulligan felt most melancholy. Rita never gave him so much as the time of day anymore, and he missed their bracing sessions in the upstairs lounge, even if he did not miss Rita. He didn't even have the consolation of Imelda's visits to cheer him, but of course, poor Imelda had too much on her plate now to drop in for a vodka and lemonade. He wished her well.

He leaned against the bar in the crepuscular and nearly deserted public room at the precise moment when Cats Phelan was passing into deep sleep. He would have to find new lodgings. Mrs. Joyce was making things unbearable for him. Ever since the gardai had chosen to investigate his activities on the night of May 12 his landlady had treated him like a dangerous criminal, a pariah. She shrank back with exaggerated dread if they happened to meet in the corridor, and no longer changed his bed linen with any kind of regularity. Twice he had returned to find things in his rooms subtly disarranged, as if she had been going through them in his absence.

At the end of the summer he would go over to England to see his son for a week, but of Nuala he was beginning to despair. She sounded more and more American, and less and less eager to return to Ireland. And why should she be? What could he give her but his bed in the dismal lodgings—a little prison for her to inhabit while her da slept on a cot bed in the other room— and meals from tins, prepared over the hot plate? He no longer even owned a car. He had seen an ad for an old clunker, a '75 Renault going for £400, but even that seemed too much. Everything he had managed to save was ear-marked for his children, for the sudden emergencies and acts of God he had learned to fear.

He took his paper from beneath the bar and spread it out, turning to the sections that advertised rooms and lodgings to let. It would be convenient to find a place closer to Balgriffin, but it would also be more expensive. The prices in Clontarf staggered him, and he was wondering if he might be better off with the horrible Mrs. Joyce, after all, when an unexpected customer came in.

There was something familiar about the substantial figure making its way toward him, but the light was dim, and Tom's eyes had to adjust after reading such fine print. "Afternoon," he said pleasantly, and then—just as the words had left his mouth—he recognized who he was addressing. It was the Garda sergeant who had brought all this calamity down upon him.

Lynch sat on a stool across from Tom and asked for a pint of Guinness.

"I hope my presence doesn't make you anxious," Lynch said, while Tom set the pint to level. "I suspect you of nothing, Mr. Mulligan. I merely need your help this one last time."

Tom topped the pint, leveled it, and set it before his tormentor with steady hands. Lynch produced two pound notes and Tom went to the cash register, aware of the sad, doggy eyes that followed his every movement.

"You don't have to speak so low," he said, returning with the change. "Cats there is out for the count."

"Ah yes, I remember Mr. Phelan." Lynch sipped his Guinness, nodded happily, and then produced something from his pocket. He pushed it across the bar and said, "Take a look at this man, Mr. Mulligan. Study him as long as you please."

It was not a conventional photograph, or even a police photograph. It was a picture printed on thick, glossy paper, and the photographer was credited along the border. It was very small, no more than four inches by three, and it showed the smiling face of a man in early middle age. He looked innocent and harmless. Laugh lines radiated from his guileless eyes, and his forehead was lofty and full, the result of a receding hairline. As if to compensate for the defoliation of his pate, the man in the photograph had let the rest of his hair grow rather long—little tendrils showed around the lobes of his ears.

"Who's this supposed to be, then?" Tom asked.

"Have you ever seen him?" Lynch countered.

"Don't think so," said Tom. And yet something haunted him about the face in the photograph. It reminded him of something.

"Doesn't he remind you of anyone?" Lynch took a long draft of his Guinness and looked from the mysterious picture to Tom.

"He does that, but I can't think who," said Tom.

"Try the American the children said came in here to buy crisps," Lynch said. "Or the man who was killed on the racecourse. They weren't all that different to look at, and you've got to remember this photo is five years old. Yer man lost more hair."

"There's a certain resemblance to the man who was murdered," Tom said, "but about the man who came in here I couldn't say."

"Well, of course you couldn't, man, because you never saw him. The children made him up and then you were obliged to lie. He never existed—not that man. But this one?"

"They lied?" Tom said, feeling a dull, trapped interest.

Lynch sluiced his hand in the air, to show it was of no importance now. "Just study that face, if you will. He won't have come into the pub at all. Think of him on the Gilligan Road, or slinking past when you were waiting at the bus stop, after closing. Or *on* the bus earlier, journeying into Balgriffin from Dublin."

"I don't understand."

"And neither do I, but give me your best effort, Tom."

Tom stared at the crinkled eyes, the balding dome, and could find no recognition. He tried to turn the photo over, but it was mounted on cardboard, and there was no information to be had.

"I draw a blank," he said. "Sorry."

Lynch sighed and drained his pint. "Thank you, son," he said. "I had to try. All the best."

When he had left, Tom acknowledged that his anger had been misplaced. Lynch was not to be blamed for his current misfortunes. Neither was the killer, since you couldn't blame an unknown entity. The man who was responsible for Tom's misfortunes was the poor sod who had met his death in the grandstand. It was all his fault.

TWENTY-ONE

On the following morning, Frank Browne went to all the auto rental places on the north side of the Liffey, while Lynch visited those on the south bank. At the very first place, the one nearest the address of the man he was investigating, Lynch was shown the copies of transactions dating from the first two weeks in May.

The day of the twelfth yielded nothing, but on the eighth, a Saturday, he found the name he was looking for among the five people who had rented a car from Terenure Auto Rental.

"Do you remember this man?" he asked the young girl behind the desk. "He rented a dark blue Ford Escort from you on the ninth of May."

The girl squinted at the photograph. She seemed to be nearsighted. For no very good reason, he noticed the quantity of shiny green goo on her eyelids.

"Sure, it's a funny kind of a photo," she said. "Why is it stuck up on cardboard?"

"It's clipped from a book jacket," he explained. "It's a picture of the author."

"Is he famous?"

Lynch said he didn't think the author could be called famous, and waited patiently for the girl to say whether she remembered the face in the photo. "Can't say I remember him," she said at last, "but that doesn't mean anything. Will I call Des? He shows the cars and all—I just do the paperwork. Ordinarily, I'd remember, but he just looks like anyone, if you get my meaning."

Des remembered, although he allowed as how the photograph must be a few years old. "That's himself," he said cheerfully. "He paid with American Express. What's he done, anyway? He didn't look like a criminal type. What's he wanted for?"

"Nothing, it may be," said Lynch. "This is a routine investigation."

"Well," said Des with insulting cheeriness, "you'll find no evidence in the Escort. He returned it all clean and nice, and it's been hoovered out and wiped down a dozen times since then."

"What'd he write?" the girl asked.

"A scholarly work," said Lynch. "An academic biography."

"Oh," said the girl. Politely she lowered her iridescent eyelids to conceal her boredom.

Professor Connors was enjoying a break when Lynch arrived at the National Library. He was standing on the portico, hands thrust into the pockets of a lightweight gray poplin jacket, surveying the courtyard. Except for the fact that he did not smoke a pipe, he seemed the epitome of professorship. His kindly face was creased with lines denoting intelligent good humor, and there was an endearing smudge of ball-point ink on his left cheek, as if he had swiped at it with a hand that held a defective pen. He did not see Lynch at first, and by the time Lynch stood two feet from him on the sheltered portico, he had sighed and turned, as if willing himself back to his interminable Yeats studies.

"Good morning, Professor Connors," Lynch said in a too loud voice.

Connors wheeled about in confusion. This was only the second time they had met, in person, but Connors recognized him immediately. His face split in a wide grin of delight. No doubt he thought that the Garda sergeant had come to thank him for speaking at the book club circle in Blackrock. Lynch had made the suggestion over the telephone, and on the actual night he had been—as always on Una's literary hostess nights—at Slattery's music pub on Capel Street.

"Hello there," said Connors, beaming. "I can't tell you what a pleasure it was for me to lecture to your wife's circle. To be welcomed into a real Irish home! Una, if I might call her that, is a most delightful woman. You are a fortunate man, Sergeant."

Lynch bowed his head, to show his good fortune. He wondered if Henry Connors had a wife and children, back in the States, and hoped it wasn't so.

"I'm divorced, myself," said the professor. "Unfortunately, Mrs. Connors —Patricia—and I never had any children. She wanted to put it off, you know, and then we split up. She remarried, and now she has two young ones in San Luis Obispo. That's in California."

A whistling wind was stirring in the courtyard of the National Library, and all the warmth was being sucked out of the day. The young gardai who stood at the portals were hunched into their jackets.

"Damned strange weather for early July," Connors said.

"It's about to hail."

"How would you know a thing like that?"

"Experience," said Lynch. "I want to thank you for lecturing at Una's book club. She said you were splendid."

Now it was Connors's turn to bow his head. "My pleasure," he said. "Absolutely."

The sky darkened, and within minutes, as Lynch had predicted, hailstones came pelting down, pinging against the cobbles of the courtyard. "Oh, magnificent!" shouted Henry J. Connors. "Nature at her absolute, vindictive best!"

When the thrilling, diamondlike hailstones melted into a drumming rain, they passed into the main hall of the National Library, admitting defeat. They passed the tragic famine posters, and walked into the dim gallery where James Connolly's bloodstained tunic could be viewed, under glass. They were the only English-speaking people in the room; farther up, before the Emancipation Proclamation of 1916, three Germans had embarked on hot debate.

Connors seemed, not uneasy, but curious about Lynch's presence. "What brings you here, today, Sergeant? Investigating another crime, or did some other visiting American get his pocket picked?"

Now, in the American's company, Lynch remembered how difficult it was to associate him with crime of any kind. He also felt—and he knew it was absurd—that it was rude of him to question a man who had so recently done him a favor. Nonetheless, there were the earrings, mailed from London while Connors had been there. Since Bergit had so conveniently burned the wrappings with the blurred postmark, there was no evidence of any kind. The photocopied car rental document was burning a hole in his pocket, but even that could be explained away.

"Professor Connors," he said, studying the seventy-year-old bloodstain on the patriot's tunic, "did you ever rent a car while you were here in Dublin?"

"Yes," said Connors, after a slight, surprised pause. "Several times. I revisited Sligo, Yeats's grave, you know, when I first arrived. Another time I went down to Wexford, I have an acquaintance living there, fellow I knew a long time ago. He married an Irish girl."

Lynch noted the awkwardness with which Connors had said "a long time ago." He had been about to say something else, something which would reveal more of his history, and thought better of it. "Was that in May?" he asked. "The jaunt to Wexford?"

"Late June, if I remember correctly. I got my first car straight from the airport, but when I went down to visit my friend I rented from a place on the Terenure Road, near my lodgings. Young fellow there, Des, most helpful."

"But in May?" Lynch pressed. "Did you rent a car in May, Professor?"

"I wish you'd call me Hank," said Connors, wrinkling his forehead and massaging one earlobe in an effort to remember. "May, May." He snapped his fingers. "Of course. I had an urge to go driving through the Wicklow Mountains, and I rented the car, an Escort, and then I came down with that god-awful flu. I had the car for a week, you see, and I kept thinking I'd get better, but I only got worse. The truth is, by Monday I felt so sick I didn't have the energy to turn it in. I think it was Wednesday when I finally brought it back. Not a mile on it, Sergeant. Not so much as a mile!"

For the first time, he seemed to lose his composure. He listened to what he had just said and corrected himself. "Well, there may have been a few miles from that first day, but you know what I mean."

Lynch fancied the scent of lemons had sprung up in the gloomy gallery. He remembered pouring the boiling water over the powder in Una's cup, recalled her assertion that Lemsip probably did no good but certainly made her feel better. It was advertised so widely, both in England and in Ireland, that any right-thinking citizen of either of those countries automatically reached for it whenever the symptoms of a cold threatened. Lynch had had it only twice, quite enjoying the tang of lemon as filtered through liberal lacings of whiskey.

"I remember now," he said. "Lemsip saw you through that bout."

"Yes, that's right," cried Connors delightedly. "Good old Lemsip!"

The Germans were drawing near, still arguing. "I beg your pardon," said one of them abruptly. "Have you the correct time?"

Henry Connors gave them the time and then launched into a torrent of German. Lynch watched, fascinated, while Connors and the Germans appeared to trade ideas. The American spoke slowly, but he was understood and listened to. It occurred to Lynch that he should simply steal away, leaving his suspect in his element. Henry J. Connors would go back to America, harming no one, and continue to live a productive life; he would educate the young and enthrall book circles and spend much time and effort in producing yet another book on William Butler Yeats.

"Just in case you care," said Connors, when the Germans had departed. "Those blokes were on your side, but they were disturbed by the number of martyrs in Irish history. They said you made a cult of martyrs."

"Perhaps we do," said Lynch. "You speak German very well. I admire your command of a foreign language."

Connors shrugged. "I had to learn it for my Ph.D. I don't really speak it very well, but I make the attempt. Now, what were we talking about before I so rudely interrupted us?"

"Lemsip." Lynch smiled sadly, knowing how preposterous his next question would seem. "Did you take it hot or cold?"

Henry J. Connors smiled back and, after a slightly strained silence, said, "Room-temperature. I just swigged it straight from the bottle."

"I'm very sorry about this," Lynch said.

"Excuse me?"

"I'm going to ask you to come with me to Fitzgibbon Street, Professor Connors."

A look of disbelief came into the American's eyes, but it vanished quickly, to be replaced by one of dismal surrender. He seemed to shrink, deflate, before Lynch's eyes, and when he spoke his voice was devoid of the bluff, hearty tones he had employed with Lynch before. It was as if, in their other encounters, he had been playing the role of an American professor. Now he simply was one.

"I see," said Connors. "I'll just get my briefcase." In an odd sort of way, he sounded relieved.

Technically, of course, Connors was not being arrested, as Lynch explained to him. They were in the interrogation room, and every effort was made to put the professor at his ease, if ease was a state that could be achieved in such circumstances.

A comfortable chair, Lynch's own office chair, was brought in for Connors, and a black coffee, two sugars, given him. It was a cheerless room, designed to offer no comfort, but Connors showed little apprehension. He sat stolidly, drinking his coffee, and occasionally flicking his gaze from Lynch to Browne, who sat writing in his notebook. He declined to remove his poplin jacket and Lynch realized that, for an American, it was doubtless chilly in the room. It was July, but the rain that had caught them on the portico of the National Library continued to sluice down. The room was windowless, but they could hear the grumbling of thunder from time to time.

"It seems to me," Connors said, "a lot of fuss is being made over a patent remedy. Okay—let's suppose I lied about the Lemsip. I did, of course. I had no idea you had to boil water and mix it up, that much is clear. But that doesn't prove I didn't have the flu. I only added the touch about the Lemsip because it seemed the friendly thing to do. I'd seen ads for it, you see, and I thought, 'when in Rome,' and it seemed so much more the thing to *do*. Doctor myself with an old Irish remedy."

"It's English," muttered Frank. Only Lynch heard him.

"A lot of fuss is being made," said Lynch, "because on the night you professed to doctor yourself with Lemsip, a man was killed in Balgriffin. You say you haven't a soul who can vouch for your whereabouts on that night. Balgriffin is seven miles from the center of Dublin, and you had rented a car from the Saturday before his death, on Wednesday. Several children claim to have met with an American on the afternoon of May the twelfth. Surely, Professor, you must see why I feel the need to question you?"

The children's lie served him in good stead, for Connors actually blustered in his denial. As well he might, since he had never met them.

"Let me just state, here and now, that I never met any children that afternoon, because I was not *in* Balgriffin that afternoon!"

"But later? That night?"

"Certainly not," said Connors. "If I were to hire a car to commit a crime, do you think I'd be so foolish as to walk into a rental place and give them my right name? Pay with my American Express?"

"Why not?" Lynch craved a cigarette. He craved it as an actor might a prop. "You would never have come to my attention if your wallet had not been found in a rubbish bin on O'Connell Street. You couldn't have foreseen that, Professor. If you hadn't been the victim of our skillful pickpockets, I would never have made your acquaintance or heard of you. There was nothing to connect you to the act on the racecourse."

"Precisely," said Connors in a friendly way. "There is, indeed, nothing."

"And yet a pair of topaz earrings was mailed to Mr. Murphy's widow, from London. During the time you were over, sir. Pursuing your studies at the British Library. Sure, you'd grant a coincidence there?"

Connors was unable to prevent a look of interest from flitting across his features at mention of the earrings. He hadn't known what was in the little package, Lynch thought.

"Good lord, man. Anyone could mail the widow some earrings. Anyone in London. Perhaps some jeweler she'd ordered them from, or however such things are done. I read the piece about her in *Countess Cathleen*, the name, you know, and Mrs. Whatsis is famous! Admirers all over the world! What would I know about women like that?"

Lynch let thirty seconds elapse, for effect, and felt more than ever like an actor. Frank was scribbling away at a great rate. He had not touched his coffee, and Lynch saw the fine scum that swam over the top. By contrast, Connors had Hoovered his own coffee up, sucking greedily at the last, sugary drop.

"More coffee, Professor? No? It's well within reach, you know, very easy to procure. Well then, to clear up the business about the earrings, Mrs. Whatsis has assured me they are a gift from her dead husband. They were taken from his lifeless body, along with anything else that might serve to identify him, and posted to her at a date convenient to the killer. A time when he found himself in England and could not incriminate himself."

"That's ridiculous," said Connors, with conviction. "The kind of a man a cold-blooded killer would be—would he trouble himself with mailing a package? It's a contradiction in terms, Sergeant. A savage does not adhere to the amenities."

Lynch found it fascinating that Connors, under the gun, so to speak, was sounding progressively more Irish while he, the interrogator, spoke in an English mode. There was a lesson there, somewhere.

"All men who kill are not savages," he said. "If our culprit proved to be an essentially decent, moderately civilized man, his first instinct would be to return private property. There are men who kill who would scorn at stealing, if only by accident."

"Yes, that's true," said Connors, as if addressing an exceptionally bright graduate student. The thought seemed to depress him.

"Were you ever in the American armed services?" Lynch asked.

Connors regarded him with admiration, as if he might be the devil. "Yes," he replied. "Difficult as it may be to believe, I was a marine. A member of the USMC. *Semper fi,* Sergeant."

"And during that time, Professor, did you meet with a man called Niçk the Prick?"

Connors laughed. It was meant to sound mocking and amused, but merely sounded nervous. "You astonish me," he said. "I thought you were a true Irish gentleman. I've never known a grunt, or anyone else, who went by that charming name."

"If you never met him," Lynch said, "you were lucky, by all accounts."

Frank looked up from his notebook. "Just one thing," he said, "just for my own curiosity. Isn't it rather unusual for an ex-marine to become a professor of literature?"

"Slightly unusual, but not unheard of. We had to do something to earn a living, and I'd always been fond of poetry."

"You read so much about vets who can't adjust to life, civilian life, when they return. Apparently you had no problems of that sort, Professor?" Frank was regarding Connors with evident sympathy.

"I don't believe I was brought here to answer questions about my psycho-logical state on my return from Vietnam. That is my business, surely? Let me just say that I returned in one piece, gratefully, and carried on with my life. I'm not one of those men who misses the thrill of combat, sir. I was well out of it."

And then, taking advantage of his temporarily superior position, he said, "Look, I'm free to go, aren't I? There's not a shred of evidence that binds me to the events in Balgriffin, is there?"

"You may go at any time," said Lynch. "I must ask you not to leave the country without telling me, however."

"I will be here until my sabbatical ends," said Connors. "My work is finished in England."

Frank saw him to the door and was escorting him out when Connors turned back. "You know," he said, "that article in *Countess Cathleen* was very unfair, I thought. You're not an arrogant man, Sergeant Lynch, and God knows you're not derelict in your duties. I'm living proof of that—you leave no stone unturned. No hard feelings."

"No hard feelings," agreed Lynch, "and thank you."

"He's not guilty, Sean," said Frank when he returned. "Don't you feel it?"

"Oh, but he is, Frankie. He's guilty as sin, but we can't prove it. Not yet."

"Sure I can't see him strangling yer man in the grandstand. He's not a commando anymore. That was years ago. I believed him when he was sayin' he was well out of combat, didn't miss it—that was his best moment, you could say."

"To be sure, Frank. I believed him as well. With any luck, Henry Connors might have lived out his life as a mild professor, writing on Yeats, atoning for whatever he feels he did in Vietnam. But what happens? He meets, utterly by chance, he meets Nicholas Murphy in Dublin, where he has come on his sabbatical. Murphy reminds him of all he has chosen to forget, and dies for it. That's how I see it."

"Ah, come on," said Frank. "If he was one of those fellas who did his nut every time a reminder of the past came into view, he would have committed mass carnage before now. In the States. He couldn't hold down a position in a university, Sean. And surely to Jesus he wouldn't arrange to meet Murphy on the racecourse? If he was the sort of mental case you imagine, he'd plug him right on O'Connell Street, or wherever he first sighted him."

"I don't think he's that sort of a nutter. I don't think he's mad at all. You're forgetting how unpleasant a man Murphy was reputed to be, Frank. It wasn't just *any* man who set him in motion, it was Nick. He didn't come by his nickname for nothing."

"Nick," said Frank, wheeling the comfortable chair from the interrogation room. "Nickname. That's funny, almost."

They passed Mulcahy and Ryan in the corridor. They were escorting a known arsonist, name of Brian Bohannan, toward the room Lynch and Browne had vacated. The arsonist's drawn and bony face was set in lines of irritation; he could have been a renowned golfer, disturbed at the eleventh hole—why *would* these tiresome meddlers butt in and prevent him from finishing?

"A vile day," he shouted at Lynch. "Nothin' at all but rain. Still, it's a soft rain, and we must be grateful for somethin'."

"A pyro grateful for rain," said Frank. "Now I've heard everything."

TWENTY-TWO

Balgriffin was at its prettiest when the stranger alit from the bus a few yards from the pub. The tide was fully in, and the water that lapped the seawall was silver, traced with pale green. Yesterday's rain had washed away the heat and dust, so that the old white church appeared as dazzling as those he had admired in Naples and Calabria during a long-ago holiday. The village, did, in fact, have a Mediterranean feel to it. On the bus from Dublin he had passed palm trees as they drew nearer to the estuary.

A man was selling vegetables from the back of a van, and a short queue of housewives was lined up to buy them. Some of them glanced curiously in his direction, but he was an unremarkable figure, dressed in jeans and an old combat jacket, and they quickly looked away. He took a final look at Ireland's Eye, so clear on the horizon it seemed an image painted on a drop curtain, and then he went into the pub.

Half a dozen old men sat nursing their pints; it was not, he guessed, a busy place at midmorning. A young boy served him a Guinness and then went back to the saloon bar.

When a grown man, a man a few years younger than he, and very good-looking, came through with a tray of glasses, the stranger smiled. The other barman had been scarcely older than a child—this was the one he would talk to.

"Hello," he said. "You serve a fine jar here."

And then a curious thing happened. The barman, his face smiling in a professionally friendly way, said, "American, are ye? Enjoying yer stay?" It was not the words that were peculiar, but the changes that took place in the barman's face as he got the words out. In the course of the two simple questions, his eyes had gone from a jovial, bright expression to one of caution and extreme bewilderment.

"Have I met you before, then?" he asked.

"No," said the stranger. "I've never been here before." He drained half his Guinness and, fiddling with a cardboard coaster that advertised Harp Lager, said, "Lovely little spot this is. That view from the estuary, well, it's priceless. I imagine you're quiet here, even though you're so close to Dublin. Quiet and peaceful, here in—what's this place called?—Balgriffin."

"You'd be surprised," said the barman, "what can happen in quiet, peaceful places."

"Oh, go on." He had hoped to draw the man out with his implied disbelief, but the barman was too intelligent for such a juvenile game. He efficiently sterilized the glasses, his head caught in a cloud of infernal steam, and then went down the bar to refill the glass of a man who called him "Tom."

"Another, please," he said when Tom was once more in his general vicinity. "Another, Tom."

The barman filled his order, and he was able to say, lowering his voice, "I've got to apologize, Tom. I remember, now, there was a terrible thing here earlier in the year. A body on the racecourse. I read it in the papers."

"You've been here some time, then," remarked Tom, leveling the foaming head of the stout. Engaged in such a familiar task, he still seemed furtive, and ill at ease.

"Yes, since March. I read the papers every day, and I've never seen any mention of the murderer being caught. Will they just forget it, do you think?"

"No," said the barman, with an odd intensity, "they never forget. Only yesterday a garda was in here on related matters, but he hadn't a clue. He was carrying a photo of a man, wanted to know if I'd seen him the day of the killing. Some of the kids round here, good kids, told him they'd seen the man. An American, they said, and he came in here and bought them crisps."

"A photograph?" the stranger asked, feeling confused. "Where did he get a photograph, this garda?"

"Don't know. It was queer, taped on a bit of cardboard. A wee picture, it was. But the really fantastical slant to it all was—the kids lied! They invented the Yank, excuse me, the American, and even so the sergeant is ploddin' in with his likeness."

"Why would they lie? What earthly reason would they have for lying?"

"I've asked myself the same question. They found the body, you know. Six of them, it was, and it must have been a terrible thing. They're only small, and nice wee children. Finding that man, it must have upset their lives in various ways. Who can tell with kids? Maybe they invented an American to take suspicion away from someone they loved?"

The stranger frowned, staring down into his dark Guinness. "But surely," he said, "there wouldn't be anyone in Balgriffin who'd come under suspicion. The man, as I recall, was a foreigner."

Tom snorted. "Yours truly was a hot suspect for a while there, and I can tell you it was no picnic. I'll probably have to leave my lodgings because of it. When a man is killed in a place, it isn't just those who knew him that suffer —the whole bloody *place* suffers." He strode off to do something in the saloon bar, and when he came back he continued, as if incensed by his own words.

"I lost a very pleasant, ah, *connection* because of that bloody killing, but never mind me. One of the children who found the body is a young lad from Belfast. His family moved down here because he was shot in the head with a plastic bullet, shot by the army. They're a good, decent family, the Keegans, and now the Special Branch keeps tabs on them, in case there's some connection between the killing and the war up North.

"Bein' a barman, I tend to find out things I don't even want to know, and one of the things I know is that Mrs. Keegan had a breakdown after the boy was shot. They came here to get away from death."

"Keegan? Would the boy's name be Matthew? Matt?"

Tom looked at him with astonishment and nodded.

"I met him, then."

"Where would you be meetin' Matty Keegan?"

"On Ireland's Eye," said the American. "Quite by chance. No wonder he stared at me."

Tom lowered his head and bent very close, speaking now in a low murmur. "Look, mate, if I was you I'd clear out of Balgriffin. The photo yer man brought round yesterday? It could have been your younger brother. I'm after warning you."

"Thank you, Tom." He drained his Guinness and produced two more pound notes. "I'd like six packets of those crisps, please. All different flavors will do."

He left the pub, carrying the crisps in the paper bag Tom had provided. He was sorry that Tom would have to leave his lodgings, still sorrier about his broken "connection." He turned at the church and walked up the Gilligan Road. He passed some children, scurrying along in a tittering cluster, but they were too young to be the ones who had invented him. He stood by the wall of the racecourse, looking out at the grandstand. The only shapes moving in the long grass were a herd of black-and-white cows. It was probably not a good place for children to play, today; yesterday's rain would make the racecourse squelchy. He tried to remember where it was the sergeant had told him the children said they'd encountered the Yank, but it all seemed so long ago.

Matty and Gervaise were leaning on the seawall, trying to find the fossils Janie always insisted were embedded there. Terry was riding his bike on the pavement, doing wheelies. The wheelies drove Wolfe Tone mad, and he yapped with disapproval. Janie, who had just left the library, was waiting for the traffic on the estuary road to thin, so she could cross over and join them.

"That man's watchin' us," Gervaise whispered to Matty.

"What man?"

"Just there." Gervaise jerked his head.

Matty turned and saw a man in jeans and an old U.S. Army jacket, or something, familiar from movies on telly. He thought he might know him, and just as he was wondering how, the man's face became lit with recognition.

"Matt Keegan!" he shouted, walking toward them. "Remember me?"

He heard the American voice and thought: Ireland's Eye.

"Hello, Hank," he said, feeling acutely uncomfortable at using the man's first name. He did not know his other name in any case. He was approaching, coming closer and closer, and Terry, made curious by the sound of an American voice, cycled back to join the group. Janie arrived just as the man was pumping Matty's hand.

"How're you doing?" Hank asked.

"Great. Yerself?" He had noticed that both Janie and Gervaise had grown very pale and were scarcely breathing. Meeting Hank on Ireland's Eye was all very well, but to meet him here, on the seafront, was so close to what they had imagined, it was eerie.

"Will you introduce me to your friends?" This was such a great breach of etiquette, he hardly knew what to do. He had never been called upon to perform introductions.

"This is Gervaise," he said, nudging him. "That's Terry, with the bike, and the girl is Janie."

Hank shook their hands, one by one, and then said, "Where are the other two?"

"Which other two?" asked Terry in his authoritative voice.

"Well, I was told it was six of you that invented me."

"Oh Jesus," said Gervaise and Janie simultaneously. Even Terry's jaw hung open.

"Well, here I am," said Hank, still smiling. "Tallish-sized, middle-aged, and going bald. I'm sorry about the plaid trousers, though. I don't own any."

Janie held her library books over her face and wailed softly. "Holy Mother —I'm goin' mad."

This seemed to distress the American. "No, no," he said quickly. "Please, Janie, don't be frightened. You're not seeing things—I'm real enough, and I'm not angry at you, either. This all has a perfectly logical explanation."

The four children listened while the amazing apparition told them of how the police, believing their story, had questioned him. It was perfectly all right, he said, because the police had not suspected him of anything. But now, he said, he knew the truth. It was all as simple as that.

"Why did you come?" Terry asked.

"Lots of reasons. I was curious to see you. Wouldn't you be, in my shoes? And then I wanted to tell you there were no hard feelings. But most of all I felt the need to find out why—with all the types of people in the world to choose from—you picked someone just like me?"

"Not just like you, ah, Hank," said Matty, feeling deeply shamed for reasons he could not articulate. "You don't own any of those plaid trousers, now."

"I'm the one," Janie burst out. "We were all tryin' to decide on a mysterious stranger, and I was the one said it should be a Yank. An American, excuse me. We didn't want an innocent man to be accused, and I thought no way would an American be the real killer, so you seemed just perfect and all."

"I see," said Hank, nodding. "That makes sense, I suppose. But why go to the trouble of inventing me at all? Were you protecting someone?"

"Ourselves," said Terry. "We had to get the pressure off. Sure, we couldn't play on the racecourse anymore, and our parents were that nervous. And one of us, he's not here today, he thought his mother had taken to drink because of it, but that turned out to be quite a different thing."

"And Matty's Uncle Tommy, in Australia," mumbled Gervaise.

"Australia!" Hank looked at Matty incredulously. "You don't mean to say a death in Balgriffin stirred up waves in *Australia?*"

"Yeah," said Matty nervously, launching into deepest Belfastese, "me Uncle Tommah, he went te Australyuh, he went dine there when he was after gettin' out of the Kesh. Me mam, she's his suster, she was worrit they'd thunk there was a connecshin, all on account of some arms was shipped te Balgruffen while back from Dine Under."

Janie began to make a translation, but Hank held out a hand to show that he had understood. "Your Uncle Tommy?" he asked. "Did he get in trouble?"

Matty shook his head.

"And how is your mother?"

"Grayut, thank ye."

"See, it's like this," Terry said officiously. "Even though they haven't caught the fella, it's all blown over. We didn't need to make you up, but we didn't know that then."

"You are a very talented little group," said Hank. "You convinced Sergeant Lynch, and he is an intelligent man."

"We're sorry, mister," said Janie. And then, unaccountably, she giggled. "There was another thing we agreed to say about you, but then we forgot. We were goin' to say you were sneezin' a lot on account of having a shockin' cold. Americans always get colds over here."

"Isn't that funny," said Hank, speaking in a small, chastened voice. "That's what I thought, too. Great minds work alike."

Before anyone could ask what he had meant, Hank opened the paper bag he carried under his arm and began to distribute the packets of crisps.

"I thought it was only right," he explained, "to do what you imagined."

They walked him to the bus shelter halfway up the sea road. Terry, pedaling slow, explained that Wolfe Tone had been the one to discover the body. Hank shook Wolfe Tone's paw, to please Terry. In the bus shelter, Hank said an odd thing. He said they were all good kids, and whatever happened, in the days to come, they should remember it.

His words shook Matty Keegan, who perceived, although dimly, that he was once more encountering grief. He noticed that Gervaise and Terry had opened their crisp packets and were munching greedily. Janie had not opened hers. She also held the packets intended for Rory and Kevin, along with her library books. He didn't know about Janie's intentions, but as for himself, he knew he would never open his. He would keep them, no matter how long he lived, as a memento. When he was Mr. Halloran's age, he would still have them, disgusting and moldering as they would be by then, to remind him of an event he could not understand now.

Una was delighted to discover Dr. Connors on her doorstep, in Blackrock. He had known she would be, even though he was no longer dressed in the good, professorial tweeds she expected him to wear. He remembered the inscription he had penned on the flyleaf of his book, the night he had lectured to her circle: *To Una Lynch, with all affection for her Irish hospitality.* It was the sort of fatuous sentiment he had displayed when he had been Henry J. Connors, Yeats scholar. Yet he was genuinely fond of Una, a sweet, once captivating woman who had found herself washed up on the shoals of late middle age without adequate preparation.

"Actually," he told her, "I've come to see your husband."

"Oh, Sean won't be back home for an hour or more," she said. "Come into the garden, and we'll have a drink, will we?"

"That would be very pleasant."

He sat in the fragrant garden, comfortable in a low-slung plastic lawn chair, regarding the peonies. They appeared to be dying, their season past. One in particular intrigued him, because the petals had fallen away in such a manner as to suggest a face. There were dark gaps, like crescent eyes, and another, oval in shape, to suggest an open, screaming mouth. The peony was screaming, without hope, and as he stared it became the face of a Vietnamese woman, or perhaps she was Cambodian? Viewed at other angles, the flower was less oriental, assumed the look of a dying Irish child, or an American tourist in a pub in Nottingham, discovering that she was, in fact, about to be blown up. Just possibly, he thought, she might have been near the scene of greatest damage and been killed immediately, known neither pain nor fear.

"Well, here we are, then," cried a woman's voice, and he looked away from the faces of death and saw Una approaching with a tray. He knew it would be polite of him to jump up and take the tray for her, but he seemed unable to move. He glanced back at the peonies to hide his confusion.

"Aren't they nasty?" she said, as if reading his mind. "Never mind, they were lovely for such a long time, before that monstrous rain. If only I'd cut them, the night before, and brought them in for a bouquet, but a person can't have foresight, wouldn't you agree?"

"With all my heart," he said.

He was thinking, now, of the beautiful little Vietnamese girl. He could remember the precise hue and texture of her apricot skin, and the way her black hair fell, like curtains of some priceless silken fabric, when she bent her neck. Some of the guys said you couldn't tell them apart, but that was not the case. This girl of nineteen, who could have passed for a child, was as radiant as a burning village. She had only three colors—apricot, black, and blue. The blue flashed in her hair and appeared, in her eyes, as occasional flecks of grape. She smelled of spearmint, and there was no mystery about it because in her tiny shoulder bag she carried several packs of Wrigley's Spearmint Gum. He had only spent the one night with her, but he remembered everything about her but her name.

She had told him her real name, but he had forgotten. Around Saigon, as he later discovered, she was referred to as "Elsie." How flattered he had been by her refusal to take money from him! She had convinced him, an older-than-average soldier of twenty-four, that she "fancied" him. That term—"I fancy you"—told him only that she had slept with Englishmen.

He saw her once again, but by that time he knew she was married to the man who called her Elsie, because he could not be bothered to pronounce her real name. He also knew that the man encouraged his wife to pose as a prostitute and gather information—an old trick, the oldest in the world. But for whom was the information intended? It seemed insane to him that an Englishman, with no stake in the conflict, should run his wife as a whore in Saigon.

"He *is* insane," a recon man called Anders, a boy from Toledo, Ohio, explained. Gus Anders, that had been his name, and despite the Scandinavian name, he had been black. *Are you alive, Gus, or is your name inscribed on that fancy, austere new monument they've erected in D.C.?* "He right round the bend," Gus had said. "All that man knows is games. Dirty games, dirty tricks, that his specialty. His whole world! He warped, know what I mean?"

"Will I put on some music?" Una was saying. "I have a great craving to hear a bit of classical at the moment."

"Yes, yes," he said, feeling like a great fish speaking underwater, "that would be splendid."

Where was Elsie now? Was she a dark and slender shade, plying her trade in London's Greek Street these days? Had he passed her, all unawares, in the streets of Soho? Something told him that her fate had been worse than that, but he did not wish to dwell on it. In the nightclub, where he had last seen her, she had been wearing a minidress and Dr. Scholl's sandals. She did not acknowledge him, but after a time her husband made his way to where Hank had been sitting with friends. He was an unexceptional-looking man, except for the deep lines that split his face, radiating from his eyes when he smiled. He was only a few years older than Hank, and it seemed odd that he should be so scored.

"Here, mate," he had said, handing over a small card. "We might do business sometime."

The card contained no name, only a string of telephone numbers, and the countries they derived from. He had been able to read, in the flickering light, exchanges in Rhodesia and London, but there were more. By the time he looked up again, the man had returned to Elsie. What was he to make of it? Was there some case of mistaken identity, and did Elsie's husband imagine Henry Connors to be someone of importance?

He SAS, said the long-ago voice of Gus, intruding in the Lynch's garden. *They responsible for evil all over the place.*

He became aware of the sounds of chamber music wafting out to the garden, played softly so as not to annoy the neighbors. He thought it might be Schubert and asked if that were the case.

"Indeed it is," said Una happily. "The quintet, you know."

On his second tour, he had seen the man again, in Cambodia. Or thought he had. It was hard to remember, because Cambodia was something he had tried to expunge from his memory. By that time he had heard enough about him, too much, in fact. Elsie's husband had profited enormously by cooperating with the CIA and selling surveillance equipment—electronics—to Idi Amin. He had been an enthusiastic trainer of torture techniques in the Shah's Iran, tutoring the secret police, SAVAK. He had been protected from standing trial for atrocities in Aden, and then cashiered by the British Army. He was a mercenary, a criminal, an international careerist. If he had been a party to all the adventures ascribed to him, the man would have to be more, or less, than human.

To Hank, he had become a symbol of the cheerful corruption and rot the world will sometimes create. He did well on the misfortune of others. His sharp nose sniffed out the areas of suffering and death, and it was to these areas he was drawn—for thrills and profit.

"I have never believed in capital punishment," he heard himself say out loud. "But there are cases . . ." His voice drifted off, a thing of no importance.

"I'm with you there," said Una, eagerly taking the topic up. "But no one's fit to judge—isn't that the thing, surely?"

"Drugs in Cambodia, torture in Africa and Aden, rape and bombs in Northern Ireland," he said, unable to control himself. "God knows what-all, and never mind that little Vietnamese girl, she was just a whore, I suppose, but still. And what made it all worse was that he was such a shadow. And legally sanctioned, once, oh yes, a member of the so-called elite squad. He could swim in and out of countries, in and out of legality, and he was protected. Anonymity is only granted to the worst men of our times. . . ."

Una was looking at him with concern, her mouth slightly open.

"Forgive me," he said, reverting to his old, professorial jollity. "I've been working very hard, and I'm so tired."

"Of course you are," said Una staunchly. And then they sat in silence, listening to Schubert.

TWENTY-THREE

"They caught the racecourse killer," Imelda told Jim, visiting him on remand.

"Good," said Jim gloomily, "at least they can't pin that on me."

"Go on—as if they'd ever! But aren't you curious to know who he is?"

Jim nodded sheepishly. Imelda knew he was not all as desperate as he pretended to be. What with the partial restitution she had made, he would probably end up serving no more than two years. She saw that he would be a model prisoner, ingratiating himself with everyone, and end up feeling quite the fella—important and glamorous in his outlaw's role.

"Would you ever part with the information, Imelda?"

"As much as anyone knows is that a man has confessed to the crime. It said in the papers he was under surveillance for a good bit of time, and they're questioning him now. They didn't give the name, but what do you think? He's not one of ours at all, he's an American citizen. The whole thing's nothing to do with us."

"That's pretty bloody useless. A Yank kills a Brit, and he has to do it on *our* racecourse?"

"I suppose we'll find out more as time goes by and all."

Imelda could not prevent herself from feeling hopeful. She knew it was an inappropriate feeling—a woman who is visiting her husband in prison should be in despair, by rights—but she had taken a part-time job in a cleaner's establishment out at the big shopping complex in Donabate, and found that the work suited her. She enjoyed the multitudes of people who streamed in to the cleaner's each day, carrying their soiled jackets and dresses and trousers. She liked being able to hand back clean, rejuvenated garments, and sometimes pass the time of day in a harmless fashion. She even liked the way she looked today, was proud of the way her no-wrinkle pink summer dress—chosen to cheer Jim with its innocent brightness—had lost none of its crisp freshness throughout the bus ride to the city.

"What're ye thinkin', legs?" It was his old, affectionate term for her.

"Ah well—Rory. I was thinkin' of Rory."

"You already told me he was grand. Is there something ye're holding back?"

Imelda considered. In actual fact, Rory did seem to be in fine spirits. But there was something—yes, something she could pluck out and hold up for Jim to scrutinize. In the usual order of things, she wouldn't have thought to mention it, but she could hardly admit to thoughts about something so trivial as her pink dress.

"Kids are so queer," she said, hardly knowing how to begin. "They live in a different world, like. When I told our Rory about the bit in the paper, how the man was a Yank, he laughed and laughed. I sez, 'Well, don't kill yourself with hilarity, son. What's so damn funny in it?' Rory just looks at me, cool as you please, and then he licks some H.P. sauce off his fingers and sez, 'Nothin', Mam.' "

"And did you let him off with that?" Jim asked, furrowing his brows in the old, threatening manner, as if he were still lord of his manor.

"I did not," said Imelda. "You know me, Jim. I kept on after him, but I came up with nil. I expect it was a wee bout of hysteria."

"Right," said James Kennerly sagely. "When I was a lad his age, I remember it well, I would laugh at the strangest class of a thing. It's hormones, likely, Imelda, and you've nothin' to fret about. Kids are on a different planet, altogether—it's almost like they're blind."

"Oh, that reminds me," cried Imelda, intending to mention the odd alliance between Matty Keegan and Mr. Halloran. Just then the guard told them their time had run out. The visit was over.

Relief seemed to be the dominant principle that guided Professor Connors at Fitzgibbon Street. In an ecstasy of catharsis, he poured forth a stream of confessional material so copious that Lynch could not help but feel that he had heard more, in several hours, from the lips of one man, than he might have heard, as a priest, from a lifetime of miscreants.

A tape machine had been set up to catch every last word that Connors chose to spill, but Browne still scribbled away, in the background.

There's something wrong with Dr. Connors, Una had said. *He's out in the garden, talking about peonies and Cambodia, Sean. Also bombs and anonymity. He came to see you, but there's something gone wrong, there.*

"Flotsam and jetsam," said Connors, now. "That's all we were—flotsam and jetsam, the rejects of the sane world. We drifted in on a crazy tide, back and forth, back and forth, ebbing and flowing, beaching at the right moment, wouldn't you agree? Why else would I meet Nick on Capel Street?"

To Lynch's question of why, if Murphy had been roaming Dublin openly, nobody responded to his photo in the papers—even subtracting those who were unobservant, and those who didn't want to get involved, there must have been dozens of people who'd seen him—Connors had a ready answer.

"Hair makes the difference," he said, "and I should know. He always wore a cap, the flat cloth kind, and it made him look years younger. Nobody would connect the man in your photo with him."

It came to Lynch that Robert Malone, once freed from prison, also wore a cap, even in the summer. Yet Connors did not. The fact that Malone and Murphy were vain men, proud of their looks, and Connors was not, saddened him.

Connors didn't know what Murphy was doing in Capel Street, but there was nothing unusual about that. "He loved mystery," Connors said. "You'd no more expect a straight answer from him than milk from a chicken. You wouldn't even ask."

The two men had gone for a drink in a bar along the quays, where they had remained until the Holy Hour forced them out.

"Can you explain why you would go for a drink with a man you so disliked?" Lynch asked.

"For one thing, I was so surprised he remembered me. I'd changed so much, but: 'Hello, mate,' he said, just as if no time had passed, 'remember me?' He seemed tickled to death at his memory for faces. 'I never forget a face, never.' He seemed so pathetic, somehow, so shaky and nervous and tense. I thought, in my naïveté, that he'd been broken by—his past, by things. In the end, though, I suppose I went out of simple curiosity."

Connors lapsed into silence, at that point, as if he were reconstructing his time with Murphy at the quayside bar in his own memory. He wore a dark lightweight suit today, and a white shirt with pale blue stripes. He looked every inch the Yeats professor, unlike the man who had cowered in his combat jacket in the garden in Blackrock.

"And was your curiosity gratified?"

"No," said Connors, regaining the composure which slipped away from him so often now. "It was not gratified but piqued. There are never any explanations with that man, only possibilities. He talked quite freely, but then he would contradict himself. He had a huge roll of bills and insisted on paying for every drink."

"That can be an insult," observed Frank Browne sympathetically.

"Yes, can't it?" Connors spoke automatically, recalling slights from another life. "He told me he was rich, and planned on getting richer. Sometimes he said he was milking the man in Libya—Qaddafi, I supposed—and other times he said he was in the electronics consulting business in the Middle East. He showed me a photo of his new wife, Swedish bird, he called her, but when I asked after Elsie he seemed not to remember her. Another time he said, 'Elsie? Water under the bridge—probably dead, old son.' By that time he was quite drunk. He seemed under the impression we'd met for the first time in Iran, only he kept calling it Persia. I remember, because he pronounced it Per-sha, the way the English do."

As the Holy Hour drew near, Nicholas Murphy had seemed fumblingly, embarrassingly inebriated—the sort of drunk a boy of ten might rob of his enormous bankroll. He had left the money lying on the table, and once a great wad had been dislodged by his flying elbow and dropped to the floor, from which Connors had retrieved it. "Hold it for me, there's a good lad," Murphy pleaded, "and this as well. All of it. Otherwise I'll lose all my bloody pocket money to the thieving Paddies round here."

At the word *Paddies* several heads in the bar had raised themselves with belligerence. Professor Henry Connors, profoundly ashamed, took the money and put it in what he called his "billfold." It was awkward, fitting it all in, and the surplus he shoved into his jacket pocket.

Outside the bar, in the glaring light of midafternoon, he had tried to hail a cab for Murphy, but no cabs were available. They proceeded as far as Eden Quay before a taxi drew up.

"Give me a ring," Murphy said, lurching into the taxi's backseat. At the same time he passed a card to Connors, a card strangely like the one he had possessed in Saigon. There were numbers, but all had been blacked out but one, a Dublin exchange.

"Your money," Connors cried, trying to extricate his billfold and at the same time dredging bills from his pocket, but the taxi sped on, caught in traffic. An oddly sober-seeming Murphy smiled back at him, giving the Marine salute, and then the car turned north, and he was lost. Vanished, as if the odd encounter had never been.

"In the men's room, at the National," Connors told them, "I counted the money. It was more than five hundred pounds, some sterling, some Irish. So, you see? I had to call him back. On my life, Sergeant, I didn't want to see the man again. Not ever! But I had to return that money, didn't I? I couldn't function, knowing I had—oh, what's the exchange rate? Never mind, I couldn't rest easy with all that money that didn't belong to me."

"That would have been on the Thursday," said Lynch.

"If you say so."

"And on the Saturday you rented the car. What happened between the two days?"

"Blackmail, Sergeant. That's what happened—blackmail, pure and simple."

Henry Connors looked about in dismay. Then he buried his head in his hands. "No use asking me for answers," he said. "No use, because I can't remember. I don't remember anything I did—do you recall? Don't tell me, if you do, because I don't want to know."

"Where?" said Lynch. "Where is it you don't want to remember, Hank?"

"Cambodia," said Professor Connors, whispering.

"It says in the paper they've got the man who did that business on the racecourse," Mrs. Halloran told her husband.

She always referred to the murder as "that business," as if the killer had merely relieved himself in the fields. Ordinarily, Scobie found it amusing, but now that he was a small player in the drama he felt uneasy. It had happened too soon after his phone call to the gardai.

"And oh, would you ever? He was an American. That's what it says."

"No, by Jesus! That can't be!"

"Andy," cried his wife in alarm, "what's wrong with you?" He felt her drawing nearer, preparing to fuss at him. He heard the sharp crackle of her discarded paper, and now her hands were patting at him, searching for his distress.

"Now, Ellen, nothing in this world. It was only the surprise, finding him after all this long time. Sure, I thought they'd given it up."

While she went to put the kettle on for their tea, he sat and fidgeted with impatience. It was still a good hour until the news, and he longed for more information. There were at least four hours before he could decently go to the pub, but no one in the pub would have the details he craved.

He lit one of the longish butts he kept in his jacket pocket and inhaled deeply. "Smoking these sixty years," he told himself. "At least I have good lungs." If he were ten, even five years younger, he would be able to saunter over to the Crescent, or even all the way to the shop, where there was a selection of newspapers. In the midst of his feelings of impotence, a comforting thought arrived. Although Matty would be too shy to pay a call at his house again, there was every opportunity of seeing him tomorrow. It would be a Thursday, and the vegetable man would have his van parked in the road. Matty almost always came over to say a few words, and tomorrow there would be important material to be discussed.

He would practice his opening sally, so as to strike the perfect note. He had heard a radio program where some eejits were talking about something called . . . Never mind, it would come to him. It had to do with knowing the future, and as far as he was concerned it was a load of bloody old tripe, but it would be the perfect opener for his conversation with young Matty. If Matty knew about it, it would make him laugh; if he didn't, he, Scobie, would have the pleasure of explaining it. H.P.? Ah, Christ, no, that was steak sauce—rotted the belly out of poor Christy Slattery, who had too great a liking for it. ET?

"ESP," he said aloud, triumphantly.

He would say, "Why did ye never tell me ye had the gift of ESP, young Matty? Sure, you'll be a millionaire before the winter comes."

Oh boys, oh boys.

The Professor had fallen into his confused mode with his talk of blackmail and Cambodia. The blackmail he had referred to was that of the money. Nick had gauged him well, knew that Hank Connors could never pocket another man's money, simply because it was easier than seeing him again.

"It's almost funny," he told Lynch and Browne. "Sometimes he could read a man's character so well, even if he didn't know who the man was. To the end, I swear he thought I was someone else—someone much more influential —but he knew I'd never walk off with his damned five hundred pounds. He had me pegged, gentlemen—good old American simp. The man he had me down for might have been the most cold-blooded killer in the world, but he sure as hell would never take advantage of a drunk in peacetime. A code of honor, I guess."

"Very English, that is," said Browne. "Very public school."

"Much more diabolical than that," said Connors. "I didn't go to public school, or anything like it. I went to the Woodrow Wilson High School in a small town in Indiana. We had no official code, sir, none at all. But Nick could see straight through to my soul. He knew I was, at heart, what we used to call a straight arrow. When I called him, on Friday, he knew I'd come to the Balgriffin racecourse on the day he said. He told me he had a proposition I would find irresistible."

"Did you ask what the proposition was?" Lynch asked.

"Of course not," said Connors. "I didn't want to know. I hung up and went out to the place on the Terenure Road and rented a car. I drove to Balgriffin, and familiarized myself with the racecourse, so I'd know how to get there. He told me to park my car on the Portmarnock–Balgriffin road. He gave me explicit instructions on how to gain access to the grandstand from the road. No one has used it in years, and it's very dangerous."

"Dangerous?"

"It's falling down," said Connors plaintively. "There are warning signs."

"Now, I am assuming," said Lynch, "that you took Murphy's request to meet in the grandstand of a disused racecourse as just one more example of his eccentricity? His love for melodrama?"

"Well, actually, it's yes and no," Connors responded, brightening. He was back in the classroom again, enlightening a student who had brought up an odd but interesting point. "Like everything about him, it was half-crazy and half-understandable. His father took him on a sentimental pilgrimage to Ireland, when Nick was just a young boy. The high point of this trip was a day at the races in Balgriffin. Back when the racecourse was a going concern, of course. He told me all about it. Really, he waxed poetic. Apparently it was the finest day in poor Murphy's young life, and he thought it would be a wonderful adventure to see it again."

"At night?" Browne asked. "There's nothing to see."

"Ex-*act*-ly! That's his other half speaking, the one that hasn't made sense for years." Connors smiled, happy with this thought, content for the time being.

"If he wanted melodrama so much," said Lynch, "why didn't he lure you up to the North? Belfast, or Derry, or the border?"

"Oh, he's been there," Connors said in a pained way. "Don't worry about that."

And then, in his new disjointed way, the professor told them what had happened in the grandstand. Nick had wanted a contact in America, someone used to the ways of the secret armies, familiar with deep and covert methods of accomplishing death; he had thought Hank the very man to help him, because Hank labored under a cover of great respectability. He had mentioned money, and when money did not seem alluring enough, he had summoned up power. The power to manipulate.

"You can watch the news, mate, and know you made it. Whatever they say happened, it's because you *made* it happen," the half-crazed voice had droned in his ear, there, in the darkness of the derelict grandstand. The voice had gone on, threatening about deeds done in Cambodia, things mercifully forgotten in Henry Connors's point of view, but proud and brilliant in the eyes of Nicholas Murphy.

"That was his first mistake," Connors said. "He had begun to read me wrong."

"You mean?"

"He thought I was excited by that kind of talk. He thought he could seduce me with the concept of making news. My eyes had adjusted to the dark by then, and I could just make out his face when he made his second mistake. He told me about a bombing, an event he had engineered. With every word, he thought he was pulling me in."

"Like a marlin," said Lynch, thinking that the professor would appreciate his allusion to Hemingway.

"A marlin is a worthy adversary," said Connors. "No. It was his obscene, pale face, the way his lips stretched while he related the story, Sergeant. Are you familiar with the Nottingham bomb?"

"As it happens, I am," said Lynch. "A lady in Cork told me all about it. It seems things were not what they appeared to be."

"But I never suspected," Connors said, as if to himself. "I believed what I was told. Isn't that what we're supposed to do—believe what we're told?"

He was looking at Lynch, but not seeing him. Connors was not insane, Lynch thought, nor was he trying to appear to be. He was a man under pressure, relieved to have come to the end of the road. He would no more have left Ireland, once suspicion had been cast upon him, than he would have failed to return the five hundred pounds belonging to Nicholas Murphy. It was his very decency that had trapped him—the impulse to mention Lemsip, the mailing of the earrings, the trusting way he had left his billfold in an unprotected position at the GPO.

"There was supposed to be a warning," Connors said. "Goddamn it, there was supposed to be a warning."

Browne handed Lynch a note which read: *Who did he lose?*

The idea was not a new one for Lynch. He was quite sure a grotesque coincidence had placed someone dear to Connors inside the pub in Nottingham. He would have read of the death or maiming, back in America, and felt great sorrow. He could not have known that the sorrow would turn to cold rage some years later, when the culprit announced, so pridefully, that he had been responsible. More than anything, he thought, Connors had killed Nicholas Murphy for thinking they were the same kind of man.

He nodded at Frank.

"By any chance," said Frank, "was there anyone you knew in that pub, sir?"

Connors looked up and nodded. "You've got it figured," he said. "You tell me."

"Someone in your family?" Browne suggested. "Wife? Sweetheart? Fiancée?"

"No," said Connors. "Nothing so close as that. It was just Miss Moffat. Blown to confetti."

"Miss Moffat?"

"She was my eighth-grade English teacher. Nice woman—she used to say teaching was a fine profession, because you could travel in the summer. She gave me A's."

Lynch saw that the time had arrived to break the mood. Disliking himself, he said, "So there you were, Professor, in the grandstand on the racecourse, waiting to hand over five hundred pounds to a lunatic who wanted to recruit you for some nefarious activity. I can see how tedious it must have been—you wishing to get away, and he trying to prolong the dubious contact to the utmost limits. You must have felt confused, what with his blathering of blackmail and Cambodia, and longed to be miles away. You despised him, and yet a part of you felt sorry for him, isn't that so?"

Connors smiled.

"And then he made that mistake you mentioned. He bragged about the bombing in Nottingham, and making the news, and you saw that he was not only worthless, but evil?"

"That's it," said Connors. "That's roughly it."

"You weighed him in the scales, as opposed to Miss Moffat. What did you do then?"

"He turned his back. To light a cigarette, I think."

Lynch tried to imagine it. Murphy's barking, slurring voice; the pathos of the deadly junket to the racecourse; the irreconcilable natures of the two men in the darkness of the ruined hulk; and the hated back, turned, defenseless. Perhaps, all along, Nicholas Murphy had wanted to be killed.

"And what did you do, when Murphy turned his back to you?"

"Terminated him," said Professor Connors smartly. "With extreme prejudice."

TWENTY-FOUR

Soon after the children had returned to school that autumn, Kate, Imelda, and Nora discovered they could not do without each other. Somehow they had all become true friends, and no weekday passed when they did not assemble—however briefly—in one of their three kitchens. Paul Keegan affectionately referred to them as the Triumvirate and others, less tolerant—women in the Crescent who suspected close friendships and were jealous of them—called them the Holy Trinity.

Yet there was nothing holy in their relationship, even though they were constantly performing good works for one another. Nora didn't knit slippers for Imelda to take to Jim in prison out of a sense of Christian duty, any more than Imelda's minding of Kate's wee Juliet was inspired by a desire to be seen as selfless. When Imelda was working, there was always someone to see to Rory's tea, and when Imelda's married daughter made a brief, humiliated visit, it was Nora and Kate who made much of her and managed to dissolve the girl's pain over her imprisoned father by praising him.

They engaged in these small and large services because it pleased them to do so, and made life sweeter. They had no secrets, and quite openly discussed forbidden topics. Kate, the most innocent, confided her unworthy feelings of suffocation in the tiny Crescent house. Imelda spoke openly of her flirtation with vodka during the height of the Florrie Devine affair, and confessed her complicity in the matter of Tom Mulligan and his unknown lady friend. Nora not only admitted to her suspicions about Jim because of the night of the escaped cows, but went as far as it was possible to do, describing her nearly fatal decline in Belfast, after Matty had been shot.

"They're not able for getting it straight," said Kate.

"Who's that, then?" Imelda broke off a bit of rusk and gave it to Juliet, who was teething.

"Papers. They say one thing and then another. It's altogether maddening."

They were sitting in Kate's kitchen, among the ruins of a copious breakfast. Nora was removing a plate of half-congealed egg from the table and scraping it into the rubbish. Wolfe Tone, bounding at the garden door, seemed nearly mad with interest. It was a warm, gilded day in early autumn, but the sun fooled nobody. Occasionally the sight of the coal scuttle near the hearth reminded them all of the time when a fire would be desperately necessary.

"*Green Beret admits to slaying on Balgriffin racecourse,*" said Kate scornfully. "That's what one of the tabloids said. Sure he wasn't a green beret at all —they're army, I believe. He was a marine."

"Where's the difference?" asked Imelda. "They're all the same."

"The truth is the truth," said Kate. "How're we ever going to know the truth if the journalists just twist things round to make a good headline?"

"Sometimes ye're as simple as a baby," said Nora in her up-and-down Belfast voice. "Honest, Kate, I don't know what ye're on about. Ye'll *never* know the complete truth so long as ye live."

She separated a buttered crust of toast from the plate and opened the door, tossing it to Wolfe Tone. The dog tried, and failed, to catch the crust in midair.

While Tom Mulligan sterilized glasses and cut bread, Scobie lounged in the doorway, close by the vegetable van, and found himself sliding into a waking dream. He was a nimble-footed boy of ten, running over St. Stephen's Green, hunting out empty cigarette packets the gentry might have discarded. The pretty kind, with grand pictures. He collected them. Now and then he found a half-smoked butt in the grass, one with life in it yet, and he bent in a fluid gesture, effortlessly, for he was ten, and placed it in his jacket pocket.

Yeats was thought to be a difficult poet, Matty knew that much. The poem they had been given to analyze was a simple one, specially picked out for children. It was called "An Irish Airman Foresees His Death," and it was sad, when you thought about it. Here was this Irish pilot, flying missions for the British during the war, and thinking to himself that nothing that comes of the war will do his own people a scrap of good. *My country is Kiltartan Cross, My countrymen Kiltartan's poor. . . .*

Rory was trying to engage his attention, over in the next row, but he didn't acknowledge him. He was really interested in the poem and wanted to see how things came out for the Irish airman. Things looked bad, to judge by the title.

He read the last four lines, then reread them, holding his breath.

> I balanced all, brought all to mind,
> The years to come seemed waste of breath,
> A waste of breath the years behind
> In balance with this life, this death.

Matty expelled his breath slowly and looked up. Brother Malachy's flinty eyes were scanning the room, but he didn't really notice Brother Malachy. He was seeing Hank, standing with his binoculars on that ledge above the sea on Ireland's Eye. Of course, they weren't going to put Hank to death, but he would go to prison after his trial came up. How could he not, since he had confessed everything?

Matty lowered his head again and pretended to be puzzling over the poem. He did not want Brother Malachy to call on him just yet, because he was formulating a plan. As soon as school was over, he was going to call a Council. There would be obstacles to his plan, of course. He wasn't sure if they let kids in without their parents, but maybe Sergeant Lynch would be able to bend the rules. They would take turns, all of them, visiting Hank in prison.

It seemed the least they could do, for having breathed him into being.

ABOUT THE AUTHOR

Mary Bringle was born in Racine, Wisconsin, and lives in New York. THE MAN IN THE MOSS-COLORED TROUSERS is her sixth novel, and her second with the Crime Club. She lived in Ireland for six months in 1983, traveling frequently to all parts of the Republic and Northern Ireland.